CAST THE FIRST STONE

A MEDIAEVAL MYSTERY

Cast the First Stone

A Mediaeval Mystery

C.B. HANLEY

For Emily,
a historian (and editor) in training.

First published by The Mystery Press, 2020

The Mystery Press, an imprint of The History Press
97 St George's Place
Cheltenham, Gloucestershire, GL50 3QB
www.thehistorypress.co.uk

British Library Cataloguing in Publication Data.
A catalogue record for this book is available from the British Library.

ISBN 978 0 7509 9195 7

Typesetting and origination by The History Press
Printed and bound in Great Britain by TJ International Ltd, Padstow

He that is without sin among you,
let him cast the first stone.

John, ch.8, v.7

Praise for C.B. Hanley's Mediaeval Mystery Series

'*The Bloody City* is a great read, full of intrigue and murder. Great for readers of Ellis Peters and Lindsey Davis. Hanley weaves a convincing, rich tapestry of life and death in the early 13th century, in all its grandeur and filth. I enjoyed this book immensely!'

Ben Kane, bestselling novelist of the *Forgotten Legion* trilogy

'Blatantly heroic and wonderfully readable.'

The Bloody City received a STARRED review in *Library Journal*

'The characters are real, the interactions and conversations natural, the tension inbuilt, and it all builds to a genuinely satisfying conclusion both fictionally and historically.'

Review for *The Bloody City* in www.crimereview.co.uk

'*Whited Sepulchres* … struck me as a wonderfully vivid recreation of the early thirteenth century … The solid historical basis lends authenticity to a lively, well-structured story. I enjoyed the plight of amiable and peace-loving Edwin, trapped by his creator in such a warlike time and place.'

Andrew Taylor, winner of the 2009 CWA Diamond Dagger and three-times winner of the CWA Historical Dagger

'It's clever. It's well written. It's believable.
It's historically accurate. It's a first-class medieval mystery.'

'*Brother's Blood* [is] a gift for medievalists everywhere …
Hanley really knows her stuff. Her knowledge of life in a
Cistercian monastery is impeccable. More please.'

'British author Hanley's enjoyable fourth medieval whodunnit
will appeal to Ellis Peters fans.'

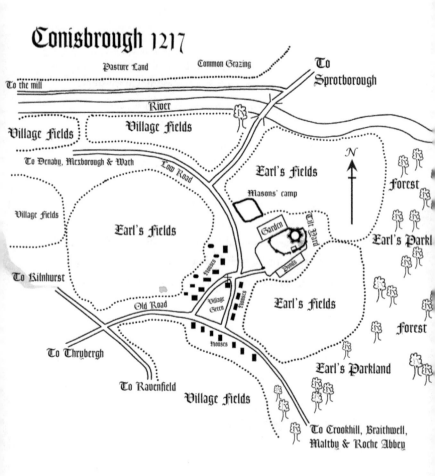

Conisbrough 1217

Pasture Land   Common Grazing

To the mill

River

To Sprotborough

Village Fields

Village Fields

To Denaby, Mexborough & Wath

Low Road

Earl's Fields

Masons' camp

N

Forest

Village Fields

Earl's Fields

Village Fields

Garden

Tilt Yard

Earl's Parkl

To Kilnhurst

Houses

Bowls

Old Road

Village Green

Houses

Earl's Fields

Forest

To Thrybergh

Houses

To Ravenfield

Earl's Parkland

Village Fields

To Crookhill, Braithwell,
Maltby & Roche Abbey

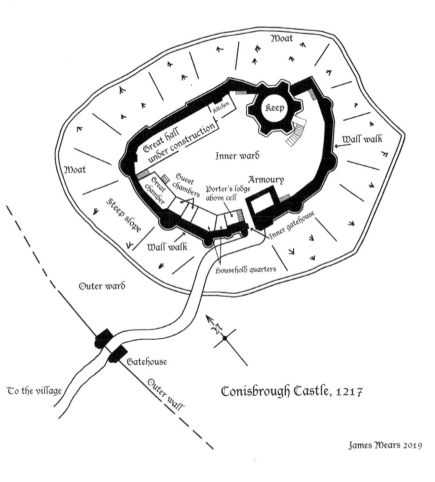

Moat

Kitchen

Keep

Great hall under construction

Inner ward

Wall walk

Moat

Guest chambers

Armoury

Great chamber

Porter's lodge above cell

steep slope

Wall walk

Inner gatehouse

Outer ward

Household quarters

N

Gatehouse

To the village

Outer wall

Conisbrough Castle, 1217

James Mears 2019

Chapter One

Conisbrough, November 1217

Rivulets of blood were trickling down Conisbrough's main street, and Edwin picked his way across them so that his new boots wouldn't get soiled. He was almost home, where a wife and a hot meal awaited him, and once again he had to remind himself that he wasn't just imagining his good fortune. He was –

'Master Edwin!'

He turned, peering into the early dusk, to see that he was being hailed by the fast-approaching Hal. He stopped and waited for the panting boy to catch him up.

'They're at it again. Father says you're to come.'

So much for the hot meal and the quiet evening with Alys. Edwin followed Hal, though there was no need: he knew where they were going.

In a village of wooden buildings, the new stone house under construction stood out. Ivo, the recently appointed bailiff, had insisted upon it as a condition of his moving to Conisbrough, and Sir Geoffrey had received the earl's permission to have the masons work on it in addition to their duties at the castle. A stone house took longer to build than a wooden one, and it was still not complete although Ivo had been here several months; in the meantime, he was temporarily lodged in guest quarters at the castle. However, he visited the site frequently so he could check on progress and argue with the masons, and Edwin heard the sound of raised voices as he approached.

Hal stayed just outside with his father as Edwin stepped through the open doorway and into what would be the main room.

There was as yet no proper roof, but half of the wooden trusses had been placed and canvas laid over the top, so that one end of the space was sheltered; it was under this cover that four men were standing.

This time it wasn't the masons who were on the receiving end; the master and one of his men were off to one side, tools hanging unused in their hands, glad to be out of the way for once as Ivo engaged in a furious stand-up row with the reeve.

'I'm telling you, that's not the way we do it around here.'

'And I'm telling you that that's the way you're going to do it from now on!'

'But you can't just –'

'Oh yes I can, and –'

They both broke off as they saw Edwin. He had learned that the best thing to do was not to say anything, so he simply folded his arms and looked at them.

It was the reeve who broke first. 'Edwin. Can't you just …' He flapped his arm in a helpless gesture.

Ivo looked down the considerable length of his nose. 'I fail to see what it's got to do with him.' He turned to Edwin. 'But now you're here, perhaps you can talk some sense into him. I'm the earl's representative, so I can overrule any man here, and the sooner he realises it – the sooner you *all* realise it – the better for everyone.'

He stalked out, and there was a long moment of silence.

Edwin addressed the masons first, switching to their native French. 'At least it wasn't you this time.'

Philippe, the master, inclined his head. 'This time, no. But it will be again, no doubt, as he has no conception of how building work is done. I did not catch all of their argument, but it would appear that our friend here is having a similar experience. Monsieur Ivo is good at giving orders but has little idea of practical matters.'

'I'll talk to him. Perhaps you'd better go for now.'

'Yes. It is getting too dark to work anyway. I will send two men down tomorrow if I can spare them from the castle. Come, Denis.' He nodded at his man and they departed.

Once they were gone, young Hal opened his mouth to speak, but his father, who was still hovering by the door, shushed him. 'Quiet, boy. It's not your place.' He bobbed his head at Edwin and the reeve. 'We'll be off then.'

'Thank you for calling me, Alwin, it was the right thing to do. Hal, be a good lad and run to Alys for me. Tell her I'll be a little while more but I won't be too late.' The boy nodded and turned. 'Oh, and you look hungry – ask her if you might eat yours while you're waiting.'

Hal's grateful smile was visible in the gloom as he departed, and Edwin was left with the reeve. If this was going to be one of *those* conversations, he thought, he may as well sit down; he made his way past more roof beams stacked waiting to be used, and found a couple of blocks of stone packed in straw at the far end of the dry space. He sat and gestured for the reeve to do likewise.

'So, what was it this time?'

The reeve expelled a long breath. It was funny, reflected Edwin, that he always thought of the man facing him only by his job. He did have a name, but unfortunately for him it was Theophilus, far too much of a mouthful for most of the local folk to bother with, so they tended just to call him Reeve, as though that was his name. In any case, he'd held the position so long – being elected unopposed by the villagers every year since Edwin could remember – that he was now indistinguishable from it anyway.

'It's nothing too big – not yet, anyway – but it's just this constant way he has of picking up on every small thing, wanting to change the way we do it. Yesterday he was all for having the widow Mabel up at the manor court for grinding a bit of grain between two stones, when we all know she can't afford to pay the miller, and she hasn't got half a sack to take to him anyway. And today it was Osmund for using the wrong type of snare for rabbits. Lord knows what it'll be next, but I'm honestly starting to get the feeling that he's doing it on purpose just to rub people up the wrong way.'

Edwin reflected that there might well be a grain of truth in that: maybe Ivo was trying to impose himself in his new position, but just going about it badly. He'd certainly made enough mistakes in his own unfamiliar role over these past months, so he was hardly in a position to criticise. But there was something rather … *petty*, was the best word he could come up with, about Ivo.

The reeve was continuing. 'Can't you have a word? Can't you do anything?'

Edwin shook his head. 'You know I don't have any authority.'

'You have, though – everyone knows it. You're not just Godric's son any more – you're the earl's man, and Sir Geoffrey's stepson now, to boot. And Ivo's trying to get rid of me, after all the years I've worked in peace with your father.'

Edwin opened his mouth, but he didn't get the chance to interrupt.

'And look, if we can't rely on you to help, you being one of us – supposedly, anyway – then who *can* we ask? He's the bailiff, we have to do what he says, but he's going to make everyone's life a misery. And if we have a hard winter, I'm telling you he might even cause death.'

That was not a word Edwin liked to hear, having seen so much of it during the past year. He didn't really want to get involved in this, but what choice was there? Eventually he nodded. 'All right. I can't promise anything, but I'll see what I can do.'

The reeve stood. 'You have my thanks. And, you know, it might do you some good round here too.' He passed out through the doorway, leaving Edwin to ponder his cryptic parting remark.

Edwin remained where he was for a little while, certain that nobody would enter to disturb him. Life was meant to be simpler now that the war was over, and he had looked forward to coming home to enjoy peace and quiet for a time while the earl was far away at his castle of Lewes, at the other end of the realm. He'd even arrived as the bringer of good news, for he carried with him the earl's permission for Sir Geoffrey, Conisbrough's castellan, to marry. And marry he had, to none other than Edwin's widowed mother, whose life and status had altered to a dizzying extent as soon as they had made their vows. Sir Geoffrey, of course, would return to continue his duties at Conisbrough, but he was currently away: he had taken his new wife to visit his own manor so that she could be seen and recognised by his people there, and they were not due back for another two or three weeks. In the meantime, the Conisbrough garrison was in the temporary charge of Sir Roger, another of the earl's knights, but he was … well, best not think of that now. Suffice it to say that Edwin would very much have appreciated having Sir Geoffrey's firm and familiar hand and iron discipline looming over the castle and the village at this point.

As it stood, then, the only voice of authority about the place was Ivo, the new bailiff, who was responsible for law, order and the good running of all the earl's Conisbrough estates, just as Edwin's father had been for many years. And this was where Edwin's own position had become awkward. For most of his life, Edwin had expected to be appointed bailiff whenever his father should die or become too old or infirm to hold the post. And the villagers had expected it, too; his sudden promotion to an ill-defined position as 'earl's man' and the consequent imposition of a stranger upon them had taken them all by surprise, and they weren't reacting to it overly well. Throw into the mix that Ivo himself was confused about – and therefore probably suspicious of – Edwin, and there was bound to be trouble ahead. Ivo could not quite clarify to himself whether Edwin outranked him or not, so he veered between appealing to his authority with the villagers and treating him with a sort of jeering superciliousness.

Anyway, the current situation was that the bailiff and the villagers had been in constant low-level conflict for three months, that boiling point had not yet been reached but probably would sometime soon, and that in the absence of any higher power and with nobody else to complain to, both sides had got into the habit of coming to Edwin with grumbles and requests for arbitration.

But sitting here in the gathering dark wasn't going to help anything, and he was hungry. He peered out. Ivo was gone, everyone was safe in their own cottages, and Edwin was thankfully undisturbed as he made his way home.

———

Alys had the meal prepared and the table set. She had also checked on the animals, cleaned the house, remade the bed – twice – and gone through the stores, which she already knew down to the last grain. She stood at the door for a while, looking out at the small village and the empty street, and sighed. But it wouldn't do to let the cold evening air in, and the draught was starting to make the fire smoke, so she came back and sat down to stare at the four walls.

Her hands moved without thinking to tuck the distaff in her belt; she took up her spindle and started work, the rhythmic movements the only thing that remained familiar from her previous life. Of course she had done the right thing in uprooting herself to come here and marry Edwin, and *of course* she loved him dearly, but after a lifetime in one of England's biggest and busiest cities, being stuck in this cottage, in this village, cooking and cleaning and caring for just one person, was just not enough. At first she'd had Mistress Anne, Edwin's mother, to talk to and show her around, but in the three or so weeks since Anne's wedding Alys had enjoyed no meaningful conversation with anyone except Edwin, and he was out most of each day.

Some of the other villagers tried to help, telling her to enjoy the peace while she might. Wait until you have children, the older women would say, nodding to each other sagely. Then you'll know what busy is. And each time Alys forbore from noting that she had already brought up three children, while running a shop at the same time; she just smiled, nodded, pushed the scream down inside and went back to her spinning. Looking now over the yarn she'd produced since her arrival, and on the slow journey before that, she saw that there was now a good amount, and that anger and frustration hadn't spoiled its quality. As she waited for Edwin to come home, she eyed a corner of the cottage. Might a loom fit there? Would anyone here know how to build a proper one?

The door banged open and she looked up to see young Hal. He at least was a welcome and useful addition to the household. Alys had not yet grasped the complexities of rural work – words like oxgang and virgate meant nothing to her, much to the amusement of the local girls – but she knew that Edwin had more strips of land than could be worked by one man, especially when that man wasn't free to toil in the fields most of the time anyway. The family had for some while employed a landless labourer to work for them, but since Edwin's father's death and his own new duties even that wasn't enough, so he'd taken on a boy as well. Hal was twelve years old, and he helped out not just in the fields but also around the house; in return he received fourpence a week and ate his evening meal with them each day, a Godsend to his own family who were relieved of one mouth to feed as well as benefiting from the income.

He always entered the house as though a whirlwind was behind him, but he had at least now learned to stop and shut the door. He did so now and came forward to rub his hands together in front of the fire as he bobbed his head.

'Master Edwin says he'll be late, but not too late.' He licked his lips, and Alys heard his stomach rumble. 'He said I could ask if I could have mine now?' he added, hopefully.

Alys smiled and put down her spindle. 'Sit down, then.' She ladled a generous helping of pottage into a bowl and placed it in front of him with a hunk of bread, then started work again as he shovelled it in.

She produced several more yards of yarn. Hal finished his meal, wiped the last of the bread around the bowl, ate it, and then picked up all the crumbs from the table and licked them off his fingers. And still Edwin had not returned. Alys sighed. 'Off you go, then.'

The spindle was nearly full by the time the door opened again. This time it was Edwin himself, and Alys's heart lifted as he smiled at her. She helped him off with his cloak and laid it over the kist in the corner as he splashed water over his hands and face and sat at the table.

They ate, and as usual he complimented the meal and thanked her for it – something few men did – but she could see that there was something on his mind. She waited to see if he would mention it, but instead he looked about him and shook his head in disbelief. 'It looks so different in here.'

Alys had to agree, for the cottage was much improved since she had first seen it on her arrival in the summer. There had been some previous agreement between Edwin and the earl regarding their marriage, and not long after Edwin had returned from the south coast a number of items of new furniture had been delivered, along with a heavy bag of pennies that were to serve as her dowry. This last was most welcome, as Alys felt embarrassed that she had brought nothing to the union except a few bolts of cloth; the coins were now safely buried against a time of need. The furniture was as fine as Alys had seen in some of the merchants' houses back in Lincoln: a carved kist in this main room and another in the bedchamber; a sideboard that was too large for their collection of plates and cups; a new table, bench and stools; and Edwin now sat at the head of the table on a real chair, one with a back. He seemed constantly overwhelmed by the new surroundings, and to be honest some of it – particularly the sideboard – did look out of place in the simple cottage. Neighbours had made regular visits to view, gossip and then grumble under their breath about luck and how some people were getting above themselves.

The evenings were Alys's favourite time; the day's tasks were done and she had Edwin all to herself. Unlike many other couples, they hadn't grown up in the same place, so there was still lots to learn about the other's previous life, their likes and dislikes, their hopes and fears. And with the door shut and the fire glowing, the cottage was a safe little haven from all that might be outside; it was theirs, and theirs alone. Alys's discontent, as it did every day, faded with the light.

The next morning started like any other. The air was chill and the bed was warm, and Alys was loath to get out of it, but the fire needed reawakening and there were tasks to be accomplished. Edwin set off for the castle, as he normally did; it was teeming down with rain so she warmed his new fur-lined cloak near the fire while he readied himself. Then, with a kiss, he was gone, and she was alone once more.

Keep busy. That was the thing to do. She had already made the bed, scrubbed the table and swept the floor of both rooms when she heard the call of the swineherd outside, so she pulled up her hood, wrapped a shawl about her and stepped out into the weather. Gyrth was making his way along the street, collecting the pigs from each house and herding them along in the direction of the woods. He waited, patiently and vacantly, as she unfastened the stiff and soaking gate to let out the two they were keeping for the winter. He mumbled something and passed on his way. He was a large, strapping youth, but a simpleton who understood little and said less. Still, he was a good hand with the village pigs, spending so much time with them that he knew them all individually, and taking care to move them around the woods to where the best acorns could be found to feed them up. She watched him as he trudged on, an occasional tap from the stick in his left hand keeping the pigs in order as they grew in number on their way out of the village.

By now Alys was wet through, so she might as well go to fetch the water before she went back inside to dry off. The buckets were heavy, and left her no hand free as she walked to the well; the hood started slipping off her head and she could feel the rain seeping through her wimple to soak her hair. The sky was grey and looked full; the rain was probably set in for the day, and it would never get fully light. She stepped in a puddle, drenching her shoe and the already heavy hem of her gown. The mud was particularly bad as she approached the well, as so many other feet used the same path, and she trod carefully to avoid falling and making a spectacle of herself.

A gaggle of girls and married women were already there, gossiping cheerfully in a manner that tailed off when she reached them, turning into whispers and giggles behind their hands as they stared at her. Alys tried to ignore it, but couldn't help comparing the friendly greetings she would have received back at home – *back in Lincoln, where she used to live*, she reminded herself – and it stung. When her turn came, she let down the pail and then concentrated as hard as she could on turning the wet, slippery handle to raise it. As she heaved the full container over the lip of the well to pour it into her own buckets it slipped, and for one moment she thought she was going to tip the whole lot over herself. The humiliation might even have been worse than the soaking, but fortunately she was saved from both by a pair of work-reddened, friendly hands that steadied the weight.

They turned out to belong to Rosa, the only girl who had ever given her anything approaching a friendly look; she was Hal's sister, though, so Alys wasn't sure whether she really was welcoming or whether she merely felt obliged. 'Don't mind them,' whispered Rosa under her breath, making sure nobody else could hear. 'They'll get used to you in time.' And then she was gone, pulled away by the others, but Alys felt a little more cheerful as she made her laborious and muddy way back to the empty cottage.

The rain was pelting down as Edwin made his way up the path to the castle. Unusually, it was rutted and full of holes; that did happen in this kind of weather, of course, but in normal times repairs were carried out swiftly. He passed through the main gate and into the outer ward, waving at the smith in his bright forge as he passed, but not stopping as he hurried up to the inner gatehouse, dripping all the way.

The armoury was his first point of call in the inner ward, and he entered over a pile of assorted equipment that had been left lying. 'Do you know where Sir Roger is?'

One of the soldiers rolled his eyes – not something anyone would have dared when speaking of Sir Geoffrey – and replied, 'Where do you think?'

Edwin nodded and made his way to the keep, where, as he expected, he found Sir Roger on his knees in the chapel.

Following the events of the campaign on the south coast in August, Edwin had not seen the knight for a couple of months, but he had arrived at Conisbrough in time to stand at Sir Geoffrey's side during the wedding, and had then taken command of the castle garrison while Sir Geoffrey was absent. In theory this had been an excellent plan, but Edwin had been shocked and disturbed at the knight's altered appearance and behaviour. He looked like he'd aged ten years, dark-circled eyes staring out from a haggard face; the spring had gone from his step and the joy from his demeanour. He'd always been devout, but now he seemed hardly ever to leave the chapel, spending so many hours on the stone floor in fervent prayer that Edwin wondered his knees could stand it.

Edwin hesitated to disturb a man at his devotions, but after a short while he realised that Sir Roger was oblivious to his presence and would continue to be so unless he did something. He tried clearing his throat, which had no effect, so he stepped forward and laid a hand on the knight's shoulder.

One thing Sir Roger hadn't lost was the reflexes of a trained warrior, and he shot round and seized Edwin's wrist in an iron grip, twisting it painfully, before he noticed who it was. Then he dropped it and stood. 'Sorry.'

Edwin flexed his fingers. 'I came to see if you had any orders for me today.'

Sir Roger looked about him abstractedly, as if only now remembering where he was. 'Orders? Oh, yes, orders. Some letters have arrived. I need to take out a patrol, so why don't you read them while I'm gone? And then if you have time …' he tailed off, waving his arm vaguely. 'I'm sure you can find something to occupy you.' He turned to make a final genuflection to the altar and was gone.

He hadn't said where the letters were to be found, but Edwin didn't bother calling after him, guessing – correctly as it turned out – that they would be in the earl's council chamber here in the keep. The room was cold and dismal, no fire in the hearth and just enough damp light drifting in through the one small window for Edwin to see his breath clouding. As he was on the earl's business he took it upon himself to light a candle, although with no fire from which to take a spill he was forced to strike a spark himself, which took some time. Still, there weren't all that many letters, and he wasn't in a hurry.

He kept his cloak on and tried to pull the sleeves of his tunic further over his cold hands, blowing on them before he broke the first seal.

It was all the usual sort of routine correspondence, and – as far he could make out in the murk outside the window – it was not yet noon by the time he had finished. He stood, stamping his feet and glad to move, the sound echoing about him. It was still odd, being in the council chamber by himself. The first time he'd been left alone in here, shortly after his return from the south coast, he'd felt as though he was trespassing, and was ready to jump up with an explanation every time he heard a foot on the stair. But today he'd walked in as though he was born to it. Strange how so much could change in such a short while.

But now was not the time to start thinking about everything again. He left the sorted correspondence ready for Sir Roger, blew out the candle with care and made his way down the dim and echoing spiral stairway, ignoring the ghosts that threatened to rise up if he would only let them.

The inner ward was chaos these days – one of the reasons the earl had chosen to stay at one of his other residences for the autumn – as the masons were rebuilding the great hall in stone. The old wooden building that had stood for a hundred years, with its smoke-blackened roof beams, was just a memory; in its place bright new walls were rising. Good progress had been made, but as Edwin had soon after his return calculated the number of stones in each row, the number of rows needed to take the building to its full height, and the amount of time it had taken to get thus far, he thought that the earl's estimate of it being ready by Christmas was overly optimistic. Besides, the masons would halt construction over the winter, spending their time carving and stacking new blocks ready for the spring but not laying them while the weather was cold. They were at work now, in an area of the ward between the hall and the great chamber; it was covered with a temporary wood-and-canvas roof that kept the rain off as they maintained a constant tap-tap-tapping with their hammers and chisels.

To be more precise, most of them were at work; one of them was otherwise engaged being shouted at by Ivo. Edwin didn't know many of the masons by name, but this was one he recognised – a small Frenchman with gold rings in his ears, the one who had been in the house with the master on the previous evening. Philippe was currently nowhere to be seen, so the poor fellow was enduring the tirade as best he could without responding. It was honestly the last thing Edwin wanted to get involved in just now, but he'd promised the reeve, so he made his way over.

Of course, as soon as he got near them they both turned their attention to him and appealed for his intervention. Ivo was angry about some of the previous day's work that had not been carried out according to his exact specifications. The mason went off into a rapid explanation that contained such a flood of technical vocabulary that Edwin couldn't keep up, but he was willing to believe that the man knew what he was talking about. He tried to calm them both down without overtly taking sides, but was not entirely successful; Ivo strode off muttering dark threats.

The mason swore under his breath – Edwin understood *that* – and raised his hammer with a clear desire to smash something. Fortunately, he retained sufficient wit not to bring it down on the almost-square block on the table in front of him, and instead thumped it into a pile of chippings, scattering them far and wide and breaking some into further pieces. Edwin was surprised at the violence of the reaction, and also at the man's strength. He looked more closely: the mason might be small, but his forearms were the size of hams.

For the want of anything else to say, he asked, 'Why is it round?'

The mason, calming as quickly as he had become enraged, was now making 'tsk' noises to himself and examining his hammer for damage. Unlike those used in the village or fields, its head was not square but rather a sort of tapered cylinder. 'It makes it easier to use when you need to strike at different angles. Look.' He picked up a chisel and demonstrated as he spoke, manoeuvring to chip more small pieces from the block to square it off. 'And of course, you have it in your hand all day every day, so it needs to be comfortable or you can't work.'

Edwin nodded. He reached out to run a finger along the smooth edge of the stone block. The work was delicate and certainly a very different thing from, say, hammering in a fence post, for which a crude square hammer would be perfectly adequate.

The mason looked at him properly. 'You're the man who tries to help master Philippe when that ... when *he*' – he gestured at Ivo's back – 'argues with him.'

'I try.'

'That's more than most.' He held out his hand. 'Denis.'

Edwin took it. 'Edwin.'

Denis made an effort to pronounce the unfamiliar combination of letters. '*Edouin.*'

Edwin laughed. 'It's an old English name – you probably don't hear it very often.'

'But you are an important man in the earl's service? You speak French? Was your father married to an Englishwoman, that you have this name?'

'No. I mean yes, my mother is English, but my father was too. His name was Godric – you probably don't hear that very often where you're from, either.'

'No, but it is easier to pronounce.' A puzzled look came over his face. 'But how did an Englishman rise so high in the service of the earl?'

It struck Edwin that he wasn't really sure of the answer to that himself. Luck? The will of God? He shrugged. 'Great men choose their servants where they will.'

Denis nodded. 'This is true. Anyway, I am glad to know you, Edouin. I will look for you when I go down to the village later to work on monsieur the bailiff's house.'

'Good to know you too.' Edwin left him to get back to his block of stone, wondering at his own lack of perceptiveness. The masons had been at Conisbrough for many months – years, even – and yet he couldn't remember ever really speaking to any of them, except for the odd distant greeting. If asked, he wouldn't be able to say which ones had been there all along and which had come and gone. But they were men like any other when you spoke to them.

Dinner was being served in the inner ward, but it was a very brief affair. With the earl away, the garrison was much depleted, and some of those left had gone out on the day's patrol with Sir Roger, so there weren't many to feed. There was also, of course, no hall, so another temporary shelter had been rigged up in the lee of the keep, near to the kitchen, containing some of the displaced trestle tables and benches. It kept most of the rain off, but it provided little shelter from the wind that always whipped around up here, so the men huddled near braziers as they ate their hot pottage. Ivo sat alone at one end of a table; the selection of dishes in front of him indicated that he had at least managed not to antagonise the castle cook, a wise move under the circumstances.

The afternoon was short at this time of year, and Edwin managed to find enough business to occupy him until it was time to go home. He was waved through the inner and outer gates by the porters and was halfway down the pockmarked path before he sensed – and heard – that something was wrong. Squealing pigs were careening everywhere through the streets and gardens, shouting villagers chasing after them. What …?

Edwin broke into a jog, but as he reached the church he heard a different noise. He stopped and peered into the churchyard as he tried to make it out. The sound distilled itself into a sobbing, and Edwin moved towards it.

Curled up in a corner against one of the walls was the swineherd. He had both hands pressed tightly over his ears and was rocking back and forth as he whimpered.

Edwin knelt in front of him. 'Gyrth?'

The youth opened his eyes wide. 'The blood. There's blood everywhere, so much blood. I've seen it. I don't like it. Make it stop!'

Chapter Two

Alys had been drawn out by the commotion and looked on in dismay at the pigs running wild through the village. She gathered that this wasn't a planned occurrence; everyone else was darting around waving their arms and shouting as they chased down the animals in an attempt to catch their own. She stepped out of the garden to see if she could identify theirs, and was almost knocked off her feet by a large, squealing sow panicked by the noise and fuss.

Eventually order was restored. Once most of the noise and panic was over, talk naturally turned to how this had happened, and Alys soon found her answer in the sight of Edwin walking along the street with a weeping Gyrth, talking quietly to him and patting the much larger youth on the shoulder as he did so. She assumed that Gyrth had somehow lost control of the pigs on his way back from the woods, and winced at the thought of the reception he would receive, but strangely the villagers restrained themselves to shakes of the head and tutting noises.

Edwin delivered the swineherd to the man Alys recognised as his father, and then approached her. He took her hand. 'Are you all right? You didn't get trampled or hurt?'

She was pleased at his consideration. 'No, I'm fine, and the pigs are safe. But …?' She indicated Gyrth.

'Oh, of course, I forgot you haven't been here at pig-slaughtering time before. It makes him upset. He's with them all day every day of the year and thinks of them as his friends, and then most of them have to go to the knife in November. The noise frightens him and the sight of blood makes him panic. We try to keep him away from most of it, but they haven't been too careful the last couple of days and it's been running down the street.'

They watched as Gyrth was led away by his even burlier father, who had an arm about his son's shoulder and was casting apologetic looks and words at everyone else as he went.

Edwin continued. 'It's ... well, you've seen what he's like. He's not all there, and it's like he forgets that it happens. He's been the swineherd for years but every November it's the same, it's a surprise and a shock to him.' He shook his head. 'The Lord must have made him that way for a reason, so we try to keep that in mind, and everyone just accepts that he goes mad at this time of year.'

The following day was the day of the monthly manor court, so instead of heading out to work, the villagers made their way to the green. Thankfully it was not raining, but the ground was wet and a chill wind blustered around Alys as she stood with the other women to view the proceedings. She found herself between Edwin's aunt, Cecily, and Rosa.

In the centre of proceedings was a single chair that had been brought down from the castle. It was currently empty; Ivo would wait until everyone else was assembled before he made his own appearance. Near it was a table and stool, at which Father Ignatius, the priest, was sharpening a quill; to one side were a number of benches where the village jury would sit. The jury comprised every able-bodied and able-minded man and boy over the age of twelve, and Alys saw Rosa beam with pride as Hal took his place for the first time alongside his father and elder brother. Edwin was also there. Alys had asked him that morning about his role in the court. When his father had been the bailiff Edwin had been the one at the table writing the notes, but he was not going to position himself as Ivo's assistant, so he deliberately took a seat on the bench at the back.

Alys ran her eye over the benches as they filled. She recognised most of the men, even though she didn't know all their names: the labourers, the carpenter with half a dozen of his many sons, the miller, the reeve. But a few were strangers, presumably men from outlying farms.

Rosa was staring at one of them, so Alys took the opportunity to ask who it was. A heartfelt sigh accompanied the answer. 'That's Aelfrith.'

Alys looked more closely. The young man was tall, straight and well-muscled, with dark curly hair, a short, well-kept beard and a handsome face. Rosa wasn't the only girl gazing at him dreamily as he greeted the men around him; Alys smiled to herself.

When all were assembled Ivo made his entrance, flanked by two guards from the castle who took up position behind and to either side of his chair. Alys heard Cecily's sharp intake of breath and looked enquiringly at her.

'Let's just say that Godric never had to do that.'

Alys watched the bailiff as he in turn observed the villagers. His gaze swept over them – counting? Marking absences? – but lingered on some of the younger and prettier girls in a manner Alys didn't quite like.

Further questions to Cecily were forestalled by the start of proceedings; evidently no other person from the castle was expected. Alys was a little disappointed not to see the young knight who was standing in for Sir Geoffrey; she hadn't met him before but Edwin spoke of him warmly, and she knew that he was also a friend of the two knights who had saved her life during that dreadful day back at home – *back in Lincoln* – in the spring. Still, there would be plenty to interest her even without his presence. She turned with the other women to watch in silence, although she was observing them as much as she was the main event.

The first few items seemed to be routine, and did not arouse more than a passing interest from those around her. A woman had sold ale that wasn't fresh; a boy had caught a rabbit with the wrong sort of snare. They were fined, the coins placed on Father Ignatius's table, and business moved on swiftly.

The first darker tone came when Ivo called forward Gyrth, accusing him of dereliction of his duty and damage to the earl's property. The swineherd didn't know how to answer, and stood bemused and blank-faced in the middle of the open space until both his father and the reeve came to stand beside him.

The father took off his hat and twisted it in his hands. 'If you please, sir, he didn't mean no harm. He's always been simple, but he's a good boy.'

Ivo was not impressed. 'A good boy wouldn't let a whole herd of pigs run riot through the village, causing damage and danger.'

The father looked like he was trying to frame a reply, but the reeve was quicker, speaking in a tone that was perhaps a shade more belligerent than it needed to be. 'And what damage was that? The only garden trampled was Osmund's own,' – he gestured to Gyrth's father – 'and when we caught the pigs and counted them they were all accounted for.'

Ivo was not to be drawn, and he replied smoothly. 'Osmund's garden? He is unfree, so that land belongs to the lord earl. As does the fence around the churchyard, which I have just examined and found to be damaged.'

There was a murmur of discontent at this, as all knew that only a single wattle panel had been knocked awry.

'Please, I'll mend the church fence myself.' This from Osmund. 'And I'll sort out the garden and we'll still pay the same rent and tithes that we owe, even if there's less to harvest.'

Most of the jury were nodding their heads, and an unidentified voice noted that this sounded fair. Ivo looked inclined to argue, but Father Ignatius put down his pen and stood. 'On behalf of the Church, I accept this offer,' he declared.

Alys had never really spoken properly to the priest, seeing him as part of the background of the village, but now she looked at him sharply. That was clever. He might have no official authority but he was a clergyman and thus – however humbly – represented the might of an institution that Ivo wasn't prepared to take on. He nodded grudging assent, Osmund and Gyrth made good their escape from the centre of the open space, and the court moved on.

But Ivo wasn't pleased, and there was an edge to his voice as he made his next announcement. It was the seemingly inconsequential information that the site of the large autumn trading fair would be moved from one field to another. Alys was surprised to find not just murmurs but actual cries of dissent, with an undercurrent of real anger.

Cecily saw her confusion. 'It's the dung.' She smiled. 'I suppose there's no reason for you to know. When the fair comes, there are lots of horses and oxen, and the droppings they leave are good for the ground; once the fair leaves, it can just be dug in. But he wants to move it from a village field to one owned by the lord earl so that we won't benefit.'

Alys watched as the reeve argued animatedly that this was against local custom and practice, but Ivo was sitting with folded arms and shaking his head with an expression so smug that she was sure he knew something. To her consternation she saw that a number of villagers were looking at Edwin, some of the men urging him openly to do something. He too was shaking his head, but with a much more pained expression, and he stayed where he was.

The priest had no grounds to intervene this time, the matter being nothing to do with the Church, and so the reeve's lone arguments were batted away, and then silenced completely as Ivo held up a document covered in close writing, which he said was the original charter allowing the fair to be held. 'And there is nothing in it that stipulates which field; only that it shall be held outside the castle on the manor of Conisbrough. So if I – on behalf of the lord earl – decide to move it, I can.'

Only two other men present could read, and the reeve was looking from one to the other. The priest made a helpless gesture and went back to his writing, pressing so hard that he splattered the ink and had to stop to blot it. All Edwin could do was nod, his face now even more distressed, to indicate that the charter – which he must have looked at himself at some time in the past – was genuine and that the bailiff had the right to do what he was doing.

The matter was thus passed, but the mood in the court was heated as Ivo moved on to the last item of business. Alys was forewarned that something serious was about to happen by the way he looked at his two guards before he spoke, and they grasped their spears more firmly. And the blow, when it fell, was a heavy one.

All the villagers, began Ivo, were obliged to have their grain ground into flour at the lord earl's mill, and to pay a fee for doing so. This was met with acceptance and nods, for all knew it. Some of the women around Alys started to look relieved. Was he just about to haul someone up for having a hand-mill? Alys could tell from his face that he wasn't.

The bailiff's voice carried across the green. 'Until now, the lord earl has given gracious permission for the bread to be baked in an oven used communally by the village. But with times being hard and he being burdened with many expenses due to the late war, he now decrees that, as soon as it shall be built, an oven belonging to him shall henceforward be used, and that a fee shall be payable for each loaf baked therein.'

There was a slight pause while everyone worked their way through the deliberately formal language, and then there was uproar. Bread! He wanted to charge a fee on bread! It was the great staple of life, with the poorer among the population eating little else. How could he possibly …?

Angry words were being exchanged, with the reeve and a couple of others even taking a few steps towards Ivo. He was having none of it, standing and moving briskly off with his armed guards even as he declared the court closed.

Nobody else dispersed; the green was a sea of shouting, gesticulating men, with women joining them too now that the official business was over. Everyone had something to say; everyone had someone to complain to. The reeve, the priest and Edwin were all surrounded, and Alys's alarm grew as she saw that some of those around Edwin seemed to be enraged with him rather than with Ivo. 'You should have said something!' and 'Your father would never have stood for this!' were just two of the accusations she caught, as she tried to fight her way through the crowd. She had no idea what she would do when she reached him; she only knew that she had to stand by his side.

Edwin himself was saying something that looked like it was meant to be placatory, but this only seemed to inflame some of the men

more. Now he was moving, trying to walk away, but he was surrounded and being jostled. One shove even made him trip, and she
began to feel fear as she fought her way towards him.

'Stop that right now!'

The voice was the priest's. There was a pause, a few shame-faced
looks, and then people started to fall back a little. Alys again mentally
reassessed his status and authority in the village. If there was going to
be trouble, he would be an ally worth having.

Father Ignatius made his way to the centre of the group. 'Edwin
and I will discuss the legal matters in detail and see if there is anything
to be done. In the meantime, the court is over and there is work to
be done, so I suggest you all get to it and cool your heads for a while.'

He led Edwin through the press as they stepped back. But although
nobody shoved Edwin again, there were many dark looks cast his way,
and somebody – Alys couldn't make out who – even murmured the
word 'coward' under his breath. She was glad when he reached her,
and she walked on his other side away from the village green and the
angry people upon it.

Many thoughts had gone through Edwin's head as the court pro-
gressed. It was odd, to start with, to be viewing it from this angle: he'd
been his father's scribe and assistant since he was twelve, and had never
sat on the jury itself. If he'd had the leisure, he might have appreciated
the sensation of not having to scrawl to keep up with the cases, not
needing to sharpen a quill constantly, not ending up covered in ink and
with an aching hand. But events had precluded any such relaxation.
What was Ivo thinking? Not just to announce what he had, but in the
way he had done it. Did he honestly not care that he was antagonising
the whole village, or that this was just going to make his own life more
difficult and unpleasant in the months and years to come?

He'd been relieved when Father Ignatius and the reeve had managed
to sort out the situation with Gyrth. A charitable interpretation would

be that Ivo simply didn't know him, and that he would be more lenient next time, but Edwin wasn't sure. The moving of the fair site was petty and mean, but unfortunately Edwin had read that charter several times and he knew that Ivo had the absolute right in law to decide exactly where it should be held. He also knew that people had been looking at him to make a stand, but what was the point? Any appeal was bound to lose, so better to save his efforts. The bread, though – that was another matter entirely. He wasn't sure of the legal position there, as such a thing had never even been considered before, but it could cause great hardship.

The subject occupied him as he followed the priest, oblivious to anything else going on around him. They reached the cottage, and Edwin offered Father Ignatius the chair and took a place on the bench against the wall, holding out his hand to Alys as she hovered. She sat next to him and they both looked expectantly at their guest.

Edwin had known Father Ignatius all his life, and this was as near as he'd ever seen him to being angry.

He was virtually spluttering. "'I am the bread of life," says the Lord. And bread means life. How many will suffer if this comes to pass? How many will go hungry?'

Alys spoke. 'Is there anything that can be done?'

Edwin had to admit he didn't know. 'I'd have to check. But Sir Roger wouldn't be familiar with the details either – I'll have to wait until Sir Geoffrey gets back and ask him.'

Father Ignatius was tapping one ink-stained finger on the table. 'But it doesn't take long to build an oven, surely – this may well have been pushed through by the time he returns. And I foresee suffering for the poorest.'

Edwin sighed. 'Yes. But Ivo has charge of all the charters and parchments now – I'd have to beg him to let me see them.'

'If we have to humble ourselves to help, my son, then we must do it with a good heart. When he has had time to reflect, I will speak to him – not legally, but in the name of God and charity. Maybe –'

They were interrupted by a knock at the door. Alys got up to open it, and Edwin knew who it was before she showed him in, for Aelfrith had a startlingly deep voice. Alys was looking him up and down as he came in, and Edwin tried to recollect whether she'd ever met him before.

Aelfrith nodded at Edwin but addressed the priest. 'If you please, Father, it's my mother, she's taken bad again. Will you come?'

Father Ignatius hauled himself to his feet. 'Of course. Edwin, we'll discuss this further and ask the Lord for guidance. Alys, I bid you good day. Come, Aelfrith, and we'll stop at the church to collect the oil.' He continued as they went out. 'We can pray for your mother on the way. Take comfort that ...'

Alys shut the door behind them and came to sit close to him again. She always carried with her a fragrance of flowers, even at this time of year.

'I was worried about you out there,' she said.

He shrugged. 'It wasn't pleasant, but it's fine. I've known these people all my life.'

'But couldn't you see how angry they were?'

'Of course they were, but not with me. It was about the bread.'

'I'm not so sure.'

He was surprised. 'Why do you say that?'

'The way they were shouting at you and pushing you. That came after the announcement about the bread, but it started earlier, when they were talking about moving the fair. Why didn't you say something?'

'There would have been no point. The charter is clear.'

'Yes, but they didn't know that. What they saw was you not standing up for them, as though you couldn't be bothered, as though you sided with the bailiff. That's what made them angry.'

'But –'

'It's not what you did, it's what's they *believe* you did. That's what they'll remember.'

'How do you know so much about it when you haven't known them long?'

'I don't know. I can just see it, that's all. Can't you? Or perhaps it's because I've spent my whole life working in a shop – you get to know about people. I could always tell who was going to buy and who wasn't, before they even opened their mouths.' There was a pause before she spoke again. 'So, that young man. Aelfrith.'

Edwin was taken aback by the abrupt change of subject. 'What about him?'

'Tell me about him.'

'He has a farm about three miles away. Father Ignatius will earn his dinner by the time he's been out there and back on these roads.'

'No, I mean tell me about *him*. Is he married?'

'No, he isn't, and – but you're married to me!'

She laughed. 'Oh, Edwin, of course I am. And I love you. I wasn't asking on my own behalf.' She leaned forward and kissed his cheek. 'So do carry on. I'll tell you why later.'

'All right. No, he's not married, and not likely to be while his mother is still alive. She absolutely rules the place, I don't know how he puts up with it, and there's no girl willing to risk being her daughter-in-law for years on end.'

'But she's ill?'

'Ha. She's been convinced she's dying for years now. She sends for Father Ignatius at least twice a month to give her the last rites, and he, bless him, goes along with it. She never comes here – he has to walk out to their farm every time. Then he comes back, she doesn't die, and it all starts again.'

'And let me guess – every time he goes, there's a queue of girls waiting to hear the news when he gets back?'

'Now you come to put it like that, yes, although I hadn't thought of it before. Now tell me why you want to know.'

'No particular reason. I just wonder who might be put at the front of the queue.'

Edwin had no idea what she was talking about, and he wasn't sure he wanted to know. 'Anyway, we shouldn't be sat here chattering in the middle of the day. I'd better get up to the castle.'

'And I need to go and collect the flour from the mill.' She made a face. 'Then I'd better make some dough and get it baked in the village oven while I still can.'

He hastened to reassure her. 'If it comes to it, we'll be able to pay the fees. I earn more even than my father did. And we've got those coins as well, remember.'

'I know. But others won't. Anyway, next time you happen to know that Aelfrith is coming into the village, why don't you ask him to eat with us here?'

'Yes, of course, if you like.' Confused again by her insistence about the man, and with a tiny finger of suspicion poking into the corner of his mind, he went out.

The wind was picking up as he reached the castle, hitting him with particular force as it funnelled through the inner gatehouse. The men were at their dinner, minus Sir Roger, and Edwin wondered if he dared have a word with the knight about the situation when he returned.

Ivo was sitting by himself at one end of the table, and Edwin hesitated on his way to the keep. Perhaps he should have a quiet word here, while he could, away from the villagers and their rising tempers. It wasn't a conversation he could look forward to, but Alys's words and the priest's had convinced him that he should at least try. He took a seat on the bench next to the bailiff.

Ivo looked at him but did not speak or stop eating, chopping his meat into fastidiously small pieces before popping each one in his mouth without spilling any sauce.

There was no point prevaricating. 'About today's manor court.'

The long, thin fingers stopped. Knife and spoon were placed on the table with precision.

'It's just … I wondered if you'd really thought through your proposals before you announced them.'

'And you think this is your business because … ?'

It was going to be that sort of conversation. Fine, if that was the way he wanted it. Today's Edwin was not the Edwin of a year ago.

'Because I work for the lord earl, I am his man, a member of his household, and I care that matters here run smoothly while he's away.'

Several of the nearest soldiers stopped what they were doing and turned round to look at him. Surprised at his tone, no doubt, particularly if they had been here throughout the spring and summer rather than on campaign, and hadn't seen him for a while.

Ivo's eyes were cold. 'And I am the bailiff on these estates. Responsible for law and order, raising revenue and reporting to the lord earl.'

'So it would seem that we both want the same thing.'

'I'm not sure that we do.'

Edwin felt the first stirrings of irritation. 'Explain that, please.'

Ivo dabbed at his mouth with a napkin. 'I want to serve the earl. You seem to want to harm his interests by undermining my authority.'

'Harm his interests?' Edwin was incredulous. After he'd spent the last half a year risking his life over and over again in the earl's service?

The men had finished their dinner. Most had drifted away but those closest were in no hurry to leave. Edwin tried to push down his anger. 'That's not true and you know it. My lord's interest is best served by having well-fed labourers who can go about their work in peace.'

'No. My lord's interest is best served by everyone – *everyone* – recognising his authority in the person of his bailiff.'

'Not if the bailiff isn't doing his job properly.' Edwin's tone surprised even himself. *Getting heated rarely helps the situation*, said his father's long-ago voice in his head. But people's livelihoods were going to be at stake, and besides, it was too late to take the words back.

Ivo almost spluttered. 'How dare you!'

The sergeant-at-arms was calling the last of his men away, and they got up with reluctance. Edwin and Ivo were alone at the table under the canvas roof, the wind swirling around them. He tried to keep his voice low, not entirely successfully. 'I dare because I know what the work entails,' he hissed, 'and I know that the estate has been run well these thirty years, and I don't want my father's life's work destroyed!'

'Oh, your father. Yes, I hear about your sainted father wherever I go. It seems to me that he was lucky to retain his position if he was as lax as he seems to have been.'

Edwin felt the rage rise. He needed to leave, needed to get away, before he really lost his temper. That wouldn't help anyone. He stood, almost tripping in his hurry.

But Ivo wasn't finished. 'And you, "knowing what the job entails" – you want it back, do you? You want to step into my shoes? Well, you're not going to!' He banged his hand down on the table, not noticing that some of the utensils were rather nearer the edge than he had thought. He bent to retrieve his cup from the ground. His knife had landed by Edwin's foot, and Edwin couldn't help but pick it up and hand it back.

He pointed a finger in Ivo's face. 'We will speak more, but let me tell you, if you *ever* insult my father again –' He forced himself to move away. Furious both with Ivo and with his own inability to make any progress, he pushed past the group of surprised men forming up outside the armoury and made his way up the steps that led to the walk around the top of the inner ward's stone walls. He paced up and down for a while and then sat down in what had always been his favourite embrasure to try to calm himself.

It was more peaceful up here, the sounds and smells of tightly packed humanity and animals lost in the clean, cold air. He took deep breaths and looked out over the village. It was going to be one of those days where it never got completely light, but now at noon he had the best of it. He could see the men at work in the fields, although rather more of them than usual seemed to be collected in unmoving knots. And in the distance he could make out Alys, passing the great oak at the edge of the village and crossing the bridge to walk along the opposite side of the river towards the mill. There was no point in waving; she was facing away from him. Now she was on the far bank and starting to pick her way along the muddy path. She had her shawl drawn tightly about her, but hopefully the walk of half a mile or so would warm her up. She passed into a clump of trees and he lost sight of her, but they would be together again later – and there would be fresh bread to look forward to at home this evening or tomorrow morning, depending on when she could get her turn in the village oven.

Oven. Yes. Reluctantly he turned his mind back to the question that needed addressing. Now that he had provoked Ivo, there was little chance that a polite request to view the relevant documents would be successful, so what was he to do? And he had a nasty feeling that the antagonistic situation between bailiff and villagers was going to be a long-term one; there was no reason to suppose that Ivo would be replaced or that his appointment was anything other than lifelong.

The water was high and fast-flowing as Alys crossed the bridge. They would all do well to fetch their flour before it got any worse; as well as the rain itself there would no doubt be much water draining off the fields into the river, and the bridge might soon be impassable. The path on the other side was muddy, and once more she felt a pang of loss for Lincoln's cobbled streets.

As Alys neared the mill, she met a group of wives coming back – they must have set off straight after the court, while she had been at home talking. They were burdened with their flour so she stood to one side of the path to let them pass, receiving nothing more than a look of suspicion in return. She sighed and supposed it was natural that those who had lived here all their lives should be wary of a newcomer. It wasn't like the city, where merchants, travellers and pilgrims came and went constantly; these people had their ways and didn't like them to be upset. But hopefully they would grow used to her as time went on. She resolved to be polite and pleasant to all to speed the process.

She heard a rhythmic banging before she saw the source of the sound; the carpenter's eldest son was sitting on the mill's roof mending some shingles, with one of his younger brothers passing things to him from a point halfway up a ladder.

Alys dredged through the many names she had learned in the last few months. Robin the carpenter was a widower, his wife having died in giving birth to their youngest, Barty, five years ago. His eldest was also called Robin, generally known as Young Robin even though he was a grown man. Then there was an unmarried sister, Avice, who kept house; but between them and Barty there was a crowd of nine or ten others whom Alys had not yet succeeded in telling apart, not helped by the fact that at least three of the middle boys all appeared to be called Bert.

However, she was confident in Young Robin's name so she began her new resolution by calling out a greeting to him. He had several nails in his mouth but nodded, while the younger boy stared.

Her business was soon completed, the fee for the milling paid at the door, and she was handed her sack of flour. She checked it over, having been warned early on by Mistress Anne about possible sharp practice, but it was her own with the mark in the corner, it was full and the weight felt about right.

The miller had already disappeared back inside as she lifted the sack a little awkwardly. She had forgotten to bring a spare one: a half-full sack in each hand was much easier to carry than one full one that overbalanced her.

'Hold on there.' Young Robin was sliding down the roof towards the top of the ladder. 'Out the way, Bert.' He landed with a thump and strode over to her. 'You can't carry it like that, you'll hurt yourself.'

Alys stood back as he took the sack. 'Turn round.' He hefted the weight easily and then settled it sideways across her shoulders, pushing two corners forward. 'Now put your hands up and take these.' She grasped one in each hand and was surprised to find how much lighter the flour seemed.

He still had hold of her, making sure she was balanced. 'All right?'

Alys bent her knees, straightened them and took an experimental step. 'Yes. Thank you.'

His hands were still at the top of her arms, gripping them firmly. 'Sure?'

'Yes.' As well as she could under the weight, she gave a slight shrug to indicate that he could now let go, which he did after a pause that was a little longer than she was comfortable with. He stepped away and she set off, aware that he had not climbed back up the ladder but was watching her as she walked.

Once she had rounded the corner and heard the banging noise starting up again, any remaining uneasiness faded. He had only been trying to help. She would get home, and then the afternoon would be spent in making dough and in baking. Edwin would be pleased when he returned, for he loved fresh bread, and she might even use the small packet of cinnamon she had managed to source from the last travelling fair.

———

A delicious smell assailed Edwin's nostrils as he made his way through the darkened garden and opened the door, letting the bright firelight spill out on to the path. But it wasn't bread; it was meat.

Alys was stirring the pot over the fire. 'It was our turn at the slaughter today, so I've started the smoking' – she pointed up at the new hams hanging from the rafters – 'and there's some to eat fresh.' She gestured towards the window. 'There will probably be chicken in the next few days, too – one of the older hens stopped laying well before the others this year, so she's next for the pot.'

Edwin washed his hands and sat in his chair as she placed a bowl and plate down in front of him. 'The bread is old, but it will be fine if you dip it. I couldn't get to the oven today but it won't do the dough any harm to stay overnight.'

The pottage, with the pork to flavour the leeks and barley, was delicious. Edwin savoured it while he watched Hal gulping his down. He felt a momentary pang of sadness as he remembered other boys in other places who had enjoyed a similar healthy appetite, all cold in their graves now, and a shiver passed over him despite the warmth of the fire.

Hal finished his before Edwin had barely started, and looked sorrowfully at the empty bowl. Edwin smiled. 'Might he have some more, do you think?' He had a sudden urge to look after the boy while he could.

Alys, who had younger brothers of her own, seemed to understand. She ladled out some more and put it in front of Hal, who could hardly believe his luck. 'Eat up, now, or you'll never grow up strong like your brother.'

Edwin suppressed a laugh. Ned reminded him of nothing so much as an ox, and the chances of his wiry, lively brother ever resembling him were remote, to say the least. He watched as the boy finished his second portion, finally slowing down as he wiped a last piece of bread around his bowl. Then he sat back with a belch. He looked tired: after the excitement of sitting on his first jury that morning he had spent the whole day in the fields, and the earth was wet and heavy at this time of year.

'Off you go, then. There's still enough firelight about the place for you to see your way home.'

Hal stood, swaying a little. Those cold and tired muscles had warmed into comfort with the food and the fire, and he looked dead on his feet.

'Go on now, before your mother worries. She'll have a fire of her own, and you can lie down to sleep.'

Hal nodded and reached the door. He turned with his hand on the latch. 'Thank you, Mistress. I'll see you at dawn.'

Edwin knew it wasn't the way to get the most work out of labourers, not when you were paying them, but he couldn't help it. 'Leave it until a little after dawn tomorrow.' He was rewarded by a weary smile and a draught of cold air as the door opened and closed.

The evening passed pleasantly, and soon he was drifting off to sleep with Alys in his arms.

He was woken with a jolt by shouts and cries from outside, and then someone started hammering on the door so hard that he thought it might break.

Chapter Three

'All right, all right – I'm coming!'

A rush of cold, damp air hit Edwin as he scrambled out of bed. Alys was by now also awake, looking alarmed. Her hair tumbled about her as she sat up. 'Edwin? What …?'

'I'll go and see. Stay there.'

The thumping was still going on, but the high voice was one he recognised. As Edwin opened the door, Hal half-fell on to him. It was indeed past dawn – it appeared they had all slept in – but there was really no need for the boy to behave like this. He opened his mouth to chastise him, but then saw the look on his face. 'Hal? What's the matter?'

A hand grasped at his shirt. 'It's Ivo, Master Edwin.'

Edwin's irritation at being woken increased. 'What's he done now?' He brushed aside his own question. 'Never mind. Just give me a moment to put something on.' He stamped back into the bedchamber. 'It's nothing. Ivo's done something again and they want me – although who he's managed to upset this early in the morning I don't know.'

Alys was now up, and she passed him his hose and tunic. 'Don't go out half-dressed, then. I'll get the fire going and you can tell me and have something to eat when you get back.'

She was so caring. So adorable. He didn't want to leave his warm cottage, or his loving wife, so suddenly, and certainly not to deal with whatever upset Ivo had caused. His foul mood increased as he walked out of the room while concentrating on fastening his belt, and stubbed his toe painfully on the leg of the table. 'Honestly, one of these days I'm going to kill that man,' he grumbled as he hopped over to the bench and sat down. He pulled on his boots and went out.

'Come, then, what's he done now?'

Hal looked like he was about to burst with the news. 'It's not that, Master Edwin. He's *dead*!'

The world started spinning. Edwin paused to suck in great gulps of the morning air. 'Dead?'

'Yes, Master.'

'Where? How?'

'Where is in his cottage, but Reeve says the how is for you to say. That's why he sent me to fetch you.'

They had been directing their steps to Ivo's unfinished cottage as they spoke, and now they reached it. But what had Ivo been doing here so early in the morning? Surely there were no masons here yet, for they tended to start their day in the castle and then send someone down to the site in the village in the afternoons. Had he come down to inspect it before he started on his other daily duties?

A small crowd had gathered around the doorway, and it parted as Edwin approached, leaving the reeve to greet him. He jerked his thumb. 'In here.'

Edwin followed him inside the half-covered structure, where there was just enough light to see Ivo lying sprawled on the floor. There was no question that he was dead. Edwin touched the wound on the bailiff's head and then looked at the blood on his hand. Suddenly his grumble about killing him didn't seem like quite so much of a joke, and he was glad he hadn't said it in public. But one thing was for sure: this was going to cause trouble for them all.

He turned to the reeve. 'Have someone fetch Sir Roger here before we do anything else.' It wasn't up to him to be ordering around an elected village official, but he'd assumed a tone of authority without thinking, and the reeve did no more than nod and step outside to issue some instructions to Hal. More people had arrived and were crowded around the doorway, but nobody dared to cross the threshold, so Edwin was alone with the body. He crouched once more to examine it.

It seemed as though he had only been there a few moments when he heard the sound of tramping feet outside; Sir Roger's voice ordered the men he'd brought with him to clear the villagers away, and then he entered.

The sight of a dead body was nothing to a knight, and he paused only long enough to cross himself and mutter '*Requiescat in pace*' before he joined Edwin. 'Well?'

'This hasn't just happened – I'd say he's been dead several hours at least.'

Sir Roger looked down on the corpse. 'Agreed. But how?'

'That's also fairly straightforward, I think.' The light had improved further, and he only had to point at the bashed-in right temple and the blood smeared down the side of the face.

Sir Roger knelt and put out a hand to the wound, brushing back a few strands of hair from Ivo's face. 'Yes – that would have killed him at one stroke.' He looked about him. 'But with what?'

Edwin was surprised to find that he too could examine the corpse without feeling sick. How many deaths by violence had he seen in the last few months? He leaned in closer. 'I don't think that's the mark of a bladed weapon, do you? It looks like he's been hit with something blunt.'

'Yes.' Sir Roger pointed at Ivo's head. 'But there's nothing in the wound to say what, and there's no weapon here that I can see.'

'Something smooth, then – not rough like a rock, or bits would have come off it.' Edwin looked about him: as far as he could tell, all the loose stones on the floor waiting to be used in the building were still in the same position they had been when he'd last visited the house. Besides, they were large, square, heavy pieces – very difficult for one man to pick up, and if Ivo had been hit with one, the wound on his head would have been much worse.

There were a few smaller rocks over in one corner; not squared-off pieces worked by the masons, but rather bits that had been dug out of the ground as the foundations were prepared. He picked one up; it was covered in dirt that flaked off when he scratched it. He looked at the wound again: it was unsoiled. 'He's been hit with something smooth, blunt and clean, and by someone else.'

'You're sure?'

'Yes. The wound is to the front and side of his face, so theoretically he could have hit himself with something, by why on earth would he? And if he had, it would still be in his hand, or at least on the ground behind him. No, he's been attacked by someone else who struck the blow and then took the weapon away.'

Sir Roger stood and dusted off his hands. 'Murder, then.'

'I'm afraid so.'

The nearest of those outside had heard the word, and a collective moan went up. *Murder*. In Conisbrough village. Of a nobleman – well, a minor one, but nevertheless an official appointed by the lord earl himself. The consequences would be serious at best, and might end up catastrophic for the whole village, with hangings added to the fines that would be levied.

Sir Roger made no reply. He'd been a little more like himself this morning, and Edwin didn't want him to sink back into his absent state. 'Perhaps we should decide what to do next, before we go back out.'

The knight rubbed his face wearily. The dark circles around his eyes were pronounced. 'We're at peace, so the normal rules must apply, if we still have any such thing as normal rules.'

'Yes. The lord earl must be informed.'

'He's in Lewes, though – that's two weeks' journey even in summer, more like three or four at this time of year, and then the same for someone to get back.' He frowned. 'I know he doesn't like the sheriff, but we'll have to summon him, and then either he or his coroner must come.'

'And where will he be?'

'York, I would imagine. Let me think. That's from here to Pontefract and then about the same again the other side … and then the state of the roads … so if we sent someone this morning, we could expect to have the sheriff here in about a week, God willing.'

Edwin grimaced as he looked at the body. York was much nearer than Lewes, to be sure, but still … 'Will he keep a week? I mean, will we have to bury him before the sheriff gets here?'

'I think so. But you and I can bear witness to what we've seen. And there are local processes as well, surely.'

'There are. But it's the bailiff who's responsible for law and order on the estate.'

'Yes …?' Sir Roger obviously wasn't thinking straight.

Edwin pointed at the corpse. 'Ivo is – was – the bailiff.'

The knight gave a start. 'Oh yes, of course. I was still thinking … anyway, you can make some enquiries, can't you? You're the earl's man, after all.'

Edwin had known full well that this was going to be the reply, but his heart still sank. The likely outcome of any such investigation was that the murderer would be someone he'd known all his life. But his place was to serve the earl as directed, and Sir Roger had the earl's authority for now, so there was nothing for it. 'As you command.'

There was one brighter point, though. 'If we manage to find the culprit before the sheriff gets here, and present him ourselves, it should lessen the consequences for the rest of the village.'

'Yes. Good, go to it, then, and I will pray for your success.'

Sir Roger walked out before Edwin could reply, and Edwin heard him summon the guards and set off towards the castle without addressing the villagers. Marvellous, he thought, why don't you just leave everything to me, and without even announcing that you've given me the authority to do so? But that was unworthy. Sir Roger was of higher rank than he was, and was entitled to act as he saw fit. Edwin would just have to manage.

He knelt for the final time, looking as closely as he could at the body, the wound and the rest of the interior of the house, trying to burn the image on to his mind. Then he said a brief prayer for Ivo's soul, added a couple of pleas of his own, stood, braced himself, and walked out the door to face the waiting crowd.

━━━◆◆◆━━━

Alys had dressed and coaxed the hearth into life, but Edwin had not returned. She selected a large piece from the stack of dry wood in the corner, noting that the pile was getting low; she would have to send

Hal out to the woods for some more before long. She placed it on the fire so it wouldn't go out while she was away, and then went out to see what was going on.

The first thing she heard was the pigs, which hadn't been collected; and the first thing she saw, when she went to check on them, was the swineherd curled up in the corner of their open-fronted shelter. He had his hands over his ears and was rocking back and forth.

Remembering what Edwin had told her about the youth, she approached him and spoke in a gentle tone. 'Gyrth?'

He stopped rocking and looked up at her. 'Blood. There's blood.'

'I know there is. But you don't need to worry – it's nothing for you to be frightened of.'

He held out his hands to her and she could see that they were stained with red. 'Blood.'

Although distressed, he didn't seem violent. She took a step closer. 'Come with me, and I'll help you wash it off.'

He stared at her without moving, so she reached out. 'Come.'

This time he stirred, and she felt her hand being engulfed by his larger one. She let him out of the enclosure, noting that he had been sufficiently aware of himself to fasten the gate after he'd gone in, and led him to the water butt that stood outside the cottage door to catch the rain from the roof. She picked up the broken jug that was kept beside it and scooped up some water, pouring it over his hands as he held them over a nearby patch of grass. She spoke soothing words as she did so, and he remained calm as the last of the red was washed off. Then he held up his hands and looked at them as though he had never seen them before.

'Better?' Alys asked.

'Better.'

'Good. Now, you need to get to work, Gyrth. You need to take the pigs up to the woods. Are you feeling well enough to do that?'

He nodded. 'Pigs. Yes.'

She looked on the ground around them. 'Where's your stick?'

'Dropped it.'

Alys had no idea whether he needed the stick to herd the pigs, or whether he could manage without, but in any case, he could surely find a new one once he was in the woods.

'Never mind. But come on, you can start with ours and collect all the others on your way.' He would have to go in the opposite direction to the part of the village where the slaughtering was being carried out, so with a bit of luck everything would be fine. The reaction of the villagers to him a couple of nights ago had been sympathetic, but she didn't know them well enough to guess when their patience might wear thin. If she could get him going now, just a little later than usual, she might be able to save him further trouble. Especially if they had all been distracted by something else, which seemed to be the case judging by the number of curious people who all seemed to be heading in the same direction. No doubt that was where she would find Edwin.

She watched Gyrth as he set off with their own two pigs and then safely collected two from the next house. He would be all right. But what on earth was going on up the street? She could now see quite a large group collected outside the partially built stone house, men as well as women and children, when surely all had work to do. She heard a kind of groan as she approached, and hoped she wasn't about to find Edwin getting pushed around in the middle of another argument.

She joined the back of the group just in time to see a blonde, well-dressed and strikingly attractive young man come out of the house. Sir Roger, evidently, for someone behind her mentioned the name and murmured about remembering him when he was a little boy. He certainly wasn't one now.

She watched him summon some guards and then move away, but she couldn't see either Edwin or Ivo. She didn't like to try and push her way through the crowd so she stayed where she was and craned her neck. People were looking sombre and whispering to each other, and she began to experience a feeling of unease.

After a few moments Edwin emerged, a worried look on his face. He stood in the open space in front of the doorway and cleared his throat. The chattering subsided.

'Ivo is dead.'

Alys gasped, though this did not seem to come as a shock to everyone else.

Edwin continued. 'There is no doubt that he was murdered.' He paused. 'Sir Roger is sending a man for the sheriff, and he will be here in about a week. In the meantime he's asked me to try to find out what happened.'

The buzz started up again, and this time some annoyance was directed at Edwin. From her position behind them all, Alys could see and hear some protests about why he should be put in charge, but others were saying it was only natural – he worked for the earl and he was Godric's son, after all. Alys tried to mark out and remember those who were openly the most hostile, so she could warn Edwin about it later.

He was gesturing for everyone to be quiet, but he was not entirely successful and he had to raise his voice to be heard. 'Because Ivo was from a noble family, and because this happened here in the village – not in the lord earl's castle – we need to be careful. There will be a fine to pay, at the very least, and we don't want it to be any worse than that.'

That got their attention, and he continued in a more normal tone. 'I know there has been some other trouble here in recent months, but it all happened either in the castle or when the lord earl was at war. Now that there is peace, all the old laws come back into force. The sheriff will want to know all about it when he gets here, so the more we can find out in advance, the better for us. If we can present him with the culprit, even better – it shows we're not all complicit.'

He had carried them with him until that last word, which marked him out again as clever, set apart, not one of them. There were some snorts in front of her about people getting above themselves.

'It must have been someone from outside,' said a firm voice. Alys looked about for the speaker, to see it was Alwin, Hal's father. 'Nobody here would have done this – we didn't like him much, but he was the bailiff and we're law-abiding folk.' There were nods and murmurs of assent so he repeated himself. 'It must have been a stranger – like them outlaws a few months ago.'

Everyone was agreeing, and even starting to put forward suggestions; she heard the word 'masons' spoken more than once. Edwin was losing control. Alys willed him on as he shouted over them once more. 'We don't know that yet. We have to start at the beginning and find out. I'll need to know who saw Ivo and when, and who found the body. I'll need to speak to you all one at a time.'

This provoked more grumbling, but Alys thought that they would go along with him for now, if only because the threat of the sheriff inflicting some kind of collective punishment was frightening.

'What's happening?' The voice from beside her belonged to Father Ignatius, who had appeared silently. 'I've just finished saying Prime and I was on my way to visit the sick. Why isn't anyone at work? Has something happened?'

She told him of what she had seen and heard, a little surprised that a man was dead and nobody had thought to fetch the priest.

He thanked her and moved through the crowd to speak quietly to Edwin, who gestured towards the house. Father Ignatius nodded and moved towards the doorway, stopping to turn and address the crowd. 'Once I have prayed over him I will need two or three men to carry him to the church. I suggest the rest of you get to work, for the sun is already high and it's a day for the lord earl's fields.'

Alys saw the reeve indicating to two others to stay, and then shooing everyone else away. He gave a few directions about who was to go to which field, and said he would be there as soon as he could. Edwin and the priest disappeared inside the house.

The crowd was thinning and Alys wasn't quite sure whether to go straight home or to wait for Edwin. She found Cecily beside her, looking sombre and shaking her head. 'Just when I thought Edwin's troubles were over.'

Alys tried to remain calm. 'He's been asked to find out what happened, but it's not all his responsibility, is it? Not with a knight here and the sheriff on his way? How would the lord earl see it?'

'From what I've gathered before, he'd be outraged at the insult to himself of having his bailiff murdered. If Edwin didn't come up with a quick answer that suited him, he'd hang the nearest obvious candidate and then blame Edwin for not sorting it out.'

'Oh.'

Cecily patted her arm. 'But there's no reason to suppose he won't find out, especially if he's got a week to work on it.' She sighed. 'I don't think William will be able to help him much, but we'll all do what we can.'

Thinking of Edwin's uncle, Alys said, 'Your pardon – I haven't seen William for a few days and I should have asked first. How is he?'

Cecily's eyes were sad. 'He tries to hide it, but the pain grows worse. Last night he barely made it home from the castle, and this morning he was off well before dawn so that nobody should see the struggle he has getting up the hill.'

Their conversation was cut short by the emergence of Edwin and Father Ignatius from Ivo's house. The priest nodded to the waiting men and they went in to fetch the body. Father Ignatius made the sign of the cross over it as they passed him, and told them to lay it in the church and ask his housekeeper for a shroud.

They all watched as the melancholy procession passed, and then Father Ignatius left and Edwin came over to them.

He took Alys's hand. 'I'm sorry you had to see that.'

She tried to appear cheerful. 'I've seen the dead before.'

It was the wrong thing to say, for it evidently reminded him of that terrible day in Lincoln, and he burst out, 'Yes, but I'm supposed to be *protecting* you from all that sort of thing now!'

She slipped her arm through his. 'I'm all right, truly. Now, come and have something to eat while you consider how best to start what you must do.'

He looked at her gratefully, and they bade good day to Cecily and went home.

Edwin's mind was shouting at him from all directions as he entered the cottage and sat down. He ate whatever it was that Alys put in front of him while he tried to think through the best course of action. As ever, the main question would be *why*, but he couldn't start to work on that until he had some more of the details on *when* and *how* and *who*.

He had heard Alwin's statement that the culprit must be a stranger, and he would very much like that to be true, but he couldn't discount anything at this stage – and especially when Ivo had been so markedly and publicly disliked by everyone in the village. As soon as he asked himself who might have had a grudge against the bailiff, he could come up with at least half a dozen plausible candidates. But were any of them really capable of murder? It seemed impossible. But if recent experiences had taught him anything, it was that –

Alys was saying something to him.

He made an effort. 'I'm sorry, my love, I didn't catch that.'

'I said, how can I help?'

'Help? No, no – I don't want you involved in this. It might turn out to be dangerous.'

'Life is dangerous, Edwin, and I should know.'

He shook his head. 'I might not be able to protect you from everything, but I can keep you away from this.' She started to protest and he held up his hand. 'I said no. And that's an end to it.'

She picked up his bowl and he heard it bang down hard on the sideboard. But he was already back in his thoughts and halfway to the door. 'I'll be back later.'

It was only after he was down the path and out the gate that he realised it was the first time he'd ever left the house without kissing her. He hesitated over whether to go back, but decided against it. He could talk to her about it later, and right now he had matters of life and death to think about.

His steps directed him to the castle, and he found himself in the outer ward before he had really thought about it. The news had spread by now, and he was soon surrounded by curious men asking him what was going on. He waved them away as best he could and headed first for the stables.

Edwin had, himself, last seen Ivo at around noon the day before, when they had spoken at the meal table in the inner ward. The body had been found this morning – *by whom? I must find that out* – and Ivo had probably been dead since sometime in the night. That left all of yesterday afternoon and evening unaccounted for.

He found Arnulf, the stablemaster, mucking out a stall, and was a little taken aback. 'You don't normally do that yourself, do you?'

Arnulf stopped and leaned on his shovel. 'Not often these days, no. But we're short-handed what with so many having gone with the lord earl, and besides, the work keeps a man warm in this weather.'

'Can I distract you from it for a moment?'

'Of course.' He whistled, and a groom appeared. He handed over the shovel. 'Here, finish this stall and the next one.' He led Edwin back outside, where the smell wasn't quite so overpowering. 'I heard,' he said, succinctly. 'What can I do?'

'I'm trying to find out what Ivo did and where he went between me last seeing him and … well, you know. I saw him at noon. Did he go out after that? Did he take a horse?'

Arnulf nodded. 'He did. About an hour after noon. Said he had business on the estate further out of the village.'

'Do you know where?'

'No. Not my place to ask, is it? The bailiff says he needs a horse and I get him one.'

'When did he come back?'

Arnulf took off his cap and used it to wipe his brow, which was sweaty from his exertions. 'Didn't see him, but the bay he took were back by dark, so it must have been before then.'

Good. That narrowed things down a little, at least. Edwin made a note to himself to see if anyone had seen the direction Ivo had taken. Or maybe he had left something that might indicate exactly where he had been – some notes or a record of payment. He would have to …

Arnulf was still looking at him. 'Anything else?'

'Oh, thank you, no, not for now. Don't let me keep you.'

'Not all that much to do this morning, once we're cleaned out. Sir Roger's horse needs getting ready – he'll want to go out like usual – but not much else. We're short-handed, like I said, with the lord earl being away, but of course that also means we're short of mounts, too. There's just the –'

Edwin had no desire to get drawn into a detailed conversation about horses. 'Sir Roger? He'll go out today?'

'Oh yes, every day. With patrols, as you'll know, but he also likes to get out on his own as well.' Arnulf smiled. 'Taught him to ride, I did, when he were little. And all the others, and the lord earl himself too, as a lad. Fine horseman.'

'Sir Roger?'

'The earl. Well, of course Sir Roger weren't bad either – always nicely balanced, though Sir Geoffrey had some problems with him at first, what with –'

He was interrupted by a call from one of his underlings. 'Anyway, best get on. Let me know if you need me for anything else.' He clapped Edwin on the back and disappeared inside the stable.

Edwin made his way up to the inner ward, where the day porter on the gate confirmed everything Arnulf had already said about Ivo, adding the detail that he had seen him return at dusk, but was equally ignorant of where the bailiff had actually been.

'And you didn't see him go out again?'

'No.'

'And you were on duty until when?'

'This time of year, about an hour after sunset – otherwise Warin's hours are too long.'

Edwin didn't relish having to speak to the night porter, Warin, who was in a permanently foul mood, and he certainly wasn't about to wake him up in the middle of the morning to ask. He would come back later to find out when Ivo had left again.

He had already made several notes to himself in his head. If he kept on this way he would be in danger of forgetting something important – he should write it down.

He was halfway across the ward when he remembered, again, that the steward's office was no longer there – it had been at the far end of the great hall, and had been demolished along with the rest of it. Many men had expressed regret about the hall, but for Edwin the wrench of losing the office had been even greater; he had spent many hours and days of his youth in there, helping his uncle William Steward with his accounts and inhaling the scent of the expensive spices that were kept locked away under his watchful gaze. The absence of the familiar space had only served to intensify the feeling of disconnect he had felt since returning home.

There would, in due course, be a new office as part of the rebuilt hall, but for now William was carrying out his duties from a room in the castle's household quarters, so Edwin turned to make his way there.

William was sitting at a table with various heaps of parchment and coins stacked in front of him, concentrating, and he didn't look up. Edwin caught the eye of young Wulfric, the boy who ran messages for him, who was perched on a stool in the corner, and put a finger to his lips, ensuring he could watch his uncle for a few moments before his presence was noticed. William was sweating, despite the cool day and the lack of a fire in the chamber, and a wince of pain escaped him every time he shifted in his seat. The twisted left leg was the legacy of a battle injury from years ago – as was the horrific facial scarring that frightened people when they met him for the first time – and he had limped and trailed it along ever since Edwin could remember. The problem now was that earlier in the year he had fallen down the stairs outside the keep and broken his other leg, meaning he could hardly walk at all; he had been bedridden for weeks. Terrified of ending up an object of pity (or, in his own rather stronger words, a 'useless cripple') and of losing his position and his livelihood, he had dragged himself up far too early with the help of a pair of crutches.

However, even that had offended his sense of dignity, so – against the advice and entreaties of his wife – he had put them aside and started using a single stick, such as anyone might carry. But neither leg was strong enough to compensate for the injury to the other, and he had been in ever-increasing pain during the autumn. He left his house in the village before dawn every day to force himself up the hill, often collapsing in gasping, grey-faced agony as soon as he reached his office, and he stayed there until after dark before struggling home. And through it all he kept the pain stamped down within him, clenched between his teeth, no word of complaint. Nobody except Cecily dared to say anything to his face or to express any sympathy, and Edwin wasn't about to start now. But if things continued the way they were going, he wasn't sure William would last another year.

He took a few steps back and then approached the doorway loudly to make it look as though he'd just arrived, and William looked up. The expression of irritation that had been forming died on his lips. 'Edwin, come in, lad. I thought for a moment you were another from the kitchen. How much ginger is that man planning to get through, with the lord earl not even in residence?'

Commenting on William's long-standing feud with the cook wasn't a great idea at the best of times, so Edwin made no reply. He pulled up another stool. 'Have you heard the news?'

William put down his pen. 'Ivo? Got himself killed, did he?'

'Yes. Between sunset last night and sunrise this morning. Sir Roger has sent for the sheriff but he wants me to look into it in the meantime.'

'Good. No doubt you'll sort it all out before he gets here, which will be all to the good.'

Edwin wished he could share his uncle's confidence. 'I've got too many things going through my head. Have you got any spare parchment? Old bits that have been scraped will be fine.'

'Over there.' He managed a smile, rare these days. 'You can have them if you add up these wine accounts for me.'

Edwin replied with the old conspiratorial grin and then pulled the lists over. He could never understand how other people just couldn't see numbers the way he did; the pennies, shillings, marks, gallons and tuns simply lined themselves up in his head and he had written the totals at the bottom of each column almost before William could explain what he needed.

He handed them back and William glanced at them one by one. 'I could check all this, I suppose, but there's not much point – you've never been wrong before. Take your parchment, then, and there's ink there. You can stay here or go somewhere else, as you please, but I've men coming in for wages soon, so there will be talking. Wulfric, fetch the first lot in.'

Edwin briefly considered the peace of working in the keep's empty council chamber, but he didn't want to sit up there on his own in the dark just at the moment. He could block out the noise here and remain in the company of the living. He shifted to the second table in the corner, pushed its scattered contents to one side, and set about recording what he already knew.

It wasn't much, and there were still men queueing up to receive their coins when he'd finished. He reviewed his rather scratchy penmanship. Ivo had been murdered sometime in the night, by being hit with some kind of smooth, blunt object. He was in his partly built stone house in the village, a place that anyone could enter freely because there was no door. Anyone in Conisbrough could therefore potentially have done it, unless they were verifiably inside the castle walls at that time. Equally, anyone else could have entered the village and done it, for there was no fence or gate. On the contrary, as the village was a fair site and the castle needed provisioning from miles around, the arrival of strangers was not an uncommon occurrence.

Edwin had personally seen Ivo antagonise the reeve and the master mason, but his performance at the manor court had angered virtually everyone else in the village as well, so that was not much help.

He sighed. In short, almost anyone could have had reason to do away with the bailiff, and almost anyone could have had the opportunity to carry through with it.

Was there anyone he could eliminate? He picked up his pen again. Children? Yes. The elderly and infirm? Yes. Well, probably. Women? He hesitated. Maybe. But some of the goodwives of the village could pack a hefty punch when their husbands were drunk or unruly, so he wouldn't discount them all straight away.

He wasn't getting very far here. He stood and pushed his way out past the line of men; William looked up long enough to give him a brief nod, and Edwin was struck again by the lines of pain etched on his face. Another thing to worry about.

Once outside, he made his way over to the masons' work area. He caught Philippe's eye and beckoned him over.

The master mason spoke first. 'A bad business.'

'It is, and I'm trying to work out what happened before the sheriff gets here.'

'A good idea. And this sheriff, he will dispense justice? The penalty here for murder is death?'

'It is. Which is why I want to make sure we have the right man.'

Philippe nodded. 'If I can be of any help …'

'It would be useful to know if you or any of your men heard or saw anything. For example, when did you last see Ivo?'

'I, personally? That would be yesterday, around noon. I think I saw you speaking to him at the dining table, and then when I looked some time later he was there alone again, and then he left the ward. I don't know where he went after that.'

Edwin nodded. 'That fits in with what I've heard already. Arnulf – the stablemaster – said he rode out yesterday afternoon and then came back before nightfall. I don't suppose you saw him after that?'

Philippe shook his head. 'No. But Denis was down working at his house in the afternoon – he might know more.' He looked towards the men working under the canopy, and then up at the others on the hall's wooden scaffolding, where Denis was nowhere to be seen. 'Hmm. He will be around somewhere.'

'And after dark? You don't sleep up here in the ward, do you?'

'No, we have our lodgings outside the walls, down between the gardens and the edge of the field. We have our own cooking fires, and it's only a short walk to the river for water.'

Edwin's heart sank. So the whole lot of them had been outside the castle walls – and away from the eye of the night porter – during the night when Ivo was killed. And, of course, Ivo had argued with them frequently.

'I see what you are thinking, my friend. But dealing with difficult clients has always been a part of our work. We discuss, we dispute, we get on with it.' He added, drily, 'If we started killing everyone who criticised our work, we would not be in business very long.'

That did sound reasonable to Edwin, but then again, he had heard reasonable statements from murderers before now, so he was ruling nothing out. There was one thing he should add in the meantime, though. 'I should warn you. The villagers are scared that the murderer will turn out to be one of them, and talk has already started that it must be an outsider or a foreigner.'

'And we masons are all the former, and some of us are also the latter.' He stopped suddenly and let out an oath. Edwin wondered at such a reaction, but then realised Philippe was staring over his shoulder. 'I think your warning comes too late.'

Denis was approaching from the direction of the gate, dishevelled and with blood streaming down his face from a cut on his temple.

Edwin exclaimed and ran over to him, followed by a crowd of masons who jostled around, demanding to know what had happened.

Denis gestured to them to calm down and then spoke to Philippe and Edwin in rapid French. 'It's nothing, I'm not hurt. A stone caught me, that's all.'

Edwin was horrified. 'Someone threw a stone at you?'

'Yes. There was a group of them, they were all talking in English so I'm not sure what they were saying. I think I heard "Ivo". And your word for *guerre* is "war", is it not?'

Philippe looked grimly at Edwin. 'Outsiders and foreigners. And some of us from a country you have recently been at war with, although that had nothing to do with us. We have been here since before Prince Louis arrived, and anyway, we understood he had been invited.'

It was more complicated than that, but Edwin didn't feel that this was the right time to explain it all. 'I will go down to the village and explain that this behaviour is unacceptable. I'll get Father Ignatius and Sir Roger to back me up.'

Denis had now been passed a rag and was wiping the blood from his face. '*Merci*, Edouin.'

Edwin turned to leave, but Philippe laid a hand on his arm. 'My thanks also. But I believe that this is only going to get worse. I hope you can find the culprit before more violence is committed.'

So do I, thought Edwin. *So do I.*

Chapter Four

Alys felt hot tears prick at her eyes as she stared at the back of the door. But she could not – would not – let them fall, however tempting it was to go back in the chamber, throw herself on the bed and sob her heart out. She told herself over and over again, as she made the bed, as she swept the floor, as she tended to the fire, that Edwin meant well, that he was only trying to look after her in the best way that he could. But it still stung that he had not discussed it with her as an equal, that he had simply issued an order as though she were a child. Or a wife.

The dough had been waiting long enough; she had to get it to the oven. She dashed some cold water on her face, hoping her eyes didn't look too red, and made sure her hair was covered. She hadn't yet got used to the wimple of a married woman, finding it restrictive around her face and throat, but the simple headscarf that kept the hair off her face while leaving much of it uncovered was no longer appropriate. She had to leave childish things behind.

The cold, fresh breeze revived her a little as she stepped out of the house. She carried the tray across the green to the welcoming warmth of the oven, where a group of other women were already assembled. They had been quicker – probably because they hadn't stopped to argue with their husbands and then do some angry housework to calm down – and they were on the verge of sealing it, but someone saw her coming and they waited.

Agnes, the priest's ancient housekeeper who was also the village midwife, and who was therefore respected by all, held the oven door open with a stick. 'Have you marked your loaves, dearie? Good, good. Just about room for them there.'

Alys placed her loaves on the flat paddle and used it to manoeuvre the dough inside. Once the door was shut, it was sealed and they all stepped back. The bread would be ready at around noon, and they wouldn't stay here to wait for it, but the group didn't disperse as quickly as it normally did.

There was only one topic of conversation. 'Fancy him getting himself murdered. Did it just to spite us all, I shouldn't wonder.'

Alys hovered. She didn't know any of them well enough to join in or interrupt their conversation, but maybe she could pick up something that might be useful to Edwin – if he would listen to her – and besides, he could hardly claim she was doing anything dangerous by standing around the oven chatting with other women.

'But what will it mean for the oven, now?' asked one. 'Will we get to keep this one?'

Agnes shook her head. 'You should have worse things to worry about.'

'What could be worse than having to pay to bake bread?'

'Many things. None of you remember some of the things that happened here years ago – oh, it would have been back in the reign of old King Henry. Crimes, houses burned. And some of them Normans hurt or killed.'

One of the others – Hal's mother – waved her hand dismissively. 'That was a long time ago. Nobody cares about that now.'

Agnes pointed at her. 'You might not think so. But when lords and nobles get hurt, the rest of them come down hard. The sheriff and his men, the Normans – they come here and they don't care who did it, they just punish the whole village. A fine that takes all you have. Hangings. Any man they can find, or a whole group of them.'

She continued, addressing them all now in her wavering tone. 'You'd better look out for your husbands when the sheriff gets here, and hide your sons away, because he'll have them all swinging before you can open your mouths to say anything. And if you try to make a fuss or fight back, he'll just hang some more.'

She had their attention. Avice, the carpenter's daughter, spoke with a shaking voice. 'Is there anything we can do?'

Agnes's speech had cost her much energy, and now she looked slumped and old. 'Pray. Pray that Godric will find out what happened, and pray that someone will listen to him.'

Hal's mother rolled her eyes. 'Godric is dead, Agnes. He died in the spring, remember? All we've got now is …' her eyes fell on Alys and she stopped. 'Well, anyway, I can't stand here talking – I've got work to do.'

The group started to disperse, sombre and talking in low voices. Alys stood for a moment and then followed Avice, meaning to speak to her father.

The carpenter's workshop was an open-fronted building attached to the side of his house and facing the green. He was in there, chiselling at something with a look of concentration on his face, while one of his sons swept up shavings. The youngest boy, Barty, was sitting on the ground just outside, playing with some odds and ends. It looked quite damp there and Alys resisted the urge to move him somewhere drier.

Avice walked straight past her father and brothers without even looking at them, and entered the house. She must have a lot to do, with all those siblings and no mother. There were two other girls in the family, but they were among the younger ones, so the brunt of it must fall on her.

Robin didn't look up from his work, so Alys waited, worried that if she disturbed him he might make a mistake with what he was doing. After a short while the boy doing the sweeping, with fewer scruples, called to him. 'Father! Customer here.'

'What?' He looked up from his close work and took a moment to focus on Alys before speaking rather quickly. 'Oh. Good day. What can I do for you? Got some new bowls here that the lads have just finished, if you need any?' He gestured to a stack.

'Thank you, no. I came to ask you about building a loom inside our house.'

'A loom?' He paused, a look of incredulity spreading over his face. 'But that's just two uprights and a horizontal bar. Surely even Edwin could manage …' Belatedly he realised he was about to do himself out of a bit of business. 'Or I can send Bert here over to do it for you. Simple job.'

Alys looked closely at the boy, reasonably certain he wasn't the same one she'd seen at the mill the day before. But that was no matter. 'No, that's not what I mean.' She'd seen some very simple looms of the type he described in other houses in the village: just like a door-frame, with warp threads hanging from the top bar and weighted at the bottom to keep them taut. But although these were all right on a very basic level, they produced a very inferior grade of cloth – not one she would really even consider for blankets, never mind clothes. What she had in mind was not quite as complex as the ones that had been housed in her father's weaving sheds back at h–, back in Lincoln, but certainly a step up from anything she had seen here.

She began to describe to him what a horizontal loom looked like, and at first he nodded, but by the time she got to beaters, shaft bars and treadles she could see that he was losing his way.

He spoke a little dubiously. 'Never made anything like that before. Reckon you could draw it, if I send Robin over later with a board and a bit of charcoal?'

'I could try. And if you're willing to make something new to you then I'd be very grateful. And of course I'm happy to pay properly to make sure it's right.'

He brightened; after all, he did have all those mouths to feed. 'That's settled then. Robin's finishing on the mill roof today. If he's back before dark I'll send him round; if not, tomorrow morning.'

Alys thanked him and watched as he turned back to his chiselling – something quite fine-looking; perhaps it was for the castle – and was soon absorbed. As she left she smiled down at little Barty, who was trying his best to emulate his father. He had a tiny knife, and now, instead of using it to whittle, he put the point into an offcut of wood and hit the handle with a hammer that had a very dirty round head. That certainly wasn't a toy, and she wondered if he would get into trouble when his father found out that he'd pilfered a tool from the workshop.

Anyway, the subject of the loom had been raised, and the bread was baking. The rain was still holding off, so she decided to get some work done in the garden while she could.

⸻

Edwin was about to leave the masons, Philippe's warning ringing in his ears, when a thought occurred to him. He turned to Denis. 'What were you doing in the village just now? Were you working on Ivo's house?'

'No. Philippe had said that we should stop work on it until we know more. After all, the lord may not want it built now.'

Edwin waited for more, but needed to prompt him. 'So …?'

'I lost one of my tools,' Denis confessed, glancing at the master mason shamefacedly. 'The hammer I was showing you the other day, in fact. When I was last down there, the bottom fell out of my bag and the tools scattered in the straw. I thought I had picked them all up but later I saw it was missing.'

'And did you find it?'

'No. It was gone. So maybe I dropped it somewhere else, or maybe someone has taken it.' He turned to Philippe. 'I can borrow another for now, so it won't affect my work.'

Philippe made a tutting noise, but all he said was, 'See that you do. And, to be fair, you are normally careful, so let this be the first and only time.'

Denis nodded and, after a pause during which Edwin did not speak, he moved away. Philippe also returned to his work, leaving Edwin standing in the ward thinking about a hammer. A hammer with a smooth round head. One that would be heavy enough to inflict a fatal crushing blow, if swung with force, but that had no corners or sharp edges to cause a jagged cut.

The body had only been taken to the church that morning; Father Ignatius couldn't possibly have buried it yet. Edwin made his way out of the castle and down the rutted path.

It was dark and chill inside the church, which made Edwin wonder, again, why Ivo might have wanted a house made of stone. He approached the body, which was lying on a trestle table, and pulled back the cloth. Someone had closed the eyes since he had last seen it, but otherwise all was the same. He bent to examine the wound more closely, but was hampered by the lack of light; the few small windows didn't let in much at the best of times, and on a gloomy day like today they were virtually useless.

He borrowed the candle that was burning on the altar – a good one, as the church received an allowance of them from the earl – and placed it on the table near Ivo's head, where it cast a steady light.

Now he could see more clearly, and what he observed confirmed his impression from early that morning. The right temple had been hit with a force that had dented the skull beneath it, but there was no sharp cut and no other residue around the wound. Blood had dripped both downwards and sideways from the injury – Edwin thought about it for a moment and then visualised the bleeding starting while Ivo had been standing upright, and then continuing as he lay on his back on the ground.

But the blood hadn't just dripped. Now he was looking in better light Edwin could see that it had been smeared. Were those the marks of fingers? He thought they were. Perhaps Ivo had put a hand up to his head after he'd been hit.

Edwin pulled the cloth away from the rest of the body and picked up Ivo's lifeless right hand. But the long, slim fingers were as clean as they had been when he'd seen them at the dining table. Odd. He moved to the other side, but the left hand was similarly unblemished. He went back to the head. Yes – now he had thought of fingermarks, he could see that that was exactly what they were. Someone who wasn't Ivo had touched the injury after it had been inflicted. The murderer maybe? To check that he really was dead?

A footstep sounded behind him and he started. It was Father Ignatius. 'Are you praying, my son, or working?' He came forward.

'The latter, Father, though I should do the former as well before
I leave.' He felt the warmth of the priest's bulk as they stood side by
side looking down at the body.

Father Ignatius sighed. 'Yes. Another life gone before its allotted
span, although in this case …'

'What do you mean?'

The priest made a helpless gesture. 'Murder is a mortal sin and an
affront to God. But I can't help wondering if this was the Lord's plan
all along, in order to save others from starving.'

Edwin was taken aback. 'Surely you don't …'

'As I say, I don't know. I cannot know. But the Lord has worked in
mysterious ways before and will no doubt continue to do so. I will
pray for guidance.'

'So will I.'

'Shall we do that now? If you have finished?' Father Ignatius started
to arrange the shroud over the body once more.

'Yes, for now. When will he be buried?'

'I'd like to do it as soon as possible, but I will leave it until Monday
in case any relatives come forward with a request to take him home.
Do you know if he had any family?'

'No. And now you come to mention it, that's something I should
check.' Monday. That would give him tomorrow and Sunday in case
he needed to come back and check anything else. And in this cold
weather – and in this cold church – the body would keep until then.

'If you find anything, let me know. In the meantime, I will have
Agnes wash him and lay him out properly. If anyone does turn up
after he's buried, they can at least claim his clothes.' He pointed at
the braiding around the wrist he was tucking in under the shroud.
'That's a very fine tunic, and it would be a shame to let it go to waste,
especially if the winter is cold.'

Satisfied that the body and its covering now looked neat, he made
the sign of the cross and began to pray. Edwin closed his eyes and tried
to join in, but it was Ivo's corpse, not his soul, that was uppermost in
his mind.

The rain had started again by the time he left the church. It was early afternoon and he hadn't had anything to eat yet; the meal up at the castle would be over by now, but maybe Alys could find something for him at home.

Alys. With a sudden lurch he remembered the way they had parted that morning. His footsteps slowed as he reached the gate, but then the delicious smell of new bread hit him. He walked briskly up the path and opened the door.

Alys was by the table, laying out the loaves to cool. She turned in surprise as she heard the door – it was unusual for him to come home in the middle of the day, after all – and then they both stood for a long moment without speaking.

'I'm sorry –'

'I didn't mean –'

They both stopped. Alys gestured for him to continue.

Edwin stepped forward. 'I didn't mean to shout at you earlier. I just … what I mean is, seeing that body. Here. In Conisbrough. I know you've seen danger before, but not here. I just want to keep you safe. The thought that somebody might be …' He broke off, unable to continue.

He felt her small hand in his. 'I know, and I'm sorry too. You're my husband, and you promised to protect me. But …'

'But what?'

She sighed. She grasped his other hand as well and looked up into his face. 'But I'm bored, Edwin. I'm *bored*. How would you like to be in this cottage all day every day, with only trips to the well and the oven to break it up, and even then nobody speaks to you?'

'I'd hate it. But then, I'm not a –' He stopped just in time.

She raised her eyebrows. 'And I should know my place, should I?'

'That wasn't what I –'

'Yes, it was. But look.' Her hands were gripping his quite tightly now. 'I don't mean that I'm unhappy – far from it. I love you, I love our home, I enjoy taking care of it for you. But it's just not enough.'

He was about to reply when his stomach gave a loud rumble.

It broke the tension and Alys smiled. 'Well, this isn't looking after you very well, is it? Did you not have your dinner up at the castle?'

'No, I was too busy and by the time I noticed I was hungry they would have cleared it all away. And I wasn't so desperate that I'd risk asking Richard Cook for something outside of hours.'

She led him to the loaded table. 'Plenty to choose from. Pick which one you want to start and I'll wrap the others to keep for the week.'

The smell of the three loaves nearest to him was unmistakeable, so he picked up the smallest and tore off a piece. It was still warm inside. 'I love cinnamon.'

'You have a very good nose for spices. My father would just eat whatever I put in front of him without even noticing.'

Edwin spoke through a mouthful of meltingly soft bread. 'I spent half my childhood in an office full of them, don't forget. You soon learn which is which.' He finished half the loaf and reluctantly put the rest down. 'Better not eat it all at once – there won't be another spice trader here until the spring.'

She wrapped it, along with the others, and stacked them carefully in the bread basket in the cool northern corner of the house. Then she came to sit next to him, with a level stare.

He'd hoped that he'd got away with it, but evidently not. 'I suppose this is all quite different from what you did before, running your father's shop as well as the house.'

'Yes. And I need to occupy myself more, do something else on top of looking after the house. And now this – I thought I could help you.' He felt himself shaking his head, but she continued. 'I don't mean that I would put myself in danger. But, for example, I might hear and see things while I'm out and about in the village, and might that not be useful?'

'Gossiping at the well? You think that will help?'

'Men do it too – groups of them standing around the carpenter's workshop or the smithy – but nobody calls it gossiping when it's men.'

She sounded cross. He would need to tread carefully. 'Maybe …
but only that, mind – you mustn't go out trying to track down
someone who's killed once and might do so again.'

He was still a little hesitant, but she jumped straight in. 'I agree to
your terms of business. And while we're both here – I don't mean
only just now; I mean in the evenings when you come home – you
can tell me what you've found out and we can talk about it together.'

He couldn't see too much potential danger in that. 'All right. In
fact, let's start now.' He pulled out the sheaf of notes from his scrip and
laid them on the table; they wouldn't be any use to her, of course, but
he could use them to help marshal his thoughts while he spoke.

Edwin went through everything he knew so far. For most of it she
merely nodded or agreed, but when he spoke of the actual body she
put up a hand. 'Wait.'

Of course, maybe she didn't want to hear the details – it might be
too distressing. But that wasn't it. 'The wound on his head. You're sure
about where it was?'

'Yes, of course. I've seen the body twice now. Why?'

She got to her feet. 'Stand up a moment.' He did so. 'Now, imagine
you've got something in your hand and you want to cause a wound
in exactly the same place you've just described.'

Edwin didn't like to be even pretending to hit her, but he obedi-
ently raised his right hand as though wielding a weapon. And then, of
course, he saw what should have been obvious all along. 'The wound
is on the wrong side.'

'Yes. And if, as you say, it's on the front of his head, he's unlikely to
have been struck from behind, isn't he?' She turned around and he
saw the impossibility of such an action. It would be a very awkward
way to strike a blow; he'd have to reach right round her and then
strike backwards.

She turned again. 'So the only viable explanation is –'

'That he was hit by someone holding the weapon in his left hand.'
He nodded. 'Why didn't I see that before?'

She smiled. 'Too many other things to think about, I would guess. And besides,' – more soberly – 'looking at someone who's been murdered, someone you knew, is enough to stop you thinking properly about anything.'

She tried to turn away to hide it, but her lip was trembling and her voice was unsteady. He put his arms around her, murmuring words of comfort. She clung to him for a few moments but then stepped away, wiping her eyes. 'I'm being silly.'

'You're not, you're really not.' He wiped a stray tear from the side of her face with the cuff of his tunic.

She nodded and, with some effort, spoke more normally. 'So, what now?'

'I have plenty more enquiries to make – I need to see the night porter at the castle, though I can't do that until later, and I also don't know yet who it was who found the body.' He paused. 'And while I'm doing all that, I suppose I should also look out for anyone who favours his left hand.'

'I can do that too.' Edwin opened his mouth to speak but she forestalled him. 'I can easily do it without anyone knowing it, and if I do see anyone, I won't speak to them, I'll just tell you at some time when we're alone.'

Once more Edwin found himself persuaded by the very reasonableness of what she was saying, although he wasn't quite comfortable with how he was being carried along. 'All right. And on that subject, why don't you tell me about everything you've done and seen since early this morning.'

It was almost a reverse of the earlier part of their conversation; he nodded and agreed, and then held up a hand. 'Stop there.'

That confused her – she evidently thought she was just giving inconsequential details about her visit to Robin the carpenter. But she hadn't made the connection with something he'd said. 'Barty was playing with tools?'

'Well, yes. I just noticed because –'

'And the hammer he had in his hand definitely had a round head? I mean, not round like a ball, but round like a pipe or like a cone with the point cut off?'

'Yes.'

He smiled. 'You're a genius.' He stood.

'Where are you going?'

'To talk to Robin about a missing stonemason's hammer.'

He kissed her and left the cottage, feeling a little cheered. It was less than a day since the body had been discovered, and he had made good progress already.

Robin was still in his workshop, and Edwin hailed him, looking around the floor for any discarded tools. 'Can I speak to Barty?' he asked. Robin looked incredulous, as well he might; Edwin supposed that not many people came over to talk to his five-year-old. 'I just want to ask him a quick question.'

'Barty! Get out here now!' The bellow could have been heard at the other end of the street, and the boy appeared from behind the house, carrying …

Edwin crouched. 'Hello. Can you show me what you've got in your hand?'

A hammer was held out for his inspection. A hammer with a rounded head. A rounded head that had dried blood all over it.

Edwin heard Robin gasp. 'Where did you get that?' He stepped closer. 'That's not one of mine.' He grabbed the boy's arm roughly. 'Have you been *stealing*?'

Barty started to realise that he was in trouble, and he squirmed. 'No, I didn't …'

Edwin tried to calm the irate carpenter. 'It's all right, I just want to know where he got it from.'

The boy looked from his father to Edwin, trying to work out which was the bigger threat. 'Papa, I didn't steal it. I just found it so I picked it up to use so I could practise.'

Robin was really angry now. He dropped Barty's arm and clouted him hard, knocking him over and making him howl. 'Do you know what they do to thieves? To boys who steal? They chop their hands off, that's what. Do you want that to happen to you?'

Barty was genuinely terrified, and Edwin stepped in between the two of them. 'It's all right. Barty, nobody is going to chop your hand off. Robin, please – I'm not accusing him of stealing, nobody is. I just want to know where he found it, because it might be important.'

'Is there trouble, Father?'

The voice that came from behind Edwin was that of Young Robin, who had appeared with a couple of his brothers in tow. Dusk was starting to fall on this short November day, and they weren't the only ones who were returning from their work. The noise had drawn something of a crowd.

The elder Robin made a visible effort to calm himself. 'No. No trouble. Barty here has taken someone's hammer,' – he raised his hand again, making the little boy cower, but made no move to strike – 'but Edwin has agreed to say no more about it.'

Young Robin, who Edwin couldn't help noticing was much taller and more powerful than himself, grunted. He folded his arms and stood to watch.

Edwin bent once more to the snivelling boy. 'It's all right, Barty, it really is. All I want to know is where you found it, and then I'll take it back and everything will be fine. All right?'

A tentative nod.

'So. You saw it lying about somewhere and you just picked it up?' Nod.

'And where was that?'

'In that house.' He pointed. 'The stone one. Where the dead man was.'

Exclamations of surprise came from the spectators. Young Robin snatched the hammer from Edwin's hand. 'Is that blood?' He held it up for others to see. 'It's covered in blood! This must be what was used to kill the bailiff!' Belatedly he realised what he was saying and looked down in horror at his youngest brother.

Edwin hastened to put matters straight before anything nasty happened. 'Barty is five years old,' he said, loudly. 'There is no possible way he could have struck and killed a grown man – he wouldn't even be able to reach! – and nobody is accusing him of anything.'

Nobody could argue with that, and there were murmurs of assent.

Barty was by now almost paralysed with fear, not really understanding what was happening but aware that a lot of people were looking at him and that something serious was going on. Edwin wasn't sure whether he would get anything else useful out of him, or whether he should come back another time. But he'd give it one last go. 'Now, Barty, I want you to think carefully. When you picked this up from inside the stone house, was there already a dead man lying on the floor?'

Nod.

'And did you see anyone else, apart from the dead man?'

Pause. A shake of the head. An exhalation of breath all round.

'All right. Now, that will do. I'm going to take this hammer – you can't keep it – but you're not in trouble. You're not in trouble for picking it up, and you're not in trouble for anything to do with the dead man. Understand?'

Barty nodded again and then fled to hide behind the skirts of his eldest sister, who had emerged from the house while all this was going on.

Edwin held out his hand for the hammer, still in the possession of Young Robin, who was examining it. 'Not one of ours, Father.' Robin agreed, and Young Robin held it up for others to see. 'Anyone?'

'Isn't that …' Everyone moved to look at the speaker, who turned out to be the reeve. 'Isn't that a stonemason's hammer?'

The murmurs, the rumbling of voices, became louder. Edwin felt he had to take control of the situation. 'It is. But that doesn't mean that one of the masons must have killed Ivo. Den– the man who owns this hammer reported it missing; he dropped it somewhere in the village so anyone might have picked it up.'

'A likely story,' came a cry from the back of the group.

Edwin could feel anger building. He tried to sound as stern as he could. 'Nobody is to take matters into their own hands, you hear?

There is still plenty more work to do to find out who killed Ivo and why.' He gazed at them, trying to look each in the eye. 'I repeat. Nobody is to do anything until I've spoken to Sir Roger. And that includes throwing stones.'

He'd slipped in the reference to a higher authority to bolster his cause, and it seemed to have worked – just. He saw a few nods, and the group started to break up as men made their way home for their evening meal, shaking their heads to each other.

Robin and the rest of his family were called in by Avice, leaving Edwin alone outside the workshop with a bloodied hammer in his hand. He heaved in a juddering breath of relief, realising that he was both shaking and sweating.

Anyway, that made his next tasks clear. As well as talking to the night porter to find out more about Ivo's movements last night, he also needed to show the hammer to Sir Roger, who could bear witness to its condition, and then to Denis and Philippe, to confirm that it was the one Denis had lost. Or claimed he had lost.

The evening meal was in progress up in the inner ward, several braziers lit around the tables against the fast-encroaching darkness. Their light was enough for Edwin to see that Sir Roger was sitting at the head of the table, picking at a dish of something.

Edwin didn't want to disturb his meal, and certainly didn't want to start waving a bloodstained implement around in front of everybody. He took off his hood and wrapped it around the hammer, putting it down by his feet as he slipped into a place at the lower end of the table. He hadn't intended to eat, but all he'd had today was that bit of cinnamon bread, and the vegetable pottage being doled out smelled enticing, though he passed on the Friday eel stew. He ate without taking his eyes off Sir Roger, and as soon as the knight had finished Edwin left the remainder of his meal – the trencher gratefully appropriated by his neighbour – and went to him. 'May I have a word?'

'Of course. How have you got on today?'

The men around were still concentrating on their food, but Edwin didn't want to risk saying too much out loud in case he started off more as-yet unnecessary bad feeling. 'Perhaps we could go somewhere else?'

'That well, already? Let's go into the keep.'

There were torches on the walls all the way up the stairwell, but the council chamber was in complete darkness. Sir Roger groped around for a candle, went out into the passage to light it, and returned to place it on the table. 'Now.'

Edwin placed his parcel in the small pool of light and unwrapped it. Once he'd explained everything, Sir Roger agreed that this must be the murder weapon and said he would be happy to bear witness to that effect.

'So, this is the weapon. But who wielded it?'

'That is the main question, of course. But first things first – we should trace where it's been. Tomorrow, if you are agreeable, I will take it to Denis and Philippe and ask them if it is the same one Denis says he lost. I am certain that it is, but I want to see their faces while they look at it.'

'All right. But in the meantime, I don't think you should be carrying it around with you – or keeping it in your house, for that matter. Leave it with me here, and then come and find it in the morning.'

'Very well.'

'Good.' The knight stretched, one of his shoulders cracking. 'And now? Are you off home to your pretty wife, whom I have still not met? Or have you time for a game of chess? I hear you were becoming quite skilled while we were away.'

Normally such an offer would have been a great temptation to Edwin, but he shook his head reluctantly. 'I need to talk to the night porter now, while he's awake, and then I must get home, or Alys will worry.'

Sir Roger sighed. 'How nice to have someone who will worry about you. All right, off you go then.'

Edwin left him sitting alone in the cold, shadowy room. Before he had reached the first flight of stairs he heard footsteps crossing the wooden floor behind him, which could only mean that Sir Roger was on his way to the chapel.

Warin, the night porter, was an odd man. Although he had worked at the castle for many years, he was little known – not unnatural, given that he guarded the gatehouse to the inner ward while most other people were asleep, and slept during the day while the place was busy. Edwin wondered what it must be like to live in a world of almost perpetual darkness; Warin only saw the light in the summer months when his shift started before sundown and finished after sunrise.

He was at his post now, sitting by the closed inner gate and warming his hands at a brazier. He stood as he heard Edwin approach and prepared to unbar the small door set into the gate. Edwin didn't think he'd been recognised yet, but of course, letting people *out* of the ward wasn't a problem; Warin certainly wouldn't let anyone in without knowing who it was.

Edwin greeted him quietly as he reached the gate. Warin stood aside without speaking to let him through, and seemed surprised – and not a little irritated – when Edwin stopped to talk.

'Have you heard about what happened to Ivo?'

'Aye. Heard it when I woke up.' He jerked his thumb at the small room in the gatehouse as he spoke, where the day porter was no doubt either asleep or preparing to be so.

'He was killed in the village last night. Do you know when he went out?'

Warin scratched his head as he thought. Time probably meant little to a man who did not see the sun. 'Well, I'd been on duty some while. Place was quiet, everyone asleep apart from whoever was on duty on the walls and the roof. Moon was up.' He spread his hands wide. 'Midnight, give or take? Yes, about halfway through my shift, I reckon, because I remember thinking he'd been out a long while and he hadn't come back. Still hadn't when I knocked off.'

'I don't suppose you know why he went out?'

'Nope. He didn't say and it's not my business to ask. He's the bailiff. Could have been getting an early start, maybe? Because he needed to be out somewhere by dawn?'

Edwin hesitated; he hadn't thought of that. But no. 'That's a good thought but I don't think it's right – I've already spoken to Arnulf and Ivo didn't take a horse.'

Warin grunted. 'Oh well. Must be some other reason, then.' He sounded monumentally uninterested, and Edwin didn't think he'd get much else out of him. He spoke a few words of thanks and stepped through the door, hearing Warin close and bar it behind him as he walked away.

That narrowed down the time when Ivo had been killed – between midnight and dawn – but why, in the name of all the saints, had he left the castle at midnight?

He was engrossed in his thoughts and it took him a moment to realise there was much more activity in the outer ward than there should have been at that time of night. Men were running around; there were cries of alarm. And what was that strange light over the north side of the outer wall?

A man came pounding up the slope, ignoring Edwin, and began to hammer on the inner gate. 'Help! Quick! Raise the garrison!'

He continued thumping. Edwin grabbed him, hearing a grumbling 'All right, all right, I'm coming!' from the other side. 'What is it?'

The man – one of the stable hands, Edwin couldn't immediately recall his name – had a look of panic on his face. 'The masons' camp – it's on fire!'

Chapter Five

Edwin ran as fast as he could down the pitted slope and across the outer ward, where men were already pouring out of the main gate. The masons' camp. It was far enough away from both the village and the castle buildings that the blaze shouldn't spread, but it was made of wood and canvas and the inferno would be intense. Anyone inside one of the lodges would be dead in moments unless he got out.

As he feared, the camp was well ablaze by the time he got there, but efforts to control it were already underway. In between bursts of fiery light he could see figures with buckets running to and from the river, their numbers soon bolstered by those who had come from the castle. In the darkness further out he could make out a group of village men, but they seemed stupefied. He ran over to them. 'Quickly – to the river and we might be able to contain the damage!'

None of them moved.

At first Edwin thought they hadn't heard him, so he repeated himself over the top of the background noise. But still nobody moved.

'Why should we?' came a voice. And 'Serve them right for coming here and murdering our bailiff.' A chorus of agreement.

Despite the fire, Edwin went cold. Surely none of them had …? But there was no time to think of that now. He, at least, could help.

He was darting away when a roar went up from the village group. 'There! That one – it's him!' They surged past him and he caught a glimpse of Denis before he was engulfed by the mob.

Edwin looked around in panic. Where in God's name was the garrison? Surely even Sir Roger would come away from his prayers for a disaster such as this? But there was nobody, so with an oath he threw himself into the press to try to protect Denis as well as he could.

He shouted and flailed as he fought his way through, feeling the heavy blows land on him and grateful that they were only using their fists and not weapons – for now. Denis was on the floor and Edwin tried to shield him, but he was going to be no match for an enraged mob, and indeed he could feel his tunic tearing as someone tried to pull him away.

More voices and shouts, and mercifully the thumps and kicks thinned out and then stopped. He stayed where he was, half-lying on top of the prone mason, arms over his head, while he tried to make out what was going on.

There were cries of pain, and Edwin could see a stick being wielded. He risked uncovering his face to see who it was: William Steward, somehow keeping his balance on both bad legs while he thrashed about him and bellowed the sort of curses he probably hadn't let slip since he was a soldier on campaign many years before.

Part of the weight on Edwin was lifted as a man was hauled off him and bodily thrown aside. His new rescuer proved to be the hulking form of Crispin, the smith.

There was a stand-off of yelling, threats and swearing, while the camp burned in the background behind them. Then the village men – and there were at least a dozen of them – seemed to get a second wind and surged forward. Edwin braced himself for a violent death.

A huge blast from a horn stopped everyone in their tracks. The castle garrison, headed by Sir Roger, had belatedly appeared. At a word from the knight half of them went to aid the increasingly futile firefighting efforts, while the other half, armed with spears and bows, formed up around him.

Sir Roger's voice was calm and level. 'I will give orders to shoot the next man who strikes a blow.' He waited in silence while the villagers stepped back and dropped their arms to their sides.

'See who that is and bring them here,' he said to the sergeant-at-arms, pointing at Edwin and Denis.

Edwin found himself being helped to his feet, and he made a mental inventory. Most of the blows had landed on his back, which was a little stiff, and he'd somehow managed to twist his ankle, which was inconvenient but not, he thought, serious. From what he could see in the flickering darkness Denis was bleeding from the head – although whether it was the same cut from earlier, now re-opened, or a new one, he couldn't tell – and he was holding his side. Both of them limped gingerly over to Sir Roger, who was horrified when he recognised Edwin.

'Who is responsible for this?' he demanded of the villagers.

They all looked at the ground and shuffled their feet, before a voice from the back called out, 'Edwin did it himself, my lord. We all saw it – threw himself at us while we was trying to make a lawful arrest.'

'Arrest?' Sir Roger's voice was sharp now.

Eager to deflect blame, several of the men were now talking over each other, the reeve trying to calm them and have his own voice heard, but the gist of it was that Denis had murdered Ivo and that they were merely apprehending him so he could be brought to justice.

'Justice,' said Sir Roger, drily. 'And just how much of him were you intending to leave in one piece to face the court?' There was silence, so he continued. 'And when Edwin – Edwin, whom I have set to investigating the matter – *quite rightly* intervened, you attacked him too.'

There was more shuffling. 'Didn't know it was him, sir, not in the dark. It could have been anyone trying to stop the arrest.'

Edwin was sure that Sir Roger could see as well as he could that that was a contradiction of what someone else had already said, but he evidently decided that now was not the time to go into it. 'Go back to your homes, all of you. And stay there. We will assemble on the green tomorrow morning and hear the case.'

There was a murmur. The reeve ventured, 'But what if the mason escapes in the meantime, my lord?'

Edwin knew Sir Roger well and saw from his face that he was displeased at being questioned. But nothing came across in his voice as he kept his tone level. 'The man will be taken to the inner ward and kept there under guard until then.'

Nobody could argue with that, so the men started drifting away, the atmosphere thankfully more subdued. Sir Roger spoke in a low voice to Edwin. 'And it will be just as well to guard him for his own safety.'

'You may be right.'

'Now, you? You're not badly injured?'

'No. I'll be fine. I'm not so sure about him, though – may I ask someone to tend to him?'

'Hmm. In some ways it might be better to let him appear while he's still bloodied, so they can get a sense of the seriousness of their actions. But –' seeing Denis wiping his face with his sleeve – 'that would not be Christian. Very well. Send up your wife, or better still Mistress Steward, whom nobody can object to, as soon as it is light. And you come to me at the same time so we can talk this over.'

'Yes, Sir Roger.'

'Now, I'll go and see what damage there is over here, and you can explain to him what's going to happen.' He moved in the direction of the masons' camp. It was now smouldering rather than flaming, but Edwin though that that was probably because the fire had burned itself out rather than because it had been extinguished. Thankfully the earth surrounding it was very wet, so it had not spread towards either the wheat field or the castle garden.

He turned to Denis and explained the substance of what Sir Roger had said.

Denis nodded. 'But, Edouin, I did not do this thing. I did not kill monsieur the bailiff.'

Edwin sighed. He believed Denis at heart, but he was unwilling to commit himself either way while he still had so little evidence. 'Just speak the truth at tomorrow's court. It will be in English, but I'll be there to make sure you can understand what's going on. But for now, please go peacefully with the guards – it will be less trouble.'

'Very well.' Denis turned to Everard, the sergeant-at-arms, and held out his hands in a gesture of compliance. Edwin watched them go: Denis was surrounded by the armed men, but he was not held or bound, so Edwin was satisfied he would reach the inner ward unmolested.

A great weariness came upon him as he stood. Had it only been that morning that he had been summoned, to find Ivo dead? He rubbed his face.

With the fire subsiding it was now almost dark except for the waning moon, but he could just make out a group of women between him and the masons' camp. As he walked over he saw that two of them were Alys and Cecily, tending to a few injured men. He might have known that neither of them would stay safe in their beds if they were needed.

He stopped them long enough to let them know that he was fine. Thankfully it appeared that neither of them had actually seen the violence, busy as they were with their tasks and with the fracas having occurred further away from the light, though Cecily would no doubt hear it from William later. He explained what Sir Roger had said about tending to Denis.

'To be honest I think he's innocent, but even if he isn't, there will be no danger to you – I'll make sure a guard stays with you.'

Cecily waved away his fears. 'Of course I'll tend to him. I'll walk up with William when he goes to work in the morning.'

Edwin nodded. 'Do you want me to stay here now so I can take you home when you're done?'

He saw Alys inspecting his appearance. 'You look shattered. And no doubt you'll be busy tomorrow. We'll be fine: Cecily and I will walk home together, and Father Ignatius is also here,' – she pointed out the priest, whom Edwin had not noticed in the gloom – 'so we'll be perfectly safe.'

Edwin was still hesitating when a rumbling voice from behind him said, 'I'll see them home safe.' It was Crispin the smith, who hadn't yet joined the men now drifting back towards the castle. 'Something isn't right around here. Don't like it. You'll need your wits about you. Get some rest.'

This was quite the longest speech Edwin had ever heard Crispin give, but he was grateful. He looked once more at Alys for confirmation. She leaned in to kiss him and then made shooing noises. 'Go now. I'll be back soon.'

Between them the priest and the smith – spiritual and physical might – would keep the two women safe, and Edwin admitted to himself that he was dead on his feet. Moreover, the bruises that would no doubt soon be visible on his back and ribs were already starting to stiffen. He accepted their assurances and set off home.

He was halfway through the village, which was empty but still awake, when he remembered his suspicions about how the fire had started.

———•———

Alys had been awoken by the sound of shouts from outside. Groggily she realised that she had fallen asleep sitting in Edwin's chair, and that he hadn't come back. An immediate sense of panic overtook her; even if the cries in the streets weren't directly about him, he was sure to be involved in it somewhere.

Someone was knocking at the door. Trying to swallow her fears, Alys opened it to find Cecily, in a hurry and carrying a bag.

'Alys. There's a fire at the masons' camp, and where there is a fire there will be injured men. I have salves here but more hands will be needed. Will you come?'

That wasn't one of the things Alys had been envisaging, but her 'Of course' was automatic as she reached for her shawl. As was the next question. 'Do you know where Edwin is?'

Cecily shook her head. 'No. But William says he saw him earlier in the castle, so we may hope he's still there.'

They joined the crowd from the village heading in the same direction, and Cecily identified a clear space away from danger. Brusquely ordering two of the nearest men to plant their torches in the ground, she began to unpack her bag.

Fortunately, the number of men injured was few and their wounds slight; most of them had managed to get out before the blaze really took hold. There was just one with a serious-looking burn to his face, an English mason who explained that he had been hit by a falling timber. Cecily examined him, warned him that he was going to be in pain for quite some time, and set about treating him, while Alys applied salve to a queue of men with lesser scorches and told those who were coughing and choking to sit down and stay out of the smoke as best they could. Father Ignatius arrived and, once he was satisfied that he would not need to give anyone the last rites, he gave thanks and stood with Alys to help her.

As Alys worked she overheard some of Cecily's questions to her patient – designed, no doubt, to keep his mind off the pain – and his answers. His name was Alban. He had no idea how the fire might have started as they were always careful, and the cooking fires had already been doused. He was glad that the roof beams for the hall had been stored elsewhere, as they'd already done a lot of work squaring them off and he wouldn't want to repeat it.

Alys's relief on seeing Edwin, when he arrived, was great. She gave him a searching look but could not see that he was burned or otherwise injured, thank the Lord. She was surprised that he should think they would need accompanying back home; it was only a fire and it was not going to spread to the village. And he needed to sleep.

Eventually their task was finished. Cecily told Alban that she would come to see him in the morning, after she had visited the man Edwin wanted her to look at, and he was grateful. Alys's curiosity had been piqued by this request, although she had been so busy worrying about Edwin that she hadn't paid it much mind at the time, and she determined to find a way to go.

As they walked back to the village, Cecily was busy discussing herbs with the priest, so Alys turned to the imposing figure of the smith, thanking him for his company. She had seen him about the place, of course, but had never spoken to him. His huge physical size was a little intimidating, but he had seemed pleasant enough when he had spoken to Edwin earlier.

'And your name is Crispin, is it not?'

Now they were away from the fire the darkness seemed even deeper, and she sensed, rather than saw, that he looked down at her. 'Aye. Known your Edwin since he was a scrap of a thing. And his mother and aunt treated me for burns often enough when I was training.'

He didn't seem overly disposed to talk, but she persevered. 'And you live in the castle, not the village?'

'Aye. Got a room at the back of my forge – comfortable enough. But I come down to the village regular to see my old Ma.'

'That's nice.'

'But look,' his voice dropped. 'Edwin's a good man. Looks after people. He ever has any trouble, or you do, you send for me.' Even in the dark Alys could sense that he had flexed his arm muscles as he spoke.

'Thank you. I hope we have no need to do that, but … thank you.'

'Aye, well. Anyway, we're here now.'

They had reached the cottage; he opened the door for her, waited while she entered, and then strode off without another word, shepherding Cecily along the street.

Edwin was already asleep, sprawled across the bed in his clothes, stinking of smoke. But Alys didn't care. He was safe. The relief brought on a great weariness, and she lay down next to him.

The next thing she heard was the normal sound of the village waking up; it was nearly dawn. Remembering her wish to accompany Cecily up to the castle, Alys rose quickly and went to check the fire. It was cold – she hadn't banked it up properly last night – and the remains of what was supposed to have been Edwin's evening meal were stuck to the pot. But there was no time to worry about that now; she would miss her chance otherwise.

She put her head around the bedroom door. Edwin was still asleep. She was tempted to leave him to rest, but he wouldn't like it if he was supposed to be somewhere and overslept. She shook him gently, and as soon as she was convinced that he was almost awake, she slipped out.

Cecily and William were just leaving their cottage when she got there. They looked surprised to see her but made no objection when she offered to help; indeed, she got the impression that William was glad his wife would have the company, although he didn't say so out loud. He was concentrating on his balance, and the three of them made their way with aching slowness along the village street.

They were passed on their way by the swineherd, and William stopped for a moment to catch his breath. 'All men are supposed to be at the court this morning, but it might be as well for him to be out the way. He'll have nothing of use to say, poor lad.' They waited while Gyrth and the pigs passed them, the pungent odour disappearing up the street, and then continued on their way.

Alys had only been in the castle's outer ward a couple of times since her arrival in Conisbrough, and had never been through the inner gatehouse at all. They left William there, white-faced with pain now they could see him properly in the dawn light, and were met by a guard. Whoever had organised this was taking no chances; the guard in question wasn't tall, but he had a neck thicker than his head and he looked as though he could snap an iron bar in half if he felt like it.

The guard, whom Cecily greeted politely with an enquiry about his mother, led them around behind the gatehouse and into a small room that contained only a stool and a staircase leading downwards. Warning them to mind their step, he descended and unlocked a door at the bottom. 'In here. I'll leave the door open so you're not shut in with him, and I'll be just outside.'

Such were the elaborate precautions that Alys was beginning to feel oppressed and a little afraid. Thus it was that the appearance of the man inside the cell came as something of a shock. She had been expecting a violent-looking criminal, but here was a small, inoffensive fellow sitting quietly in the straw with his back against the wall. He looked up and shielded his eyes as the door opened, and then stood when he saw them. It took him a little while to get to his feet, and he was holding his side.

Alys was glad the door was going to remain open, for it would have been very difficult to see, otherwise; the only other light and air came in through a small barred window high up in one wall, which must have been at ground level outside. As it was, she could see that the cell was almost bare, but the straw was of reasonable freshness, there was a bucket in the far corner, and a bowl and cup lay near the opposite wall.

The mason said something in French. Alys looked at Cecily, who shrugged. 'He's one of them foreigners,' interposed the guard outside, helpfully.

'We're here to treat your injuries,' said Cecily, loudly.

He looked at them uncomprehendingly.

'I said –'

Alys interrupted with a smile. 'I'm not sure that saying it louder will help. I sometimes had to deal with foreigners in our shop – may I?' Cecily nodded.

Alys pointed to herself. 'Alys.' She repeated her name and then pointed to him. 'You?'

This he understood. 'Denis.'

'Denis. Good.' She pointed to herself again. 'I'm Alys, Edwin's wife. Edwin.'

He looked briefly confused and then realisation dawned. 'Ah, Edouin?' He said something else she didn't understand but which she assumed was about Edwin, and he seemed cheered.

Alys repeated the performance to give him Cecily's name, and then pointed to the dried blood on his face and then to the bag Cecily was carrying. He seemed to keep up with this, especially when she opened the bag and displayed the cloths and rags.

Cecily addressed the guard. 'I will need a bowl of water.'

He began to shake his head, saying he wasn't allowed to leave them. She clicked her tongue and spoke as though he was five years old. 'Why don't you shout for someone else to bring one?' He had evidently not considered this, and thought it very clever.

By the time the water arrived they had succeeded in getting the mason to stand in the best of the light so that his wound could be seen. Or rather, two wounds: he had one on his cheek and one a little higher up on his temple. Neither was overly serious and Cecily cleaned them up before applying a little salve. Then she stepped back and smiled at him. 'Better?'

'Is good,' he managed in English. 'Thank you.'

'Now, to those ribs.'

By dint of much pointing and gesturing they managed to get him to take off his tunic and shirt, although he seemed embarrassed at doing so in the close company of two unknown women.

Alys was equally disconcerted, but she tried to copy Cecily's calm demeanour as the older woman examined Denis's bruised side, and then tried not to think too much about the touch of a strange man's skin as she helped wind bandages tightly around him.

It was soon over and he had dressed again. He started to say something, then stopped and simplified. 'Edouin? Edouin comes?'

Alys wasn't sure of the answer to that – maybe she should have waited until she could have spoken to him before she left the house – but she was saved by a familiar voice from the top of the steps. 'I'm here.'

Edwin made his way down past the guard and then, rather unexpectedly, stopped dead as he looked into the cell. It was as though something had hit him, but there was nothing there, no barrier. He did then come in, but it was like he was stepping through fire and his face held some powerful emotion that Alys couldn't identify. He was walking stiffly and with a bit of a limp, and Alys realised she hadn't yet had the chance to ask him what had happened the previous night. But there was no time now; after a brief greeting he had broken into rapid French. Anyone who didn't know him would think that his uneasiness had passed, but she could see the shadow on his face.

His conversation with Denis went on for some moments and ended with them both looking grim, Edwin reaching out a hand to lay it on the other man's shoulder and saying something that was presumably meant to be reassuring.

Edwin turned back to them. 'There is going to be another court, so you had best get to it. Sir Roger is assembling the castle men now to bring them down to the village. I'll wait here so I can come with Denis.'

'You're going to translate for him? What is he accused of? He didn't start the fire, surely?'

He shook his head. 'To be honest I'm not sure who is going to end up being accused of what. Some of the villagers attacked him, and I want to bring that up, but they say he killed Ivo.'

Alys looked in shock at the mason, who was watching their exchange with both interest and incomprehension. 'No! Surely not? I mean …'

'For what it's worth, I don't think he did, either, so I'm going to try my hardest to argue for him. But …' He turned so he stood between her and Denis, his back to the mason, and continued in a lower voice. 'Everyone's blood is up, and they're against him because he's foreign. I'm not sure what I'll be able to do, so be prepared.'

His voice was grim and Alys gasped, knowing her eyes were wide as she looked over his shoulder at the polite, appreciative mason who might soon be hanging from the neck for a crime he didn't commit.

Chapter Six

Edwin had met with Sir Roger, as agreed, before he made his way to the cell. The knight had been at prayer when he arrived. He still seemed brittle, but although he remained dead-eyed, he had so far roused himself by the time Edwin left to agree to oversee the court in person – for what other figure of authority was there? – and to bring a substantial detachment of castle men to help keep the peace. Edwin's desire was that he could persuade the jury to make no decision yet, not until he could find out more, but failing that he at least hoped, in case of a guilty verdict, to keep Denis alive until the sheriff arrived. And he hoped that Sir Roger could hold himself together for the duration of the court.

Sir Roger agreed with Edwin's plan, on the basis that it would be up to the relevant authority to pronounce the death penalty anyway. He didn't seem convinced of either Denis's innocence or his guilt, or even particularly interested, but Edwin knew he could be relied upon to do whatever would be in the earl's best interests, which would mean not allowing any summary 'justice' to be meted out. That would have to be good enough for now.

The mood of the assembly on the village green was dark and uneasy. There were a few murmurs, shaken fists and even shouts when they arrived, but with the garrison out in force nobody attempted to attack Denis or to throw anything.

Sir Roger had a chair placed and sat on it, the looming castle visible behind him to remind everyone of where the power really lay. Behind him were the ranks of the garrison, armed, but with swords sheathed, spears held upright and arrows still in their quivers. To the knight's left sat Father Ignatius, with parchment and pens at the ready; to his right were the jury, Edwin not among them this time as he stood in the middle of the central open space alongside Denis. Also missing, due to the short notice, were the jury members who lived further out of the village: Edwin couldn't see Aelfrith or a couple of others. The spectators were spread around the other two sides of proceedings: a tight-knit group of masons at a little distance off to Edwin's right, and the rest of the villagers, somewhat disconcertingly, directly behind him.

Sir Roger opened proceedings, deciding to start with the fire. When he spoke the words 'potential case of arson' there was an uncomfortable shifting around the place, for this was a serious offence. Philippe was called to give evidence; his grasp of English was a little better than Denis's, but he still needed Edwin's help with the translation of some points, and it was a laborious business. However, he did state – and Edwin wondered if he was really speaking the truth or just trying not to antagonise the villagers – that he couldn't absolutely say it was arson, and that the blaze might have been started by a cooking fire getting out of hand.

A wave of relief passed across the assembled company.

'And your losses?'

'By the grace of God, no deaths. One man too injured to work, though he will recover. Most of our tools were up in the castle, so ... our lodgings, beds, clothes, food supplies.' He spread his hands. 'It could have been worse.'

'Very well. Men,' – this to the jury – 'I put no question of arson to you. The masons are in the service of the lord earl, so his estate will see that food and shelter are provided; some of those of you who owe service will be moved from the fields temporarily and put to the task.'

There was a murmur, which Sir Roger quelled with a look. 'Next, to the attack on the mason Denis and on Edwin.'

Edwin felt all eyes turning to him.

Sir Roger continued. 'It was unprovoked. If any man wished to accuse Denis of murder, he should have done it openly. And as for attacking Edwin, a member of the earl's own household ...' He slapped his hand down on the arm of the chair. 'I tell you now, violent and lawless behaviour will not be tolerated on my lord the earl's estate.'

He was becoming angry, but controlled himself. 'Now, Edwin, Denis. Can you identify any of the men who attacked you?'

Edwin winced as he translated. If he was hoping to get the sympathy of the village once charges were laid against Denis, this was not the right way to go about it.

Denis shook his head and muttered to Edwin, who spoke aloud. 'It was dark, Sir Roger, and neither of us can say with any certainty.'

Sir Roger was now drumming his fingers on the arm of the chair in a manner reminiscent of the earl, and he didn't look best pleased. 'You cannot identify any individuals. Can you then with certainty say that the men who attacked you were not the other masons?'

There was no arguing with that. 'Yes, Sir Roger.'

'And I can bear witness that they were not men of the garrison, as we arrived to find the attack already in progress.'

'Yes, Sir Roger.'

The knight turned to Father Ignatius. 'Have there been any groups of strangers in Conisbrough in the last couple of days?'

The priest shook his head. 'Not that I know of.'

'Thus, the attack must have been carried out by men from the village. If you do not put forward the culprits, you will all be deemed equally responsible and a fine will be levied on the whole village.'

He sat in silence, his gaze sweeping the assembly. Few met his eye. He waited, and the silence grew longer and more awkward.

'Very well. A fine of four pence to every family. To be paid by next Sunday.'

Edwin heard a gasp of outrage, and he winced again. His chances of any sympathy or leniency for Denis had just evaporated. Not to mention the fact that everyone had been reminded that if they could be held collectively responsible for assault, they could be held collectively responsible for murder, if they didn't put forward a named culprit.

Sir Roger quelled the unrest once more. 'The law will be followed here to the letter, in the lord earl's name. Now, I understand that one or more of you wishes to lay a charge against Denis. Who speaks for you?'

As Edwin had feared, there was now no shortage of men willing to stand and shout and accuse the mason of murder, and Sir Roger actually had to stand up before his calls for everyone to calm down were heeded.

By eventual general agreement, the reeve was delegated to speak. 'I – we – accuse this man of having murdered Ivo the bailiff. He was known to have argued with him, and Ivo was killed with a mason's hammer.'

Sir Roger waited until the angry buzz had died down. 'Very well. A charge has been laid. First things first: who discovered the body?'

With some reluctance, Osmund stepped forward. That surprised Edwin. Why would he have been so near Ivo's house at that time in the morning?

Sir Roger addressed him directly. 'Describe for us what happened.'

Osmund looked nervous at being the centre of attention. He spoke, and Edwin translated under his breath for Denis.

'He was dead, sir, I could see that straight away, so I raised the hue and cry.'

'He was dead before you got there? You did not see the act being committed?'

'No, sir.'

'And did you see anyone else there? Or anyone running away?'

Osmund gulped and hesitated before replying. 'No, sir. Nobody.'

'So, you raised the hue and cry, and others came running?'

'Yes, sir. Reeve came first, and then the others – they were on their way out to work.' He screwed up his face. 'Alwin was there, and Robin, and –'

'All right. We don't need everyone's name. The men of the village came running, as they are obliged to do when the hue and cry is raised, yes?'

'Yes, sir. And then Reeve says we should send for Edwin, so he sent young Hal to fetch him.'

'And then Edwin sent for me. Good – I understand the sequence of events now.' Sir Roger turned to speak to the sergeant-at-arms behind him and was handed a bag. 'Now.' He brought out the rounded hammer and held it up. 'Edwin thinks that this was used to strike the blow that killed Ivo. I agree with him. Does any man wish to say differently?'

Nobody did, unsurprisingly, as the weapon fitted their preferred version of events. Sir Roger then held it out to Denis. 'Take this, and tell me whether it is yours.'

Edwin translated and then watched as Denis stepped forward and stretched out a hand to take the hammer.

His left hand.

Edwin had a sudden memory of the day he had spoken to Denis up in the inner ward, and the mason had demonstrated the use of the hammer and chisel. He could picture the scene quite clearly, and now he saw what he had paid no mind to before: that Denis had been using the hammer in his left hand.

He felt sick. Had he been wrong? Misled? Was he trying to defend a man who really was guilty?

Denis was confirming that the hammer was his, saying that he had lost it before Ivo's death. Sir Roger understood him, but he had to prompt Edwin out of his reverie to translate for everyone else's benefit. He now found himself more sympathetic to the cries of 'A likely story!' than he had thought he would.

Sir Roger called for quiet. 'This man is entitled to be heard. Denis, what have you to say for yourself?'

Edwin relayed the mason's murmured words to the assembly. 'He says he did have some disputes with Ivo, but it was just about some details of the stonework of his house, as others will testify. He says his bag broke and he dropped his tools; he thought he'd picked them all up but found later that the hammer was missing. He went back to look for it but couldn't find it. He didn't see Ivo again, and he didn't kill him.'

Denis was going to have to do better than that if he was going to prove his innocence, and everyone knew it. More accusations were being thrown, from all around the green. Denis was lying. Why would anyone want to steal his hammer? He had argued with the bailiff but nobody could confirm it was only about minor matters because they had been shouting in French. And Denis was a foreigner. Hadn't they been fighting the French? It wasn't right. He couldn't even speak English, the language of the village.

Sir Roger interrupted with the pointed observation that the lord earl couldn't speak English, either, and did they want to lay a charge against him? That calmed everyone down very effectively, and Edwin was able to attract the knight's attention.

'Edwin? You wish to speak?'

'Osmund says he found the body – and I'm sure he thinks he was the first finder – but I believe that Barty was there before him.'

'Barty?' Sir Roger evidently hadn't heard the name before. 'Then why hasn't this man come forward?'

'Er …' Edwin looked around and saw Barty hiding behind his sister. 'That's him there.'

'Ah.' Sir Roger spoke directly to the boy. 'Step forward, child, and have no fear.'

Robin the carpenter was on his feet over in the jury benches. 'You can't! He's too little!'

The knight looked at him sternly. 'He is accused of nothing, but if he has seen something of importance then we must hear it.' He relented a little in the face of such fatherly concern. 'You may step forward and stand with him if you wish.'

Robin did so, casting a look of daggers at Edwin. He placed one hand on his son's shoulder and spoke, for the benefit of the company as much as the boy. 'You're a good lad – just tell the truth.'

Sir Roger started to speak but saw Barty start backwards in fear. He gestured to Edwin. 'Perhaps you'd better ask him.'

Edwin nodded, but he began by addressing Osmund. 'Was that hammer on the floor of the cottage when you found the body?'

Osmund made an effort to recall. 'No. No, that wasn't what – I mean, no, it wasn't there.'

Edwin thanked him and turned to the boy. 'Barty, it's all right. I'm just going to ask you what happened, and you tell us. Keep looking at me and don't worry about anyone else; speak loudly and clearly and you shall have an apple with honey afterwards.'

Barty's eyes widened at the thought of such a treat, and he looked more eager.

'Good boy. Now, you were up early yesterday, playing?'

'Yes. Nobody else was up yet.'

'And you went to Ivo's house? The stone house that isn't finished yet?'

'There's stones inside to climb on. Like a castle.'

Edwin took that as a yes. 'And what did you see inside?'

Barty shrugged, too young even to be concerned. 'A dead man.'

'And what else? Did you find anything on the floor?'

Barty pointed to the hammer that Sir Roger was still holding.

'And you took it away to play with?'

Barty looked uncertain, so Edwin added, 'You're not in trouble – we just want to know.'

The boy nodded. 'Wanted to work, like papa. Then you took it away.'

Edwin looked around the green, satisfied that everyone had heard and understood. 'And many others saw me do that. So now we know what happened to the hammer. And this means that Barty was there before Osmund, though as such a young child he can hardly have been expected to raise the hue and cry. But it narrows the time of Ivo's death: after midnight, when he was seen leaving the inner ward, and before dawn.'

Nobody raised any argument, but Edwin could see that few people around him were interested in this level of detail. He persevered. 'Now, Barty, just one more question and you can go. We know that you picked up the hammer, and that's fine. Did you also touch the body?'

Robin started to protest, presumably thinking this was some kind of attempt to implicate his son, but Edwin held up a hand. 'It's important. Did you?'

Barty shook his head.

'Say it out loud?'

'No. I didn't touch it.'

Those around Edwin looked as puzzled as he felt, but for a different reason. They evidently wondered what he could be talking about, while he was thinking about the blood smeared down the side of Ivo's face. Someone had done that after the man was dead, but who? And why?

He looked down as the hem of his tunic was tugged. 'Can I have my apple now?'

A laugh swept across the green, breaking some of the tension. Edwin bent down. 'Once we're finished here, you go and find my wife, and she'll get one for you.'

'With honey?'

Despite the situation, Edwin had to suppress a smile. 'With honey. Now, off you go, there's a good lad.'

He straightened. 'I have one more question, Sir Roger, if I may, for everyone?' He received a nod and spoke to the company at large. 'Does anyone know where Ivo went yesterday afternoon?'

There were shakes of the head, and some exasperated noises. 'What's that got to do with anything?' asked the reeve. 'You just said yourself that he was killed at night, so he must have come back from wherever it was.'

Edwin opened his mouth to reply, but was drowned out by people who were losing their patience. They were standing around in the cold when there was work to do, and they knew who had killed Ivo – why did they have to listen to all this? They wanted the question to be put to the jury, and now.

Edwin tried one last appeal. 'Sir Roger, I'm sure there is more to this. Please, give me more time to find out.'

The knight shook his head. 'We must put it to the jury, but –' he raised his voice so it was clear he was speaking to everyone – 'whatever the outcome, there will be no action taken today, do you hear? The law says we must wait for the sheriff, and we will.'

As Edwin had expected, it took only a few moments for the men of the jury to cry that Denis was guilty of murder. And many of them also seemed to be angry at him for trying to say otherwise.

Sir Roger stood, causing the men behind him to snap to attention and everyone else to fall silent.

'This man will be held in a cell in the castle until the sheriff arrives, and nobody – *nobody* – will seek to harm him. However, Edwin has my permission to continue his investigations.' He spoke to Edwin. 'If you can present me with another culprit, or better still a confession, before then, I will release Denis. If not, he will be handed over to face justice.'

Edwin was forced to look Denis in the eye while he translated what had just happened, although the mason had obviously under-stood the word 'guilty' from everyone's reaction. Then he watched as Denis was taken away, arms pinioned behind him this time, up to the castle, and turned to face the hostile expressions around him.

He had hardly opened his mouth to explain when he felt himself being jostled. He wasn't allowed to speak. He became almost disori-entated: who were these people around him? These faces were not those of the men – and women – he had known all his life. They were distorted, ugly in their hate.

Edwin disentangled himself and hurried off. He was beginning to think that Alys had a point, and he wondered if he should be afraid.

———◦———

Fortunately, Edwin was the sort of husband who had at least a vague grasp of what was available in the house, for if he'd promised Barty honey and then the boy had arrived to find that there wasn't any, there would have been tears. As it was, Alys was able to take an apple from the barrel, cut it in half, smear both sides, and send the child on his way with a sticky face wreathed in smiles.

It was another late start to the day's chores, and the barley for the evening's pottage would need to soak. She used the last of the clean water in doing so, and set off for the well.

This time the group of women clustered around it called out no greetings. Instead they parted in silence, their expressions hostile, and watched without speaking as she struggled with the heavy bucket. At least she managed not to tip it everywhere this time, and she was glad to be on her way back to the house.

Setting down her burden, Alys sighed as she regarded the almost-empty firewood stack. Hal had gone out to the fields as soon as the court had finished, so if tonight's meal was going to be cooked, she'd have to fetch some more herself. Still, it would get her out for a while, and at least it wasn't raining. Taking up a piece of old rope to tie a bundle together, she set off.

To get to the woods she had to pass through the village and around the edge of one of the fields. Again, nobody spoke to her, but she held her head up high, refusing to scuttle through as quickly as possible. She stared boldly at anyone who looked at her, until they averted their gaze, and she also took the opportunity to watch what they were all doing with their hands. Robin the carpenter, for example, was definitely using his tools the normal way round, as were whichever two of his younger sons who were in the open-fronted shop with him. Avice emerged from the house as Alys passed, scattering some corn for their hens with her right hand. In the fields, too, most of the men and boys seemed to be favouring their right hands, as far as she could make out from the way they were using their tools.

The road became muddier and Alys was forced to give all her attention to watching where she was going. Eventually she reached the edge of the wood and stepped in under the trees. Although it hadn't rained today the branches were wet, and she felt cold drips on her arms as she pushed them aside. One even managed to evade all the layers of her clothing and trickle down the back of her neck, and she shivered.

There was no point looking for fallen branches here, as the village children would have picked up anything lying so close to the edge of the wood. She knew better than to try and break anything from a living tree – not only would it see her up in front of the manor court, but it would be useless for burning anyway – so the only thing to do was to go deeper.

It was not far off noon, but as the undergrowth grew thicker and the trees closer together, the light faded and soon she found herself peering through a grey-green murk. Here there were some sticks lying on the ground so, looking behind her frequently to make sure she could still locate the path, she began to gather some.

By the time she had a good-sized bundle tied together, Alys had warmed up – and had moved further from the path than she had intended. She stood still for a few moments, trying to get her bearings and unwilling to move another step until she knew it would be one in the right direction. And it was then that she heard the sound of someone else coming through the wood.

She was immediately wary, but the sound of cheerful whistling and the complete lack of stealth with which the person was crashing through the undergrowth reassured her that nobody was trying to sneak up on her. Besides, who would be in this part of the woods except for someone from Conisbrough?

Still without moving, Alys looked in the direction of the noise and soon saw Young Robin making his way through the trees.

He saw her and stopped. 'Hello. Didn't think to see you here this afternoon.'

'I was just collecting some firewood.' Alys pointed, rather unnecessarily, at the bundle of sticks. She couldn't help noticing that he wasn't carrying anything similar.

This was soon explained. 'I've been to find a couple of good trees to fell, to start rebuilding the masons' camp.' He scowled. 'That's been put on us, hasn't it – they make their own roof beams for the castle but we must be their servants to rebuild their camp. Even though they no doubt burned it down themselves.'

'Why would they do that?'

He shrugged. 'Don't know, don't care. But it means I've spent an hour when I could have been doing something else.' Then the frown left his face as he looked her up and down in a manner she didn't much like. 'Still, all the better for seeing you come out to meet me.'

'Oh, I wasn't –'

He stepped closer. 'I thought you were being all friendly the other day at the mill. Seems I was right, eh?'

Alys looked about her, wishing she could see the right path. But of course, wherever she went, he would know these woods much better than she did.

He was close to her now, close enough that she could feel the heat of his breath in the cold afternoon. He put out a hand to touch her arm, and instinctively she slapped it away.

'Now then!' He threw up both hands in a gesture of innocence. 'No need for that. We're only being friendly, aren't we? Like you wanted?' He reached for her again, this time gripping her arm quite firmly and stepping even closer. 'I know what you came here for.'

Alys stumbled back, unfortunately straight into the trunk of a tree. 'Take your hands off me. You know I'm married to Edwin.'

Young Robin laughed. 'Oh, Edwin? Fine sort of a man he is. I bet he doesn't treat you the way you want, does he?' He had one hard arm either side of her, leaning on the tree trunk, trapping her. 'Besides, married girls are the best. No accusations of taking their virginity, no proof anything was done, and no trouble if anything results, 'cause they already have a husband, and it must be his. You don't think half the brats in Conisbrough aren't calling the wrong man "father"?'

The longer he kept talking, the more chance there was that someone else would come along, but now he stopped and turned his head to look and listen. Alys could hear only the sounds she didn't want: birds calling, the faint rustlings of small woodland creatures in the undergrowth, and a breeze moving the lighter branches around and above them. They were completely alone.

He leaned in, so their bodies were touching, and breathed in her ear as he spoke. 'Besides, Edwin's not here now, is he?'

Chapter Seven

Edwin needed to get away from all these people so he could think. Home was no good, and neither was the church; they might follow him there. And besides, the village didn't feel such a welcoming place all of a sudden.

He made his way up to the castle, with the idea of sitting up in his favourite embrasure on the wall, but by the time he reached the inner ward it was spitting with rain: cold, hard drops that fell with intent and promised to get worse.

From the bustle outside the armoury he could see that Sir Roger was organising a group of men to go out on a patrol, and intending to join them himself, so that meant that the keep would be empty. He was waved in by the man on the outer steps and soon he was sitting in the cold and dark of the council chamber. This time he didn't light a candle; instead he pushed a stool against the wall, wrapped his cloak more tightly about him, sat down and tried to sink into himself.

After what was probably about an hour, maybe a little more, he was no further on. Someone had struck Ivo a blow which had killed him. The weapon had been Denis's hammer, but the killer might or might not have been Denis. After the deed was done, Barty had moved the hammer. At some point someone had smeared fingers in the blood on Ivo's head, but there was no telling when or who. Edwin had known all this already, and he'd gained nothing except a stiff neck and freezing feet, for the questions were still the same. Lots of people had wished Ivo ill, but who would want to take that far enough to kill him? Where had he been during the afternoon? And why had he left the castle to visit the village in the middle of the night?

Edwin sighed as he stood, flexing his legs and stamping his feet to try to get a bit of life into them. The one thing he was relatively sure of was that this was a crime of the here and now – nobody in Conisbrough had known Ivo before he arrived during the summer, so the answer was unlikely to lie in a secret buried deep in his past. No, he'd upset someone more recently.

That did give him a new thought, and Edwin was down the stairs, through both wards and out of the main gate before he really noticed either where he was or that it was still raining. He was stopped short by a deep voice, and looked up to see that he had narrowly avoided walking straight into Aelfrith, who was on his way up to the castle. Edwin started to apologise for his inattention but had barely opened his mouth before he slipped on a patch of mud on the steep slope. He would have landed flat on his back in the dirt were it not for Aelfrith's quick reactions; he shot out one arm and grabbed a fistful of Edwin's tunic, holding him upright until he'd regained his balance.

Edwin planted his feet carefully. 'My thanks.'

'You're welcome. Been in the ward, have you? Crispin there?'

'Yes, I've … I mean no … I mean, sorry, I didn't notice whether he was there or not. But he normally is, isn't he?'

'Ah well, if he's not then I'll wait for him.' Aelfrith hefted the sack he was carrying, slung over one shoulder. 'He's mended some of my tools so I've come to collect them. Some beans and a jar of ale in here for him in return, and Mother's mended his hood.'

Edwin enquired about his mother's health.

'She's a little better, thank you.' His voice turned softer. 'However ill she is, she makes the best of it, still running the house and helping me out. I don't know what I'd do without her.'

Edwin murmured something polite but non-committal.

Aelfrith began to move on. 'Anyway, best get on. Other things to do in the village while I'm here, after I've seen Crispin. Don't fall on your way back down – one of those holes is quite deep, and you don't want to dirty such fine clothes.'

'No, I don't think my wife would be very happy …' Thinking of Alys reminded him of something and he hailed Aelfrith's departing back. 'When you've finished your business here today, come and eat with us before you set off home.'

Aelfrith's smile was cheerful through the rain as he turned. 'That's very kind, thank you.'

'I'll ask Alys if we can have it early, so you don't have to walk all the way home in the dark.'

'Ah, that's all right – been walking that road all my life, so I could do it with my eyes closed. But Mother'll worry if I'm too late back, so that'd be grand.' He waved and began striding up towards the outer gatehouse.

Good. Right, Edwin would go home to tell Alys about their guest, and then he'd set out to discover where Ivo had been on the afternoon before his death. Someone must have seen him. And Alys had said she'd keep her eyes and ears open while she was about her chores in the village, hadn't she? Maybe there was something she could tell him.

Alys shivered as she entered the village. She had to get home, had to get there without anyone noticing, had to wash the blood off before anyone saw …

Fortunately, the village was all but deserted; the rain had started again, so anyone not in the fields was indoors. She had her shawl pulled over her head, and could hide to a certain extent behind the bundle of sticks. Besides, it wasn't as though anyone in Conisbrough liked her well enough to stop and chat.

She made it to the cottage. Once the door was safely shut behind her she allowed herself to lean against it, knees weak. But there was little time – she didn't know where Edwin was but he might appear at any moment – and she had to tidy herself up and think up a plausible story in case questions were asked, as they surely would be once Young Robin made his appearance in the village.

She poured water into a bowl and began to wash. As she scrubbed at her shaking hands, she thought more about the incident, and the more she considered it, the angrier she became. Who did he think he was? And honestly, did he think she'd been brought up in England's second largest city for nothing? Did he think she hadn't been fending off unwanted attention in the street since she was ten years old? Did he, in short, think she was a helpless village girl, to be pawed around by some yokel just because he felt like it?

She looked at her hands. Most of the blood had been his, so the damage wasn't too bad. But as she'd hurried away – leaving him groaning on the floor and unsure whether to clutch at his broken nose or the agony between his legs – she'd banged the back of her left hand against a tree and scraped her knuckles. It wasn't serious, but such things could get swollen and nasty, so she rubbed at it with cloth and water to get the bits of bark out.

She had nearly finished when the door banged open, causing her to jump almost off the floor. Her heart was still pounding from the shock as Edwin advanced towards her.

His expression turned to one of concern. 'You've hurt yourself?'

She held out her hand, willing it not to tremble. 'It's nothing – I just scraped it while I was out getting the wood.' She hoped he wouldn't look too closely at the bowl of reddened water and the blood-soaked cloths tucked behind it; Young Robin's nose had bled brightly and copiously when she'd slammed the heel of her hand into it, and there was far too much here to have come from a simple barked knuckle.

Once he'd examined her hand, though, and found it just as she said, he didn't enquire too closely. He lifted it to his lips with a smile, but at his touch she jerked it back. After a moment's pause she made a feeble excuse about it still not being clean, and wrapped a strip of cloth around it.

She needed to change the subject. 'So. What have you been doing this morning?'

He said something about the castle, but she wasn't really listening, just nodding as she thought to herself how she should be behaving.

'And so I asked him to come round and eat with us later.'

For one awful moment she thought he meant … but no, he'd mentioned another name.

'Aelfrith?'

Edwin looked confused. 'Yes. Didn't you ask me to do that, next time I saw him?'

She had to concentrate. 'Yes, yes, of course I did.' She forced a smile. 'Thank you.'

'And I wondered if we could eat a little earlier than usual? So he's not too late setting out on the road back?'

'Of course.' She wasn't really taking this in, except that she knew this had given her an opportunity to get him out the house so she could be alone. 'Off you go, then, and I'll start preparing. You'll be back before sunset?'

He leaned forward to kiss her cheek, and she forced herself not to flinch. 'Yes. I'm off to try and find out what Ivo was doing that afternoon, but I'll find Aelfrith in good time and bring him.'

Alys watched him out the door and then her knees gave way and she collapsed on to a stool. Tears sprang into her eyes and she wiped them away with shaking hands. *Stop that!* She had to compose herself, had to think. Firstly, she and Young Robin lived in the same village, and they would do for probably the rest of their lives. She must steel herself to face him again, to see him almost every day.

Secondly, and of greater immediate importance, he was at some point today going to appear in the village with a broken and bloodied nose, and everyone was going to ask him what had happened. Her best hope was that he would be too embarrassed to say that he had been thumped by a girl, and that he would make up some kind of excuse, hopefully something more convincing than she had just managed.

But what if he didn't? What if he accused her of assault? What would happen to her then? She would be up before the manor court, her reputation in tatters, to say nothing of what it would do to Edwin's prospects. Would the earl want to have in his service a man whose wife had been convicted of a violent act? And what – what – would Edwin think of it himself?

That set her off into sobs again. He must not know. He mustn't find out what Young Robin had tried to do. He'd either get angry and cause trouble, or he would just *look* at her in disgust, and she couldn't stand the thought of that.

The sound of a burning twig falling in the hearth roused her. The fire was almost out, and she had work to do. She would have to rely on Young Robin's male pride for the moment – he had plenty of it, at least – and hope for the best. Right now, she needed to work.

The bundle of sticks she had brought back with her were dry on the inside – they had been on the ground for some while so they weren't green – but they were wet from the rain so wouldn't be of any immediate use. She untied them and spread them out around the hearth to dry out, before scooping up the last pieces from the old stack to build up the fire. She checked on the barley as it was soaking in the pot, went through a list in her head of the herbs and flavourings she had available, checked to see what was left of the fresh pork and offal, and thanked the Lord that she had baked only yesterday. And dealing with that hen might give her an opportunity to work out some of her frustrations … but first things first. She squared her shoulders and stood looking at the door. She would leave the house; she would walk down the street with her head held high. Everything would be fine.

With a deep breath, she set out to find Rosa.

Edwin was wet. Mud had soaked through his boots, water had soaked through his hose, his hair was plastered down on to his head, and he could feel drips running down his back.

This was all natural for the time of year, of course, and indeed he gave thanks that it wasn't worse, for the cloak had kept some of the rain off. It was now sodden and heavy as he made his way back to the village, but it was a luxury that not many other men had. Indeed, several of the villagers had either stared jealously at it or made out-right comments as he had been questioning them.

He sighed as he sloshed through the puddles – his feet were so wet by now that there was not much point in trying to pick his way round them – feeling the water well up between his toes as he plodded and thought. It had all been for nothing, for not one man he had spoken to had known where Ivo had gone on the afternoon before his death. Either that, or someone knew and wasn't telling. The reeve in particular had seemed very evasive, but perhaps he was just busy.

Edwin hadn't needed to be very alert to sense hostility, as that was quite open in most of the faces that confronted him. Why was he persisting in questioning them, when they already had the culprit locked up? Didn't he trust them? Did he value the word of a foreigner over their own? Was he not, in short, one of them any more? This is where the sneering references to his cloak had come in, and as he'd trudged to the furthest field to make sure he hadn't missed anyone, he'd almost taken it off. But that would be silly – injuring himself just because of what others thought. What matter was it to him that they were jealous? Why should he care?

It was not quite dusk as he entered the village, but he was tired and wet and he'd had enough. He could see Aelfrith; he was standing under the lean-to shelter that was Robin's workshop, chatting and looking out at the rain. Edwin thought of Alys's comment: *Nobody calls it gossiping when it's men.*

He assumed that Aelfrith had finished whatever business he was about, so he waved and made his way over. Robin was just tidying up for the day before it got dark – or, rather, he was talking to Aelfrith while his sons tidied up around him, encouraged by the occasional back-handed slap or clip round the ear when they came within reach. Little Barty wasn't among them, and Edwin hoped he was inside by the fire with his sisters in this weather. The winter coughs would start soon and the young, as well as the old, could be carried off.

They all stood to watch as Gyrth came down the street with his herd. There was no panic today; he selected one pig and penned it safely at the house next to Robin's, and then passed by and did the same with two more at the cottage on the other side.

Once the noise and smell had receded, Robin spoke. 'Out and about today, is it?' He nodded at Edwin's sodden clothing.

'Yes.' Edwin was too tired and fed up to elaborate, or to listen to a harangue on why he shouldn't be bothering about it, but fortunately neither of the others seemed interested in questioning him.

'My eldest has been up in the woods looking for timber for the new masons' camp, so he'll be wet through when he gets back, but the others are here. Too wet today to get on the mill roof, though that's nearly done, so we've been working on these benches for the new hall.'

Edwin followed his pointing finger and saw the long, neatly squared-off pieces stacked up against the cottage wall, where they would stay dry.

'Not the beams for yon house, then?' Aelfrith's rumbling voice was curious as he looked across the green. 'Will that still be finished, now he's dead?'

Robin shrugged. 'No idea. Nothing to do with me, that – they're doing their own beams.'

'Good thing not everyone wants stone, or you'd be out of business! Anyway, I suppose there'll be another bailiff soon, so happen he'll live there.'

'Oh aye, there's always a bailiff.' Robin didn't look too enthused. 'With their rules about fairs and bread ovens.'

Edwin was cold, damp and hungry, and he didn't want to listen to any more moaning – not today, at any rate. 'Are you ready, Aelfrith? Alys said she'd have the meal ready before dark.'

Robin looked from one to the other in surprise.

'Sounds good.' Aelfrith picked up a clanking bag. 'Good cook, is she?'

Edwin extolled the virtues of his wife's culinary skills as he pulled up his hood. Robin started to say something about a loom, but Aelfrith didn't answer, so Edwin bade the carpenter a good evening and stepped out into the rain.

As soon as he opened the cottage door, Edwin's mood lightened. It was warm and inviting, and the smell was heavenly. He was a little surprised to see Rosa there as well as Alys and Hal, but Alys cast him a look that he interpreted as warning him not to say anything, so he didn't. He shrugged off his cloak and laid it over the kist, reminding himself again that he really should get round to driving a peg into the wall, and moved to the fire.

Aelfrith came to join him, rubbing his hands and looking about him. Other than his brief visit to find Father Ignatius the other day he'd never been inside the cottage before, and he made a pleasant comment to Alys about the furniture. Indeed, home looked even nicer than usual this evening, Edwin thought, for she had laid a cloth on the table and set out every dish and cup they owned.

'Aelfrith, have you met Rosa? She has kindly agreed to serve our meal so we can all sit down.'

Aelfrith frowned at Rosa in the dim light, and then his face cleared. 'Oh, Ned's little sister, is it?'

Edwin saw Alys grimace, but she didn't say anything. 'Smells lovely,' he said. 'What are we having?'

Alys stood back and surveyed everything. 'Good, we're ready. Sit down, and I'll tell you.' She gestured Aelfrith to the best of the stools and Edwin to his chair, then she sat down with them at the top end of the table, while Rosa and Hal began to bring pots and dishes.

'Barley pottage with leeks and pork,' she began, as Rosa ladled out the steaming thick mess into their bowls. 'Lucky it's not Friday.'

Edwin drew out his spoon and was about to start when she forestalled him. 'And a chicken in honey sauce' – he looked and sniffed in wonder as the pot was placed on the table – 'with raisins.'

There was also maslin bread and one of the cinnamon loaves, the scent making Edwin's mouth water even more. Aelfrith gave Alys a broad smile. 'This is a fine spread, mistress, truly.'

'Thank you. But we should also thank Rosa, who helped and who can make any dish delicious.'

Rosa had just sat down at the bottom end of the table, and Edwin saw her open her mouth and then shut it again when Alys threw her a look. He held his cup for Hal to pour the ale into it, and when everyone was served, the boy sat down too, alongside his sister.

Edwin thought that the unaccustomed formality of the occasion called for a grace, so he hastily stumbled over a few words of thanks, and then dug in. The hot, meat-flavoured and lightly spiced pottage was exactly what he needed after his cold, wet afternoon, and he savoured every mouthful, watching Aelfrith do the same as they talked of this and that. Hal, inevitably, couldn't shovel it in fast enough, but as he reached for the pot of chicken, Rosa slapped his hand away and whispered angrily in his ear.

Aelfrith saw it and laughed. 'You do as you're told, boy – the womenfolk are in charge inside the house.'

'Very true,' replied Alys with a smile. 'Rosa, why don't you help Aelfrith to some of the chicken?'

Edwin watched the girl rise and come to stand next to Aelfrith, leaning over the table to reach the pot, and then watched him watching her as she served him. Belatedly, he realised what Alys was about.

'You're lucky to have Rosa to help you tonight, my love,' he said, loudly, meeting Alys's eye. 'A good, biddable girl, that,' he added in an undertone to Aelfrith once Rosa had returned to her place. Then he turned back to his cinnamon bread, partly as he didn't want to overdo it, and partly because he didn't want to miss out on his favourite food.

Once the meal was complete, he and Aelfrith moved their seats nearer to the fire, where their boots steamed. Edwin's feet finally started feeling like they belonged to him again.

'So,' began Aelfrith. 'Tell me about the court I missed this morning? It's a shame I wasn't there, for I'd have been able to tell everyone that Ivo was out at my place all that afternoon.'

Alys was reasonably happy with the way things had turned out, but Lord, she wished everyone would just go away now. The pressure of having to act normally for the whole time was starting to tell on her; her head ached and she just wanted to go and lie down in the chamber. But she must keep going just a little longer.

As far as she was concerned, Aelfrith had turned out to be a disappointment. He had a fine figure, of course; a pleasant enough face, and there was hardly a girl who wouldn't swoon over that rumbling voice. But now she had spoken with him, listened to him over the course of an hour or so, she was coming to the conclusion that there wasn't much in his head.

She waited for Rosa to clear the dishes off the table and then picked up the cloth to shake it, the firelight catching on a few crumbs as they fell into the rushes. To be fair, there wouldn't be many men who wouldn't sound unintelligent if they had to try and keep up with Edwin's conversation for an evening, but Aelfrith seemed to her to be actually stupid. He had no thoughts, no opinions on anything outside of his own farm, and Alys reflected on how boring it would be to have to listen to that every evening from now until one of them died.

However, this didn't seem to bother Rosa in the slightest. Her eyes had been on stalks since the moment Aelfrith had walked into the house, and she'd barely looked away from him since, even when she was serving the meal. If she thought that someone like Aelfrith would do for her – and, in the light of day, it would be a good match for her family – then Alys would do all she could to bring it about.

Aelfrith was now sitting comfortably by the fire, talking to Edwin about something she wasn't interested enough to wonder about. Rosa was watching him over her shoulder while she put dishes and cups back on the sideboard. Hal, who had finished scrubbing the big cooking pot, was obviously ready to go, his eyes drooping now that he was warm and fed after a long day.

Alys attempted to pull herself together. One more effort, and then she could rest. 'Hal, why don't you go home?' she said, loudly enough to break into the men's conversation.

Hal made a sleepy move towards the door, and Rosa, as Alys had known she would, began to hurry. 'I won't be two moments – you just wait there.'

Alys looked at her but kept half an eye towards the fire. 'Oh, let him go – he's tired and he'll have plenty to do tomorrow.' She gestured and Hal, gratefully, was gone. 'Don't worry, Edwin and I can walk you home later if you're worried about going out on your own in the dark.'

Edwin was nodding as Rosa finished putting everything away and then smoothed down her apron. Now, was Aelfrith going to …? He was. 'I must be going, too, to get home before Mother starts worrying.' He stood and stretched, driving new force into the limbs and muscles that Rosa was clearly admiring, before turning to Alys. 'Thank you, mistress, for a fine meal. And I can take Rosa home to save you going out in the cold – I'll look in on Ned while I'm there.'

Rosa's smile was so wide it could barely fit on her face, but Alys was just tired. *Keep going. Just a little longer.* 'How kind.'

He put on his hood, which had been drying, and opened the door. 'Rain's stopped, and there's a bit of a moon.' He turned to Rosa. 'Ready?' She was.

Aelfrith picked up his bag. 'Edwin.' He inclined his head. 'Mistress. My thanks again.'

Then they were gone, the door was shut, and cottage, mercifully, contained only the two of them. Alys almost staggered with relief as she turned her face away from the fire to compose it, still unsure exactly what she was going to tell Edwin if he brought up the subject of her trip to the forest.

Think of something else. 'Can I ask you a question?'

'Of course.'

'Why were you so uneasy, earlier, when you came to see Denis in the cell? You looked as though you'd seen an evil spirit.' She crossed herself.

He stared into the fire for a long moment. 'Not an evil spirit, no. But maybe a ghost.' He met her eye, fiddling absent-mindedly with the leather thong he always wore around his neck. 'I've been in that cell before, just once. And –'

There was a knock on the door, making Alys jump. Had Aelfrith forgotten something? Edwin motioned to her to stay where she was, and moved to open it himself; he spoke to someone without, and Alys caught his half of the conversation. 'What? Did he? Oh, yes, he did say something about …' and then, 'Lord! What on earth have you done to your face?'

This last gave her a fraction of a moment's warning, and she whipped round to see that Young Robin was standing on the threshold.

Chapter Eight

Edwin held the door open. 'Come in out of the cold.'

Young Robin stepped over the threshold, saying again that he'd come to talk about building a loom as Alys had been to see his father about it. He carried a piece of charcoal and a flat board on which Edwin could make out some lines and sketches.

'Yes, well, there's no point asking me about that – my wife is the expert. Alys, Young Robin needs to speak to you.' He looked at Alys across the fire. She stiffened and her eyes opened wide – but no, she was fine as she stepped around the flames; it must have been the effect of the smoke on his own eyes.

Alys invited their guest to the table. 'And you sit here as well, please, Edwin. I'd like for you to know what I was thinking of.'

Edwin sat in his chair; Alys placed herself next to him and then gestured for Young Robin to sit on his other side. The board was placed on the table and Alys pushed a rushlight nearer so they could all see. She must have caught it on an uneven part of the surface, for it tipped and splashed hot fat.

Now that he could see the carpenter's son more clearly, Edwin examined his face while he started pointing at things on his drawing board. He'd had his nose broken – it was swollen and crooked, with dried blood crusted under his nostrils. His eyes were also turning puffy and black, but there didn't seem to be too much other damage – no teeth missing, for example, and he wasn't limping or groaning. So he hadn't been set on by a gang of men. But could this have anything to do with the murder?

'So, what do you think?' Alys was speaking to him.

'Er, just run that by me again? A loom, you say? Over in that corner? Plenty of room for it.'

He listened with more attention as they explained that they were talking of something much bigger than he'd been envisaging; it sounded quite complex, but Alys knew exactly what she was talking about, and she was soon smudging a finger on the drawing, making Young Robin understand more clearly what pieces would be needed and how they would fit together. Edwin was proud of her knowledge, and in an area he knew nothing about.

A hiss and a shower of sparks made him look at the fire; it was low, so he made to stand so he could put another log on it. But Alys pulled him back down. 'I'll do it. Now we've agreed on a design, perhaps you should talk with him about how much this is going to cost.'

After some haggling they fixed on a price that was probably a little higher than Edwin would have expected, but he knew the job would be done well, and besides, there were a lot of children to feed in the carpenter's family. He would pay half when they were ready to start and the other half when the loom was complete.

He was quite pleased with himself by the time he showed Young Robin out the door. Having a loom and the chance to weave would give Alys more to do, and from the way she always spoke about cloth, the different types and the way it was produced, he knew it was a subject dear to her heart. A few pennies for a loom – even if it meant losing a sizeable chunk of the floor space – was a price worth paying, especially if it kept her at home and out of trouble.

She was sitting on a stool near the fire, staring into its depths. He touched her on the shoulder as he sat down, and she started.

'You were far away. Were you thinking of everything you'll be able to make? We'll dress like kings.'

'Hardly. My father employed some very skilled weavers, but I'm both a novice and out of practice. Still, I should at least be able to make some homespun to use as blankets, or to sell for work tunics.' Her tone was light, but he could see that she spoke with some effort.

'You're tired.' She didn't argue. 'I'm not surprised – such a lot has happened today.' She stiffened, thinking no doubt of the court.

'It hardly seems possible that it was only this morning you were tending to Denis and I was speaking for him.'

She seemed on the point of saying something else, but then said, 'You don't think he did it.'

He rubbed his chin. 'I didn't – I still don't, really, but did you see that he held out his left hand to take the hammer?'

'That doesn't necessarily mean much, though, does it? It might just have been nearer.'

He shook his head. 'No. I mean – yes, but it reminded me that I'd seen him using it in his left hand when I was watching him at work the other day.' He sighed and stirred the fire. 'But I still don't think he did it.'

Alys gave a huge yawn. 'Sorry. I am listening – please carry on.'

He smiled. 'Why don't you get yourself to bed? It's been a long day, and you were up half of last night as well. I'll watch the fire until it dies down and then come in.'

She nodded and stood, dropping a kiss on the top of his head as she passed.

He took her left hand. 'Will this be all right?'

He felt her shiver. 'It will be fine. I washed the dirt out so it shouldn't swell.'

She made as if to move off, but he kept hold of it for a moment, playfully. 'I don't suppose it was you who hit Robin?'

'Of course not. Why would you think that?'

He was surprised at her tone. 'I was only jesting. I asked him on the way out and he said he got hit by a branch while he was felling in the woods today.'

He still had hold of her hand, and now he looked at it more closely – stared almost right through it.

'What is it?'

'I was just ... I remembered something ... you just reminded me of ...' He shook his head. 'No, it's gone.' He dropped her hand and watched as she made her way into the bedchamber.

Edwin heard the creaking of the ropes of the box bed as she settled herself, and then silence. He blew out the rush on the table, leaving the fire as the only light, and returned to it. He stood with his back to the flames for a few moments to warm himself, and then sat down, stirring the bright ashes. The log Alys had put on earlier was a large one, and it wouldn't do to leave the fire unattended while it was still alight. Still, he had plenty to think about – well, two things of importance – and the silence of the cottage, broken only by the crackle of the slowly dying flames, was the best thing for it.

He used his foot to push in a stick that was trying to escape from the hearth stones. On the afternoon that he had died, Ivo had been out at Aelfrith's farm. They had argued, he had learned from his conversation earlier, about the proposed new bread oven. Because the farm was three miles out of Conisbrough, Aelfrith's family had always baked their own bread there, instead of walking in. As the village oven was free to use, this had made no difference to anyone, but Ivo had apparently been so zealous about his new plan that he had ridden out there to tell them that from now on they would have to use the earl's new oven in the village along with everyone else – and pay the same fee.

Aelfrith, as far as Edwin could judge, had been quite angry. He was out in his fields every day, so the task would fall upon his mother, and he had become quite animated as he'd told Edwin how unfair this was, how she was ill and couldn't be expected to walk that far. *Another reason for him to get married*, thought Edwin, with a small smile at the remembrance of Alys's actions that evening. A fit young wife would be a Godsend out on the farm.

It sounded, however, as though Aelfrith had said some of these things to Ivo's face, and the interview hadn't ended well. Aelfrith had sworn to Edwin, however, that the bailiff had been alive and well when he left. This Edwin knew to be truth, as Ivo had been seen back in the castle later that same evening.

But had Aelfrith come to Conisbrough during the night and committed murder? It seemed a bizarre suspicion, but then, the thought of anyone in Conisbrough, men he'd known all his life, killing Ivo was equally unbelievable. It had been dark, but Aelfrith knew the road well, and there must have been some small light from the waning moon. But *why*? Surely a dispute over an oven wasn't sufficient reason for anyone to kill? And why would Ivo agree to meet him in the middle of the night to continue an argument that could easily have waited until daylight?

The fire was dying down. Edwin pushed the hot ashes from the edge to the centre of the hearth, and began to stack the turfs round it.

It took him a long time, and deliberately so, for he didn't really want to go to bed. The second matter that was pressing on him had nothing to do with the murder, but it was hurting him more. Alys had explained what had happened to her injured hand, and of course it was perfectly plausible – who hadn't, at some point, grazed their knuckles on a tree in the woods?

The problem was that Edwin had now been in the earl's service for half a year, and in that time he'd had to talk to many people in order to get the truth from them. And so he could tell when someone was lying.

━━━━◆◆◆━━━━

Alys awoke the next morning to find that the bed was empty: Edwin had already risen. Worried that she might have slept too long, she dressed quickly and moved to the main room. Edwin wasn't there – was he already at church? But a glance out of the window, as she unshuttered it, showed her that the inhabitants of other houses were only just getting up. Besides, the bell hadn't rung yet, and she would surely have heard that.

She broke off a piece of bread and chewed it as she began to steel herself for the effort of appearing normal all day. She began to plan. The whole village would attend Mass, so she would be able to hide in the crowd and wouldn't need to go anywhere near Young Robin. He would no doubt be questioned by all who saw him as to how he'd been injured, but she already knew from Edwin that he'd made up a story about being hit by a branch. That was a relief, at least.

After Mass she would seek out Cecily – she would always be safe with her, and the female company would do her good. She would string that out for as long as possible, but eventually she would have to come home; there might be no work in the fields on a Sunday, but chores in the house never stopped. Edwin might or might not be there – she had no idea where he'd gone or whether he'd be about the business of the murder. Probably the latter, so she would be alone in the house. But *he* wouldn't dare call, would he? He wouldn't dare come round while she was alone? However angry he was with her?

The bread became suddenly tasteless. But there would be plenty of people around the village. If he knocked, she would keep him outside where anyone walking down the street could see them.

Edwin came back in, breaking into her thoughts. She looked at him enquiringly.

'Just went to check on the pigs, as they won't go out today. But they're calm – now they've finished the slaughtering, most of the smell has gone so it's not worrying them so much.'

He sat at the table and took some bread himself. 'After Mass, I think I'll have to start round with more questions again.' He grimaced and spoke with his mouth full. 'That'll make me popular.'

'Do you want me to come with you?' Chores be damned; she would feel safer with Edwin.

He smiled at her. 'That's kind of you, but I think I'd better go on my own.' *Because nobody will take me seriously if I bring my wife with me*, hung unspoken in the air. 'But if you happen to hear anything useful while you're all gossiping outside church, you let me know.'

Alys nodded and tried to pretend she didn't care. *Gossiping*. Was that all she was good for? Then they both heard the sound of the church bell.

They made their way up the street, greeting and meeting neighbours as they went. They stopped at the gate of Cecily's house to wait for her and William to join them; as the couple made their way down the path Alys could see that William's face was drawn with pain, though he was walking and only leaning on one stick. Edwin held out a hand to assist him, without thinking, then quickly dropped it by his side again. Their slow pace as they followed the crowd to the church meant that others passed them, and they were almost the last to enter. The only others behind them were Osmund and Gyrth, who slipped in behind them and stood at the back.

The congregation stood, most of them paying attention but a few still chattering, as Father Ignatius entered. He made his way to the altar and then stood facing it, his back to everyone else, and began to intone the Latin of the Mass. Nobody except Edwin understood a word of it, of course, but the lines were so familiar that they slipped over Alys and she felt comforted. All over England, the same words were being spoken in churches, and her own family would be listening to them far away in Lincoln. Were any of them thinking of her?

Her mind drifted, but she was brought back to the present by William's painful shifting next to her. Standing still must be even worse for him than walking, and she longed to suggest that he should sit on the bench at the side, placed there for the elderly and infirm, but there was no point; he was too proud. Eventually, though, came the words *Ite, missa est*, and the villagers were streaming out the door before Father Ignatius had even left the altar, allowing space for William to force his stiff legs into motion.

Outside it was grey and mizzly, though not actually raining. The women gathered in a little knot, as they always did, before they had to go back to their cottages and face the daily grind again; the men did the same. Alys hovered on the edge of the women's group, listening to them with one ear but also trying to keep up with what the men were saying, for she had heard Edwin's name spoken, and as far as she knew, he was the only one by that name in Conisbrough. He wasn't there, having not yet come out of the church.

She didn't dare edge closer to them, so she caught the mood rather than the actual conversation, but it didn't sound good. Rumbling, angry tones, with even the reeve, whom she could just see if she glanced surreptitiously without turning her head, getting quite agitated.

The carpenter, who was also of the group, broke off to cuff a couple of his smaller sons, who had started fighting, and then he called over to Avice. 'Stop jangling there, girl, and get back home. We're all hungry.'

Avice bowed her head, collected two much younger sisters, and hurried off without saying anything.

The remaining group of women were broadly sympathetic. 'Difficult for her, and so young, too.' 'He wants to marry again, get a wife to sort them all out before they get too wild.' 'Aye, but who wants a man with thirteen children already in the house? You'd have to be desperate, and even then there's other men you'd choose first.' 'And maybe not so much work for him if everything is going to be in stone these days.' 'He'll have to send some of those lads out for labouring. Shame for Avice there weren't more girls, though – might share the work out a bit.' 'Well, after what happened to the older one … anyway, the littl'uns will be bigger soon, and that'll help.'

Alys drifted away from the women's talk again, because Edwin was coming out of the church alongside the priest. The men parted to let them through, staring at them in stony silence until they had passed and were out of earshot. Then the ugly buzz of complaints started again, though she couldn't make out the details.

The groups broke up and everyone meandered towards home; the men to spend a few hours in their own vegetable gardens, rather than out in the fields; the children to help or get into mischief; the women to cook and try to keep their children out of trouble. Most of the houses in the village would be full of life and noise, but Alys's would be empty.

She shrank closer to Cecily as the carpenter's noisy brood scampered past them. Young Robin wasn't among them – he was still talking to some others, evidently the subject of raillery about his injury.

Alys tried not to think about him. 'Why are so many of them called Bert?' she asked, suddenly.

William, keeping pace with them in his halting gait, snorted.

Cecily laughed. 'Yes, it was foolish, really.' She turned to Alys. 'There's no mystery. It's only three of them, and they do have different names – Herbert, Lambert and Albert – but they were all born so close together, less than a year between each and poor Hawise having no time to recover, that nobody expected all of them to survive, so Robin said he'd just call them all Bert and have done with it.'

'But they did – all survive, I mean.'

'Yes, a miracle, we all said. Fourteen children that woman bore, and never lost a single one of them. Though having Barty at such an age killed her, poor soul.' Cecily crossed herself before continuing. 'Never seen anything like it in Conisbrough, not in my lifetime, anyway. Some manage not to lose any babes, but only ever in small families, never so many. And the rest have their … losses to deal with.' She fell silent.

They reached Cecily and William's cottage, and Alys watched them go in. Then she continued on her way home, entering the empty space between the four walls, and shutting the door behind her.

Once Mass was over, Edwin waited for the congregation to disperse before he went to find Father Ignatius.

The priest was in the little sacristy, taking off his white alb and folding it with care. 'I'm on my way up to the castle to say Mass there, but this is difficult to get clean if it gets muddy.'

'You'll see Sir Roger in the chapel?'

'Yes, and others too. Why, did you want me to pass on a message to him?'

Edwin poked at a candle that wasn't straight in its holder. 'No, not really. I don't have anything new to tell him, not yet.'

Father Ignatius paused in the act of stowing his things in a scrip. 'But you don't think the mason is guilty?'

'No.'

'Then we must not let an innocent man hang. Tell me how I can help.'

Edwin made a helpless gesture. 'The only way to do that is to make sure we find out who really did it, and I'm no further on with that. Nobody will talk to me.'

'I speak with many of the villagers, so I'll bring the subject up and see if anyone says anything. It's not much, but it's a start, at least. Of course, I couldn't repeat anything anyone said in confession, but in general conversation …'

'Thank you, Father. And you could also visit Denis in his cell to pray with him, give him what comfort you may.'

The priest slung his scrip over one shoulder. 'Of course. I would do that in any case, even if he were guilty – every soul deserves its chance for repentance and forgiveness. But now I must be on my way.'

Edwin turned to walk with him. 'Well, if you're saying Mass for Sir Roger, you can at least be guaranteed one person's full attention.'

'Yes. Almost too much, indeed.' Edwin's face must have registered surprise, for he continued, hurriedly. 'I know it's an odd thing for a priest to say, and of course I appreciate any man who wishes to serve God to the best of his ability. But the rules do try to encourage us away from fanaticism, and Sir Roger is … knocking on the door of it.'

They reached the main part of the church, now empty. Father Ignatius continued. 'While such devotion, such asceticism, might be acceptable in a monk, he is a knight and therefore must serve in a different way. His continual withdrawing into himself isn't good either for him or for the men under his command.'

'I have noticed that he's been different since we came back from Sandwich. You know why, of course.'

The priest crossed himself. 'Yes. *Requiescat in pace*. But that can't be the whole reason. It's been several months since then, and I have trouble getting two words from him – or at least, two words that aren't discussions of scripture. The only animation I've seen him display since he arrived is …' he tailed off.

'What?'

'Of course, I should have mentioned it before. He overheard Ivo blaspheming, and was roused to great anger.'

Edwin stopped. 'Really? When was this?'

Father Ignatius made an effort to remember. 'About two weeks ago? Ivo came here to speak to me about tithes, and he took the Lord's name in vain when he became heated. Sir Roger was just coming in to speak of something else, and he heard. I've rarely seen him so angry. It's a sign, I suppose, of how much more devout he's become.'

Edwin considered this. Sir Roger had always been pious – much more so than any layman Edwin had ever met – but he seemed to do it in a gentle, joyful way. This sounded different. Still, it couldn't have any bearing on the murder, so he simply shelved it away in his mind.

They were now at the church door. Edwin's eye was caught by a movement in the porch, and he saw Osmund hovering there.

Father Ignatius addressed him. 'Yes, my son. Did you need to speak to me?'

Osmund had a nervous look; his eye went from the priest to Edwin and then back again. 'No, Father, no. Not now.' Then he was gone.

How strange. They made their way out of the church, where the villagers were gathered in groups as they usually were for a while after Sunday Mass. Edwin followed the priest. 'I'll walk up to the castle with you, if I may – I'll start there with some more questions and then work my way back to the village.'

Once they were through the main gate, Father Ignatius carried on, while Edwin stopped in the outer ward to look about him. There was less work going on today, of course – even the forge was unlit – but some jobs never stopped, and Edwin spotted Arnulf supervising the mucking out of the stables.

He made his way over, and stood for a moment in the patch of watery sunlight that was temporarily bathing the front wall.

Arnulf joined him. 'All right?'

'Yes and no – I'm fine, thank you, but I haven't got much further with finding out who killed Ivo.'

The stablemaster looked confused. 'I thought that were what the court were all about yesterday – I heard tell that you'd found the guilty man.'

'Not exactly.'

'Who's that locked up in the gatehouse cell, then?'

'One of the masons. The jury found him guilty, but I don't think he did it.'

Arnulf shrugged. 'Foreigner, though, isn't he? Probably best to let him swing and then we can all forget about it.'

Edwin wasn't so tired that he couldn't be incensed by this. 'But what about justice?'

'There's little enough of that in this world. If he's innocent then he'll go to heaven, won't he? And the guilty man will go to hell in the end, whatever happens now.'

'Yes, but –' Edwin's eye was caught by one of the grooms, who was carrying a bucket in his left hand. He changed the subject. 'What I'm looking for at the moment is someone who favours his left hand.'

'Oh, like Sir Roger?'

'Yes, it's not something I've ever paid much attention to before, but now I realise that some people … what did you just say?'

'I told you the other day, didn't I? Or did I – I can't rightly remember now. Sir Geoffrey had terrible trouble with him when he were a lad, 'cause he'd always hold his sword and his shield the wrong way round. But Sir Geoffrey beat it out of him in the end. Didn't make too much difference to him when he were riding, luckily for me.'

Edwin was stupefied. And to think he'd never noticed! But then again, why would he? The issue had never been of any interest before, and besides, Sir Roger held his sword or lance in his right hand, the same as everyone else.

The thought was just too enormous to contemplate, coming on top of what Father Ignatius had just said. Sir Roger? The whole notion was unthinkable, impossible.

Arnulf was bidding him goodbye as he went back to work. Edwin answered him absent-mindedly and then walked off. He needed to think.

———•◦•———

Alys stiffened as a knock sounded on the cottage door. She stood behind it, hesitating, but then heard Rosa's voice. 'Are you there?'

She forced a smile and opened the door. 'I didn't expect to see you today.'

'I'm supposed to be at home helping Ma, but I said I had to come and fetch something I'd left here yesterday. I can't be too long or she'll crack her knuckles on me when I get back.'

'Well, come in, then. Is anything the matter?' Alys noted for the first time that Rosa seemed agitated. 'Is anything wrong with Hal?'

'Oh no, nothing like that – but thank you for asking. No, I came about two things.'

Alys ushered her towards the fire and offered Rosa a seat, but she remained standing, rubbing her chapped hands over the warmth.

'The first is – thank you. About yesterday, I mean. Not just the meal but inviting me over while Aelfrith was here.'

Alys felt her lip curl up, despite herself.

Rosa saw it and rushed on. 'Oh, now – nothing like that. He didn't say nothing on the way home, but he did walk all the way with me and stop to talk with Ned for a little while. And he did say goodbye – to me, I mean – when he went.'

'Well, that's a good start. And you're welcome. If I see him again, I'll mention your name to make sure he doesn't forget.' She saw that Rosa was still fidgety. 'What was the other thing?'

Rosa's face went from pleased to agonised within a moment. The hand-rubbing became hand-wringing. 'It's about Master Edwin.'

Alys felt a weight settle in the pit of her stomach. 'What about him?'

'He's not – what I mean is – all the men are angry with him because he keeps asking questions all the time. They reckon he's trying to blame one of them for the bailiff's murder, when everyone knows it was that foreigner.'

'I don't think we do know that it was him. But carry on – is there anything else I should know?'

'Well, today after church when we got home, Pa says to Ned, we shouldn't let our Hal work for Edwin no more. But he's not much use to anyone else yet, unless we can get him a job in the castle stable. So if not, then you'll have to labour for someone else, he says, and Hal can help me.'

'I would be very sorry to lose Hal, but surely –'

Rosa interrupted her, unable to stop now she'd started. 'But it's not just that. Hal do love his job here, and I'm right happy for him, because he's well fed and he's not sick like he used to be. But you need to watch out over Master Edwin – I don't know what they're planning, but Pa says the men are going to say summat to him. Pa says he won't go along with no violence – not with Hal having worked here and it's not right anyway – but something bad is going to happen.' She dropped her hands. 'So I just thought I'd better tell you.'

Alys embraced her. 'Thank you. I'm sure it's nothing we need to worry about too much, but thank you for telling me, and I'll tell Edwin so we'll be ready if anyone comes to speak to him. Now, you'd better go before you get in trouble with your mother.'

She opened the door for Rosa and watched her hurry away.

Once she was alone, she sat down to try and take it all in. She'd noticed herself that Edwin wasn't making himself very popular with all his questions, but he'd dismissed her fears because, as he rightly said, these were people he'd known all his life. But it was easy to be jealous of the good fortune of another, and although Edwin had worked his way into his current high position – at great cost to himself – there were plenty who would see it as simple luck, and be envious. But what would they do? What could they do? Surely if they started to harangue him too much he could simply ask for the knight at the castle to intercede on his behalf? Or would that make things worse?

Another knock at the door made her start almost up off the stool. This time she peered out of the window to see if she could make out who was there before she risked opening the door. Dear Lord, between her and Edwin and all the people they didn't want to see, was life going to be like this all the time from now on?

She felt a sense of relief when she saw that it was Cecily who stood outside, and rushed to let her in.

'I've come to say that I'm on my way up to see Alban – you remember, the mason with the injured face? – and maybe also to see the one in the cell, if they will let me. Would you like to come?'

'Yes, yes I would. Just give me a few moments ...' Alys busied herself placing the turfs around the fire and finding her shawl. Anything was better than sitting here on her own the whole afternoon. 'Ready.'

The rain had started up again, and the road was muddy. They branched off before they reached the castle gate, making their way round to the remains of the masons' camp. There they found some men busy taking down any charred wood that still remained upright, and piling it up some distance away; others sorted their way through damaged cooking pots and other possessions. They had rigged up some rudimentary shelters with canvas and ropes, and a cooking fire was going with something bubbling over it, but the overall scene was bleak and they must have spent the night cold and wet.

The sight of two women approaching made a number of them stop what they were doing so they could stare, and Alys felt uncomfortable. Cecily kept going, however, with a gracious nod to one group, and belatedly they recognised her. Hostility turned to smiles, and then Philippe appeared to greet them.

'I cannot offer you any refreshment, I'm afraid, but welcome.'

'No need for apologies,' said Cecily. 'We're here to see to Alban, and anyone else who might be in need of salves.'

Philippe showed them to one of the open shelters; inside it the wind was still cold, but it was good to be out of the rain, at least.

Sitting propped up in the back corner was the mason Alban. Alys winced at the sight of his face now she could see it in daylight: raw, blistered, peeling. It must be agonising. She knelt to speak to him, to comfort him as best she could while Cecily got to work. She seemed relatively cheerful about it, telling Alban that she was sorry for his pain but that it was a good sign, as it meant the flesh was still alive and would heal. He tried hard not to cry out, but he was rigid all over, fists clenched, sweat beading the undamaged side of his brow. Only when she had finished did he expel a breath and allow his arms to fall limply by his sides.

His eyes were dry, but Alys had tears in her own on his behalf. She held a cup while Cecily poured something into it, and then lifted it to Alban's lips, helping him to sip it down.

'That won't take his pain away,' said Cecily, softly, as they rose, 'but it should take some of the bite out of it, at least, and it might help him sleep.' She turned to Philippe, who had been standing some little distance away and watching. 'Please, allow him to rest for another few days, and I'll return when I can.'

Philippe nodded, and then they listened as Alban murmured something Alys didn't quite catch. The master mason seemed to understand, and he assured Alban that he would see to it that his daily wage was still paid. 'Because,' as he said to Alys and Cecily as they walked away, 'he has a wife and children, and because it is not his fault.' He waved away suggestions of his kindness, noting with some acidity that he would make sure it was added to the lord earl's bill for the work.

They left the camp and walked up to the castle. When they reached the inner gatehouse, they were stopped by the porter; Cecily explained their errand, but he would not take responsibility for letting them see the prisoner, making them wait until a member of the garrison had been fetched, who then insisted on referring the matter to the sergeant-at-arms and disappeared again. The sergeant arrived with all suitable dignity, to be greeted by Cecily, who called him by name – Everard – and enquired after his grandchildren, at which point he thawed and let them through.

He escorted them to the top of the steps. 'Careful, now. I'll come down with you. You shouldn't have too much trouble – he's been quiet – but you never know.' They descended and he unbarred the door.

Denis was sitting in one corner of the room, knees drawn up under his chin and his head bowed. The sergeant barked something at him and he stood. He remained downcast, but his eyes were calm as they met Alys's. '*Mesdames.*'

Cecily bustled forward to examine his wounds; they were healing well.

'Don't know why you're bothering, really,' said the sergeant, who was between them and the door, left open so some light could enter the cell. 'Though I suppose we'd better deliver him to the hangman in one piece.'

It wasn't her place, but Alys couldn't help it. 'Edwin doesn't think he did it.'

The sergeant blinked in surprise at being thus addressed. Then he shrugged. 'That's not for me to say.'

Cecily turned her attention from Denis for a moment. 'But it is your place to speak the truth, is it not? And to see that others do the same?'

'Well, yes, but …'

'And to believe Edwin when he speaks the truth?'

'I …'

Even in this light Alys could see his cheeks redden. He must have been at least fifty years of age, but Cecily continued as though she were scolding a child. 'And don't you forget how honestly Godric dealt with you all those years ago. Remember those rabbits? Hmm?'

He seemed about to reply but his attention was drawn by shouts coming from above, and he was immediately on the alert. Someone was calling him. He looked from Denis to the stairs and back again.

'Go,' said Cecily. 'I'm nearly done here and we'll be safe.'

He took the steps two at a time and Alys could soon hear his voice raised along with all the others.

Cecily made a final dab at Denis's face and then nodded, satisfied. She looked into his eyes and spoke in a soothing tone. 'I know you can't understand me, but be assured that we will find out what happened. Edwin will find out.'

He caught the name. 'Edouin? *Oui*. Yes.'

Alys followed Cecily out and then hesitated by the unlocked door. But Denis had already reseated himself in the far corner, and he made a helpless gesture that she interpreted as 'but where would I go?', so she gave him what she hoped was an encouraging smile and left.

The altercation was centred around the gatehouse; they wouldn't be able to pass, so they stood to watch. A group of village men had come through the outer ward but were now being denied entrance to the inner by the porter. He in turn had summoned members of the garrison, who had shouted for the sergeant, and he was trying to get everyone to quieten down so he could find out what was going on.

'Silence, I said!' He pointed at the reeve. 'You – speak.'

The reeve stepped forward. 'We wish to see Sir Roger.'

'Oh, you do, do you? Why would that be?'

'We wish to accuse someone of the murder of Bailiff Ivo.'

That caused a hush to fall over the whole group, including the soldiers.

The sergeant scratched his beard. 'You mean the French mason? He's already here, in the cell.'

The reeve seemed nervous, but someone behind him gave him a shove in the back, and he continued. 'No. Someone else.'

'So – and let me get this straight – it was only yesterday that your jury found the mason guilty, and now you've changed your mind?'

'We're still not sure he's innocent – they might have done it together, maybe – but we want to accuse someone else, and we have evidence, so it's our right.'

'Oh, evidence, now, is it?' Alys thought for a moment that the sergeant was going to send them all away, but he sighed. 'Right then. I'm not fetching Sir Roger down here on a fool's errand. You tell me now who you want to accuse, and I'll decide whether it's worth his notice.'

The reeve was by now really uncomfortable, almost tongue-tied. Another man opened his mouth, but the sergeant shot out a warning finger. 'Not you. If he speaks for you all, let him speak.' He turned back to the reeve. 'Come, then, who is it? Who's your murderer today?'

The reeve swallowed a couple of times and then managed to get the words out. They floated across the cold, damp air to Alys. 'We accuse Edwin Weaver.'

Chapter Nine

Edwin was staring into the flame of a candle when he became aware of his name being shouted.

He was in the earl's council chamber; he'd wanted to come here straight after his conversation with Arnulf, but remembered that Father Ignatius would be saying Mass in the keep's chapel, which was on the same floor, so he'd hovered outside in the cold until he saw the priest come out. Fortunately, Sir Roger was with him; Edwin wasn't quite sure whether he wanted to speak to the knight until he'd got a few more things straight in his own mind.

He'd drawn back as they passed, and their attention was on each other anyway so they didn't see him. He caught a few pieces of their conversation. Sir Roger was saying 'He can't stop me,' to which Father Ignatius made an inaudible reply, and the knight continued with '… going there now,' and then they were out of earshot.

Edwin then slipped into the council chamber; once again it was cold and empty, and he'd lit a candle by taking a spill to one of the torches in the stairwell. Since then he'd been deep in thought, and he had no idea how much time had passed.

Now he looked up. It was around noon, judging by where the light from the window was falling, and footsteps were sounding on the keep's staircase.

A boy burst into the room, and Edwin recognised young Wulfric, who ran messages for William Steward. He was gasping for breath and his expression was serious – horrified, even.

Edwin jumped to his feet. 'What is it? Has something happened to William?'

Wulfric shook his head and gasped out a few jumbled sentences. They weren't very reassuring to Edwin, though, containing as they did the words 'murder' and 'now'.

He grasped the boy by his shoulders. 'Stop! Stop. Good. Now, start again.'

'William sent me to warn you. You're accused of murder. They're on their way to get you but I was faster. William says –' The footsteps on the stairs came closer and his voice rose to a squeak. 'Too late!'

Edwin felt strangely distant as armed men burst into the room, as though he wasn't there at all. He was surely somewhere else, somewhere where this wasn't happening. The men made no move to attack, just simply surrounded him.

He patted Wulfric on the shoulder. 'Off you go, then, there's a good lad.' He looked up at the nearest guard. 'It's nothing to do with him – he was just looking for me the same as you were.'

The man nodded and the group parted to let Wulfric through. As he left he passed Everard, the sergeant-at-arms, in the doorway.

Everard moved to stand in front of his men. 'I don't like this, Edwin, not at all. But an accusation has been made against you, and until Sir Roger gets back to tell us what to do, we'll have to treat you like anyone else.'

Edwin still felt that strange dissociation as he nodded. 'Very well.' There was a pause. 'What do you need me to do?'

Everard looked nonplussed, and then recovered himself. 'Right. You'll have to give me your eating knife and that dagger, and then we'll put you in the cell. Should only be for a few hours, mind, and then Sir Roger will clear this up.'

Edwin took his eating knife from its sheath and placed it on the table. The dagger was on a separate belt so he unbuckled it. He wound the belt slowly around the scabbard before he laid it down. 'Take care of it, please. It was a gift.'

Everard nodded. 'Thank you. Now, we'll go to the cell.' He addressed his men. 'He's not going to try and run away, so nobody is to touch him, you hear? He's still the lord earl's man.'

Edwin heard them murmur their assent, and now the initial shock was over he could feel his mind starting to work through the fog. Of course they would behave towards him with respect for now, for what would happen to them if they mistreated him on the word of the villagers, only for a knight to dismiss the charges and let him go? But Edwin knew, as they made their way down the stairs, that matters were not going to be as simple as that.

All was silence in the inner ward as they walked across it, men stopping what they were doing to watch. There was a crowd around the gatehouse, being kept back by a line of guards, and the shouts and whistles began as they crossed in front of it.

And then he saw her.

His step faltered. Standing by the gatehouse, in tears, was Alys. Edwin wanted to stop but he was surrounded, and as soon as he slowed he felt the pressure of those behind him – although no push, not yet – to continue. He tried to look at her, tried to tell her with his eyes that everything would be all right, but it was no use. He couldn't do it and she wouldn't see it anyway through her tears. All he could do was cast a glance at Cecily, who held her arm protectively round Alys, and at William Steward, who stood next to them with Wulfric hovering behind. Edwin knew they would understand his look: *Whatever happens, take care of her.*

He was shepherded down the steps; the cell was opened. The same cell in which … but he couldn't afford to think about that now or he would run mad. He stepped inside and watched as the patch of light on the floor became smaller and then disappeared, and listened as the door was shut and then barred.

Denis was in the far corner, and now he stood. 'Edouin? You have come to talk to me?'

Edwin almost laughed at the absurdity of the situation. 'I wish I had.' He explained as much as he could, although he was completely in the dark as to why he should have been accused, and what evidence anyone could possibly bring against him. But what did become clear, as he eventually tailed off into silence, was that Alys had been right and he'd been wrong: he should not have been so sure that folk in the village wouldn't turn against him because he'd lived among them all his life. A madness had overtaken them all, and there was no telling where it might end.

'Edouin. Let me ask you a question.'

Edwin forced his mind back into the cell. 'Yes.'

'Did you do this thing? Did you kill monsieur the bailiff?'

'No.' And, after a moment of silence, 'Did you?'

'No.'

'Then someone else did. And someone – whether the same man or not – has got something against both of us. And we need to find out who that is, before it's too late.'

———◦———

Alys waited until the villagers had left the castle, and then made her way down to the outer ward along with Cecily and William. After a brief discussion, the others – loath to leave her – agreed that they should go down the hill to see what they could find out. It might be of use to know who had first voiced the accusation against Edwin, who had supported it, and who had been convinced enough to suggest that the men visit the castle.

She watched them go, William seeming to walk even more slowly and painfully than ever. Then she took up a position in the shadow between two buildings, where she could gain a little shelter from the wind but still have a clear view of the stable. Nobody was quite sure when Sir Roger might return, but that would certainly be the place he would go to first, so – assuming he had managed to get through the village without being waylaid – she could speak to him first. She hoped that he would recognise her as being Edwin's wife.

It was cold, and starting to spit with rain again, but she did not move. She blew on her hands before clenching them tightly under her shawl. Please God, Sir Roger would return before dark.

After some while she became aware that she was attracting some attention. The castle was an almost exclusively male space, and although some women made their way in and out during the day, the presence of one who was merely loitering was enough to invite notice.

At first it was a couple of comments in passing, and then a few that were of a decidedly more lewd nature. She ignored them, but it didn't help, and soon there was a group of half a dozen men around her, teasing, mocking. *Just having some fun*, as they would no doubt say. She didn't want to press herself any further back into the space between the buildings, but she couldn't walk forward either, not with them standing so close. And then one of them put out a hand to touch her.

There was a sudden *smack* noise from the back of the group and they all turned in surprise. A man was lying in the mud and groaning, with the massive form of Crispin leaning over him.

'Oh dear,' he said, his voice bland. 'Didn't mean to hit him that hard – just wanted to see what was going on.' He tensed so that his shoulder and arm muscles bunched. 'Does anyone else want to get in my way?'

The men melted back, the fallen one rising to stumble after them.

Alys looked dumbly at the smith, wondering if she'd just exchanged one bad situation for another, but he nodded and kept his distance. 'Saw Mistress Cecily on my way back up from visiting my mother, and she told me what all that noise was about in the village. She said you were here so I thought I'd check you were all right.'

Relief made Alys's knees feel weak. 'Thank you.'

'Now,' continued Crispin, 'if Mistress Cecily says Edwin's innocent then he's innocent. And I wouldn't believe it of him anyway – and neither does anyone else, deep down. He has friends enough to get him through this.'

Alys felt tears springing from her eyes, and she put up a hand to wipe them away.

'Lord, you're nearly blue with the cold. Do you want to come to my workshop? I'm not working the forge today, but it's always got some warmth in it, and I can light a fire.' He glanced around at the men in the ward. 'And it's open-fronted, public.' He attempted a kindly tone as she continued to cry. 'You're not to be afraid of me.

William and Cecily would never forgive me if I let anything happen to you or the lad.'

Alys managed to choke back her sobs long enough to reply. 'I thank you, sir, but I wouldn't be able to see the stable from there. And I have to see Sir Roger as soon as he gets back.'

Crispin nodded. 'All right. Well, it's Sunday and I'm not at work, so maybe I'll wait here with you. My company isn't up to much, but it's better than some others.'

She agreed gratefully.

He lifted his face to the weather. 'Happen if I stand on the other side of you, it'll keep more of the wind off.' He moved, and Alys immediately felt the benefit of the shelter. She wiped her eyes again, told herself to summon some dignity, and stood up straight next to him.

They waited for some while, Crispin glowering at anyone who came too close. Alys was too tired and overwhelmed to make any attempt at conversation, but the smith seemed a man of few words anyway. Eventually, though, as the sun was on its way to the horizon, he rumbled, 'There he is.'

Sir Roger was entering the castle's outer gate. As expected, he rode straight towards the stable, and Alys was instantly on her way across the ward. In the gathering gloom she got mixed up with the various grooms and men who were swirling about, and she couldn't get near him. Her voice was drowned by the noise, and he was in any case concentrating on his horse as he dismounted and handed over the reins.

Someone trod on Alys's foot, and her exclamation caught the knight's attention. 'Who's that?'

'Oh, get out of the way, woman,' said a rough voice, and Alys was shoved as someone took the horse past her.

Sir Roger's voice sounded again, sharply this time. 'Unhand that woman, this instant.' He peered. 'Step forward, whoever you are.'

Alys realised she still had her shawl wrapped tightly about her and her hood up, so she pushed it back as she advanced.

'Mistress!' His tone suggested that he knew who she was. 'Are you all right?' He looked about him. 'Is Edwin here?'

She had meant to explain the situation calmly, but to her distress, as soon as she looked into his face she dissolved into tears once more, unable to speak a single word.

Everything around her was rushing, the noise crashing over her, many voices trying to speak at once, but she made out Sir Roger's telling them to be silent and then asking one to explain. The voice that replied was Crispin's, and she listened as he told the knight, in very few words, what had happened. She didn't know how much longer she could stand, felt her legs wobbling … and then Sir Roger was holding her arms, supporting her.

Even through her confusion she could hear his tone of authority as he addressed the others, and it revived her. He issued instructions to have a fire lit in the council chamber, for Edwin to be brought there, and for the reeve to be summoned from the village. 'Tell him he may bring two others if he wishes, but no more.'

Then she was moving, being shepherded by the knight's firm hand under her elbow. When they reached the keep he asked her if she would be all right to walk up the steps, and she nearly cried again, at the courtesy from a man so far above them in rank, who had the thought to care about such things. But she kept hold of herself and gulped it back. By the time they reached what Alys assumed was the council chamber she was in control of herself once more, and she could think about how to respond to what was coming.

A small blaze had been lit in the fireplace, but it had not yet got going properly and the room was chill. One servant was feeding the flames and another lighting candles; Sir Roger waited until they had left and then placed two stools by the fire. 'Now. Quickly. Before everyone else gets here. Tell me what I need to know.'

She couldn't speak quite as dispassionately as she had intended, but she managed to get it all out. Edwin had been accused of the murder. Edwin had been locked up. But Edwin was innocent. She knew it, for they – she hesitated at saying such things to an unfamiliar man, but he did know they were newly married – they had been together in their cottage on the night Ivo died.

'I believe you.' He looked directly at her, in an effort at reassurance, and even in the poor light – even in the terrible circumstances – she could not help but be aware of how extraordinarily handsome he was, how piercing his eyes. You could sink right into them. And yet, as she looked, there was something behind those eyes, something …

He broke away and continued. 'But unfortunately what I believe has nothing to do with it, and a woman may not testify in support of her husband, so we will have to find something else.'

Alys heard footsteps on the stairs, and in a moment, there he was. Never mind how handsome anyone else was, there was only one man she cared about; she ran across the room and threw herself into Edwin's arms before he had hardly crossed the threshold.

———❖———

Edwin and Denis both heard the noise coming from the top of the steps. They exchanged a glance and stood, Edwin wondering – in this world that had turned upside down so quickly – whether either or both of them were to be released, or whether a third person was about to be imprisoned for the murder. As it was, the door opened and Everard stood framed in the dim light. 'Sir Roger's back. He wants to see you.'

'Both of us?'

'No, just you. But he'll be safe in here.'

Everard stood to one side to allow him to pass. Edwin started to move but was stopped by Denis, who hadn't understood the exchange and was worried that Edwin was being taken out to face summary punishment.

'Don't worry, I'm just going to see Sir Roger – the knight – and I'll try to explain everything. For both of us.'

Denis nodded and retreated to sit against the far wall once more, bringing his knees up and wrapping his arms around himself for warmth. Edwin followed Everard up the steps.

It was almost dark as they crossed the ward, making their way by the light of the scattered braziers, so Edwin didn't feel like everyone in the castle was staring at him. He tried to gather his wits so he knew what he would say when he reached Sir Roger, but he was so cold he could hardly think straight, and besides, what was there to say? 'I've been accused of a murder I didn't commit' was what anyone would say, obviously, and 'I think the real murderer has done this on purpose' was hardly less trite.

He had at least regained some feeling in his legs by the time they had ascended to the council chamber, and the sight of a fire was most welcome. But not as welcome as the rush of movement that saw Alys in his arms before he'd taken a step towards it. He embraced her, whispering what words of comfort he could summon, and then loosened his hold and turned to Sir Roger.

The knight's greeting was both smiling and sad. Then he looked past Edwin and addressed Everard. 'Leave us.'

The sergeant's voice was uncertain. 'Sir, are you sure …?'

Sir Roger's voice took on an edge. 'In the circumstances, I'm sure I can defend myself against an unarmed man and a woman, if need be. Go out, shut the door and wait outside it. Let me know when the men from the village arrive, but knock before you come in.'

Edwin heard the door shutting behind him. He looked at Sir Roger in silence.

After a moment the knight ran his hand through his hair. 'I wish they would all just … But what in the name of the Lord is going on?' His voice was louder than usual, and not entirely steady. He took a few paces and then stopped, pointing to the stools near the fire. 'Sit, both of you. We don't have long.'

Edwin sank down and gratefully held his hands out towards the fire. 'Men from the village?'

'They are coming to accuse you of the murder. At least, I think that's what they'll do. I am told they did so this afternoon, bravely while they were in a large group, but it remains to be seen whether two or three of them will do the same, and to my face.' He stood again, evidently unable to remain still. 'But this is –'

'Sir Roger, I …' Edwin wasn't able to finish his sentence before the knight was crouching before him, his face close.

'I know in my heart that you didn't do this, but tell me now. Look into my eyes and swear that you had nothing to do with Ivo's death.'

Edwin looked into the depths. 'I am innocent of this crime, I swear it. I will swear any oath you like, and if you have a bible I will swear on it now.'

Their gaze remained locked for a moment, and then Sir Roger moved back and seated himself with a sigh. 'Good. Now, you know that I would happily throw out these men and all their accusations, but while Sir Geoffrey is absent I stand in his place, representing the lord earl and his justice, and we must see that laws are followed. They must be permitted to voice their accusations if they wish, and then they can be refuted properly, in the open, so that no suspicion remains.'

Edwin nodded. 'Justice must be done.'

He was alarmed to see that this seemed to set Sir Roger off again with another anxiety. 'Justice?' He turned his face to the fire, so Edwin couldn't read it, and continued in an undertone. 'I hardly know what justice is these days. What is justice, when … oh, if only the Lord's will was clear!'

He seemed so tense, so agitated, that it was almost in Edwin's mind to think whether he should, whether he *dared*, ask Sir Roger to swear the same oath of innocence about the murder.

Fortunately he managed to restrain himself long enough for a knock on the door to be heard, and Everard was there saying that the village men had arrived.

'One moment.' Sir Roger moved to place himself in the earl's chair. 'Edwin. Remain seated – I won't have you standing before them as though they have the right to judge you here – but move your stool a little further this way, so you can see them as well as me. And mistress, please stay by the fire.'

Edwin belatedly became aware that Alys had been holding his hand all this time, and he raised it to his lips to kiss the grazed knuckles before he moved away.

Once Sir Roger was satisfied, he raised his voice. 'Enter.'

Edwin watched as the reeve entered the room, followed by Alwin and Young Robin. They looked suitably overawed by their surroundings, and Edwin recalled the nervousness he'd felt the first time he entered the room.

The three men stood before Sir Roger, who allowed the silence to stretch before he uttered one word. 'Well?'

'We're here –' began the reeve in a high, strangled tone. He stopped, cleared his throat and started again. 'We're here to accuse Edwin, son of Godric, of the murder of Bailiff Ivo.' He wouldn't meet either Sir Roger's or Edwin's eye, although both Alwin and Young Robin glared.

'And on what basis do you make this accusation?'

They looked uncertainly at each other, so Sir Roger spoke more plainly. 'Come. Yesterday the jury found the mason guilty, and it was said before the court that nobody had seen the fatal blow struck. How, then, do you come to the conclusion that Edwin is the culprit?'

Now they all broke out at once, and Sir Roger had to hold up his hand. 'One at a time. You first.' He pointed at the reeve.

The reeve cleared his throat again. 'He was jealous of Ivo taking the job, when he thought it would be his after his father died. Wanted him out the way.'

Sir Roger looked incredulous. 'It that the best you can come up with?' He waved his arm as if to dismiss them.

Alwin cut in. 'And the bailiff wanted his house when he came, so they argued about that.'

Sir Roger turned to Edwin with a look of surprise, and Edwin realised the knight hadn't known about this. He shrugged. 'He did ask about it. But that was because he thought the house went with the position; once it was explained to him that it was my father's own, he agreed to stay in the castle until his could be built.' He tried to keep his voice level, but he remembered the cold feeling that had gripped when he'd thought, however briefly, that his wife and his mother were about to be made homeless.

Nobody picked him up on that, but unfortunately mention of the house reminded everyone of another subject.

Young Robin spoke next. 'Yes, a stone house, being built by masons. And we all thought that fellow had done it, until you stood up for him.' He was staring at Edwin with a venom that Edwin just didn't understand – what had he ever done to Young Robin to deserve this? 'So why are you so certain he didn't do it?' He turned to Sir Roger with a triumphant tone. 'The only way he could be so sure the mason is innocent is that he did it himself.'

Sir Roger made the mistake of hesitating slightly, and Young Robin pushed his advantage. 'And there's more.' He nudged the reeve. 'You tell him.'

The reeve still wouldn't meet Edwin's eye. 'He was seen threatening Ivo, Sir Roger.'

Edwin sat up straight in shock. 'No I didn't!'

The knight, too, looked shaken. 'Threatened Ivo? You have witnesses to this?'

They were all nodding now, and Alwin took up the tale. 'Yes. 'Twas after the manor court, the one about the oven – he came up here to the castle after him and threatened him. Some of the guards saw him, and one of them told my son Ned.'

The other two were agreeing, and Sir Roger looked at Edwin, nonplussed. 'You say you didn't?'

'Of course I didn't.'

'But you all say you have a witness?'

'Yes, sir.'

Sir Roger grabbed at a straw. 'But none of you saw it yourselves. What you're saying is that someone saw it, who told your son, who told you. I can't arrest a man on that.'

'But you can ask him yourself, sir. Jack, it was. Jack, the son of Old Jack.'

Edwin followed Sir Roger's gaze and saw that he was looking at Everard, who had been standing silently inside the door all this time. 'I do have a man by that name, Sir Roger, though I can't at this moment speak to the truth of anything he might or might not have seen.'

Sir Roger sighed and closed his eyes for a moment. Then he opened them and looked steadily around at all of them. 'This, here, now, is not a formal proceeding. No verdict can be brought. But,' he glanced almost apologetically at Edwin, 'I have heard enough to decide that there must be such a proceeding. Go back to the village –' this to the three in front of him – 'and tell everyone there will be another court tomorrow. Messages must be sent to the outlying farms so that nobody is absent, so we will hold it at noon rather than daybreak.'

Alwin and Young Robin smiled triumphantly at each other; the reeve was less enthusiastic. 'I'll see to it, my lord.'

'Good. Now go.'

They filed out, Everard behind them. Once the door was shut, Sir Roger collapsed back into his chair, looking younger and more vulnerable than he had in some while. 'I'm sorry, Edwin. But to dismiss the evidence of a claimed witness without even speaking to him would have been a dereliction of my duty. We will examine him in public tomorrow and should be able to get him to admit he's wrong. You will be able to come up with the right questions, I'm sure.'

'I hope so, Sir Roger.' Edwin's mind was cast back to the day of the manor court. He had spoken to Ivo, certainly, but he hadn't said anything that could be constituted as a threat. And then another thought struck him. The court. The court at which he had not defended the villagers – not to their satisfaction, anyway – and at which he had not appeared to be on their side. They, or some among them, at least, had decided that he no longer belonged to them, and was expendable. Blameable, in the same way that Denis was, in order to deflect suspicion from among their own.

He would have plenty of time to consider this overnight, because he became aware that Sir Roger was saying that he must remain under lock and key until the morrow. 'Although that's as much for your own safety as anything – I can't let you spend the night defenceless in the village.'

He did, however, give orders to the returning Everard that Edwin was to be placed in a room in the castle's household quarters rather than back in the cell.

'Excuse me, Sir Roger.' Alys had spoken for the first time.

The knight seemed only now to remember that she was present. 'Mistress. Of course … I'm sorry you had to see that.'

'I'm not sorry, sir, for now I know what Edwin is up against.' Her voice was firm, and Edwin didn't think he'd ever loved her more. 'But may I request,' she continued, 'that I bring him some supper and a blanket? I don't think he's had anything to eat all day.'

A very faint smile crossed the knight's careworn face. 'Ah, would that every man had a wife such as you. But there's no need. Edwin will get some of the castle's evening meal and he'll have a proper bed in the chamber.'

This reminded Edwin. 'But, if you please, can you do the same for Denis? It's so cold in that cell.'

With what Edwin thought was some reluctance, Sir Roger shook his head. 'The situation is different. He's been found guilty – I can't let him out. But he will get a hot meal and some blankets.' He looked meaningfully at Everard, who replied that he'd see to it.

'And now go. Think as hard as you can, Edwin.' Sir Roger's eyes were already straying towards the chapel. 'I need to pray.'

Edwin took Alys's hand and left the chamber. On the way down the stairs he had time to tell her to go straight to William and Cecily's house, to spend the night there. But could William even protect both of them? And how fantastical that he should be having to think such a thing, in his home village. It surely wasn't real. Any moment now he was going to wake up.

But he was not dreaming. The cold dash of air as they left the keep hit him but failed to wake him from any slumber; he kissed Alys goodbye and followed Everard across to the castle's household chambers.

Edwin had been convinced that he'd spend the whole night in con-templation, but despite everything he'd fallen into a deep sleep after a hot bowl of pottage, and it was dawn before he awoke.

He sat up and wrapped a blanket around his shoulders. He hadn't undressed the night before, and there was no water to wash in, so there was nothing to do but wait. The chamber was one of the ones that ran along the inside of the curtain wall, so he had stone behind him; the other three walls were of wood, with a door directly in front that led out to the covered gallery. There was a window next to it, but it was shuttered – not very tightly, as it happened, for light came round the edges, which is how he had known it was past dawn. He hadn't tried the window or the door latch, for what would be the point? If he got out the chamber he would still be in the closely guarded inner ward, and anyway, attempting to escape was the last thing he wanted to do, for his guilt would be assured by it.

As he stared at the door, it opened. Edwin stood in readiness. But it was not a party of guards, it was Sir Roger.

'I've been thinking,' he began, without preamble. Edwin could see that he had – the knight looked like he hadn't slept at all.

'Yes?'

'We don't have to have this court. The sheriff will be here within the next two days, and we could leave it up to him. You might get a fairer hearing.'

Edwin considered that for a moment. Not to be hauled in front of the whole village … but it was no good.

'Don't you remember? The sheriff is in dispute with the lord earl about his taxes. The last letter my lord sent to him was quite sharp, so he'd probably use this as an excuse to get back at him.'

Sir Roger sat down heavily next to him. 'Of course.' He crossed himself. 'A sad state of affairs that your fate would depend less on your innocence than on a quarrel between two powerful men.'

It was the nearest he'd ever come to voicing even the slightest criticism of the earl, and Edwin looked at him in surprise. 'You're worried.'

Those blue eyes met his own, and for one moment Edwin could see into the depth of the knight's soul. 'You …' he began, and then tailed off.

'Say it. Whatever you were going to say, say it.' Sir Roger was now staring straight ahead.

'You've lost your faith. After … after what happened in Sandwich, you've lost faith in the Lord's mercy, and now you don't know what to do because you thought the path in front of you was clear, and now it isn't.'

Sir Roger buried his head in his hands and said nothing for a few moments. Then he nodded and spoke, his face still hidden. 'You have it.'

Edwin wondered if the situation he was in could possibly get more bizarre, as he – the man about to face a charge of murder – tried to comfort his friend, the man who was supposedly in control of the castle, the village and everyone in it.

Eventually Sir Roger raised his head. His face was white and drawn, but it was dry. 'I must go,' he said. He gave an approximation of a laugh. 'I have a funeral to go to. Father Ignatius is burying Ivo this morning, and someone should be there.' He stood and squared his shoulders. 'We'll meet again at the court, where I hope … I hope very much that I will not lose someone else who is dear to me.'

Edwin knew that he wasn't talking about Ivo, and he nodded. 'All I can do is speak the truth, and trust it is enough.' He hesitated a moment. 'Shall we … I mean, would you like to pray together for a few moments?'

Sir Roger was still facing away, so Edwin couldn't see his expression. 'No. No, not now.'

He walked out, shutting the door behind him.

It seemed only moments before a party of guards came to escort Edwin down to the village, but in reality it must have been at least a couple of hours, as he vaguely recalled eating something at dinner time, which would have made it late morning.

He felt all eyes upon him as he came to the village green. The jury sat to one side, the benches full; Aelfrith had been summoned along with others who lived out of the village. The rest were in the usual huddle, except for Alys, Cecily and old Agnes, who stood apart. Edwin had always liked Agnes, and now he felt nothing but warmth and gratitude that she should go against the rest of the village on his behalf. Of course, given that she was both the priest's housekeeper and the smith's mother she would never be in any real danger, but there were ways of being unpopular in the village that didn't necessarily involve physical violence.

Proceedings began. The reeve, still looking uncomfortable, voiced the same accusation as had been made the previous evening – that Edwin had murdered the bailiff out of jealousy, and that, to support the accusation, a witness had seen him threatening Ivo on the day before his death.

Edwin had seen Jack Jackson among the group of guards marching down from the castle, and he expected him to step forward, but instead Sir Roger called Everard, the senior man in the garrison.

'You have heard these accusations, and specifically that Edwin threatened Ivo in the inner ward while you were there. What have you to say?'

The sergeant-at-arms stared straight ahead. 'Didn't see any of that, sir. Edwin came to sit down next to him while he was eating, and I called my men away because it was time for drill. I did look over that way some time later, but Edwin was gone and Ivo was sitting there finishing his dinner by himself, no harm done, certainly no violence.'

Edwin breathed a sigh of relief. Perhaps this was all going to blow over. But now Everard was being dismissed and Jack was standing forward. Edwin suddenly – vividly – recalled his father, Old Jack, being hauled up before the manor court some years ago for assaulting a neighbour while he was drunk. He'd had to pay a hefty fine, imposed by Edwin's father. But that had been entirely justified: surely Jack couldn't hold a grudge after all this time?

Sir Roger asked him what had happened up in the castle that day, and he was keen to speak. 'I was closer, sir, and I saw it all. Edwin came and sat next to him, spoke to him, made him stop eating. Then they had an argument. I couldn't hardly believe it at first, not Edwin – all his life he's been timid as a mouse. But there he was, telling Master Ivo he didn't know how to do his job properly.'

There was a murmur of surprise around the court.

Jack was appreciating having an audience, and now he started to play up to it. 'I know – who would have thought it? But there's more.'

The onlookers were now openly encouraging.

'So Master Ivo, he says he's the bailiff and everyone should recognise his authority. And that's right, to my mind.' He looked around for the expected nods of assent, and was encouraged to continue. 'And he says "how dare you" to Edwin.'

Edwin wasn't quite sure that was the order in which things had actually been said, but he didn't think that interrupting was a good idea. Better to listen to it all and then refute what he could, logically.

The man was in full swing now. 'But you haven't heard the worst bit yet.' He paused for effect. 'So, we had to get up and move off, but I was still close enough to see and hear it. "I don't want my father's work destroyed", he says. Then Ivo said something – didn't quite catch that bit – and Edwin stands up, leans over him, and threatens him *with a knife*!'

There was uproar. No, no, no, that wasn't what happened! Edwin really had to say something now, and he tried to interject, but he couldn't make himself heard over the hubbub.

Jack was bellowing over the noise. '"Don't you ever say anything about my father again", he says, while he's waving the knife in his face, and if that's not a threat, I don't know what is.'

The racket continued. Sir Roger appealed for calm. He didn't get it, so he stood up and signalled to the line of guards. They drew their swords, which shut everybody up with immediate effect.

The knight kept his voice level. 'But you did not see any violence? Ivo was whole and well when Edwin left him?'

'Yes, sir. But of course, he's hardly going to kill him right there in front of everyone, is he? That's why he waited until after dark when nobody was around.'

This time the shouts – of surprise, of anger, against him or in his support, Edwin didn't know – could not be quelled until the guards banged their swords down repeatedly on to their shields.

'I will have silence!' Sir Roger cast an angry glance around the court, then addressed the man. 'You may go.' He turned to the jury. 'You will remember his words about what he actually saw and heard; you will ignore his last accusation.'

Some of the men turned to each other and murmured. But Edwin knew that they wouldn't forget it: the damage was done.

Sir Roger was now speaking to the whole assembly. 'We are here to determine exactly what everyone saw and heard, what they know to be true and what they are prepared to swear on the *holy bible*, at the peril of their souls.' He spoke these last words with such force that several of those present crossed themselves. 'I should not have asked something as open as "What happened?" – from now on I will ask direct questions and those called will answer those questions, and those questions *only*. Is that clear?'

He spoke with the voice of authority and rank. Only Edwin knew how brittle it was, how close Sir Roger was to cracking; it was enough for everyone else, there were no dissenters, and it was a more subdued crowd that waited to hear how Edwin would respond.

Sir Roger sat down again and composed himself. 'Edwin. After the manor court, did you walk up to the castle and speak with Ivo, sitting down next to him at the table?'

Edwin knew that he had to set a good example if they were to avoid the court descending into chaos, so he merely said 'Yes, Sir Roger.' He expected that he would now be asked to recount the conversation, but it seemed this was not to be.

'You told him he didn't know how to do his job?'

'Well, maybe not in so many words, but –'

He was halted by Sir Roger's raised hand. 'Your exact words.'

This was not going to sound well, given the lack of context. But he couldn't lie. Hopefully he would be able to explain it properly later when everyone had calmed down.

Edwin exhaled and prepared himself. 'He said, "My lord's interest is best served by everyone recognising his authority in the person of his bailiff", and I said, "Not if the bailiff isn't doing his job properly."' He winced as he realised how that must sound, especially to those who were hostile anyway.

Sir Roger looked surprised, even pained, but they were in front of everyone and he was speaking in the earl's name, so he had to continue.

'Did you threaten him with a knife?'

This was something Edwin could answer with complete honesty. 'No, Sir Roger.'

The knight looked round at the man who had previously given evidence. 'You did not? You're sure?'

'Yes. Ivo banged his hand on the table, his knife fell off it, and I picked it up to give it back to him.'

Sir Roger spoke loudly enough to make sure all could hear. 'Very well. I can see how that gesture could have been *misinterpreted* by someone who was not close enough to see properly and who had his mind on his other duties.' He sounded easier as he continued. 'And that was the end of the conversation?' He was almost turning away.

But Edwin was on oath. Oh dear. 'Not quite, Sir Roger. I said I knew that the estate had been run well these thirty years, and I didn't want Father's life's work destroyed. And he replied "Oh, your father. Yes, I hear about your sainted father wherever I go. It seems to me that he was lucky to retain his position if he was as lax as he seems to have been."'

There was shock around the court, and an instant buzz of voices. Edwin could make out some that might be sympathetic to him – Father having been popular and well-liked, and the villagers not wanting to hear him spoken of thus – and others that were darker. Any man, on hearing his father insulted so, might be tempted to commit an act of violence.

Sir Roger sounded like the words were being dragged from him. 'And your reply to this was?'

Edwin looked at the ground and back up again. 'I said "We will speak more, but let me tell you, if you *ever* insult my father again …" and I walked off.'

'You walked off.'

'Yes, Sir Roger.'

There was conversation around the court, but Sir Roger seemed glad it was no worse. Edwin's eyes sought Alys. She tried to smile, but she was too worried. Dear Lord, what had he dragged her into?

But the worst seemed to be over. Sir Roger had no more questions for him and was conferring with Father Ignatius. 'And now, to the night of Ivo's death. We heard at the previous court of the discovery of the body, so we will concentrate now on Edwin and his movements.'

Edwin tried to unclench his fingers. This would be fine. As his wife, Alys would not be able to testify on his behalf that he had been at home with her, but there were other witnesses who knew that he had had to be summoned from his cottage. Indeed, this was surely what was going to be discussed next; Sir Roger resumed his seat and called out, 'Call the boy Hal, son of Alwin.'

Edwin watched as Hal reluctantly dragged himself forward to stand in the middle of the space. All his usual cheekiness and confidence had drained away; he was an overawed child in front of a crowd of adults and a man of higher rank than any he had ever encountered.

Father Ignatius stepped forward with the bible. Hal's hand was shaking as he placed it on the book.

The priest tried to make his tone kind as he told the boy to swear an oath that he would speak the truth, but Edwin could see that it didn't help his nervousness. But he would be fine, surely? For what could he have seen and heard that would be of any interest?

Sir Roger looked conflicted. Edwin knew that his instinct would be to comfort a frightened boy, but he also knew that the court was becoming dangerously rowdy and that the knight would be concerned above all that discipline should be maintained and authority upheld. And, moreover, he had to keep his own mask of calm and neutrality, despite his devastating loss of faith. Thus he spoke in a stern tone.

'Now, Hal. You understand what I said? I will ask you questions and you will answer them truthfully, and without adding anything?'

Hal licked his lips and nodded, too overcome to say anything.

'When the body of Ivo was found, you were sent to fetch Edwin. Is that correct?'

Hal nodded.

'You must speak, Hal, you must say it out loud for the jury to hear.'

Hal took a deep breath. 'Yes, sir. I mean my lord.'

'"Sir" will be fine. Good. And you ran to Edwin's house, you ran as fast as you could, and you knocked on the door?'

The very ordinariness of the question seemed to reassure Hal. 'Yes sir. And then –'

Sir Roger held up his hand. 'Ah! Don't add anything, remember?'

'Yes sir, sorry sir.' Hal was screwing his hat up in his hands so tightly that Edwin didn't think it would survive. Surely they could just get this very simple testimony out the way and let the boy sit down again?

'Who opened the door?'

'Edwin did, sir.'

'And what did you say? Mind – I want your exact words, not a paraphrase.'

Hal clearly had no idea what that last word meant, but he had understood the first part. He closed his eyes as if reliving the event. 'He opened the door sir, and he said "Hal? What's the matter?" And I said, "It's Ivo, Master Edwin."'

'Good. You're doing well. What did Edwin say then?'

Hal still had his eyes closed. 'He said, "What's he done now?" And then he said "Never mind, just give me a moment to put something on." And then he went back in, and he came back doing up his belt, and he said –'

He stopped dead.

Sir Roger prompted him. 'And then?'

With an agonised expression, Hal looked from the knight to Edwin and back again, and Edwin recalled once more what he'd muttered under his breath as he stepped out the door – words it now appeared that Hal had heard. He was already feeling cold, but now his body turned to ice.

Sir Roger, and some of the onlookers who were quicker on the uptake, had realised that there was something Hal didn't want to say. The knight gave Edwin a pained look that was both apology and a statement that he had to carry on now that he'd started. Then he spoke sternly to the boy. 'Hal. You swore on the bible, remember? You must tell us what you were about to say.'

Hal was still tongue-tied, his pleading face turned to Edwin. Edwin's heart went out to him and his loyalty. But this was his problem, not Hal's, and he couldn't let the boy imperil his immortal soul by telling a lie on oath. 'It's all right, Hal. You can tell them.'

The crowd had now all picked up on the situation and were leaning forward, straining to hear. 'If you please, my lord.' It was hardly more than a whisper. He paused before beginning again, staring straight at Sir Roger so as not to have to meet Edwin's eye. 'If you please, sir, Edwin said "One of these days I'm going to kill that man."'

Chapter Ten

Edwin sat on the bed in the household chamber, his knees drawn up, and stared at the walls. The thought struck him – but still did not sink in, as it just seemed too fantastical – that it might be the last indoor room he would ever see.

He still couldn't process it properly. The jury, men who had known him his whole life, had found him guilty of Ivo's murder. They must know that he hadn't done it, so how had they been persuaded? Had some disease of the mind infected the entire village?

It didn't matter. What did matter was that the sheriff would be here within two days, and that he would find both Edwin and Denis – for the jury had not rescinded their verdict on him – ready for him to take away. Would they even be transported as far as York? Would the sheriff bother to investigate the circumstances, or would he just accept what he was told? Maybe he'd simply have them taken out and hanged right here.

Edwin had seen hangings. He remembered the mass execution of the outlaws earlier in the year, and the boy who had called out for his mother before taking a long time to die. He remembered the more recent hanging in Sandwich, where he'd had to pull the rope himself. At least that one had been quick. What would happen to him, he wondered. Would he be granted the mercy of a swift break of his neck? Or would he strangle slowly, the life being choked out of him as he lost control of …

He just about made it to the slops bucket in the corner before he vomited up the contents of his stomach.

He had no thought for anything until he could stop heaving, but then the weight settled on him of all the people who would miss him. Alys, of course – what had he done to her, asking her to marry him and uprooting her from her home only for this to happen? She would be a widow of sixteen, and one who was unpopular in the village, at that. Perhaps they would even drive her out. His friend Martin would arrive back with the earl in time for Christmas, to find Edwin gone. Lord, but he wished Martin were here. All these months Edwin had been trying to stop him finding a physical, combative solution to everything, so that he – with his supposed superior mind – could think things out, but where had that got him? He would give anything, right now, to have the towering, armed figure standing between him and those who would take him to the noose.

Would the earl even care? Edwin was under no illusions that his lord had the slightest personal interest in him, but he had proven his worth over and over again, and would like to think that the earl might summon up some kind of emotion before he moved on to finding a replacement.

And his mother, his beloved mother – would she return from her honeymoon only to find that her only son was dead? Sir Geoffrey would be angry, furious enough to take revenge in any way he could, but it would be too late by then, for Edwin would be cold in the ground.

Or not. An even worse thought, which put his head over the bucket again, was that his body would not be buried, but would be left to hang, like the rotting corpses of the outlaws that had adorned the crossroads for months. And he would be denied entrance to heaven.

He heard a noise from outside the room, and straightened, wiping his face on the edge of a blanket. It wouldn't do to be found like this. He wondered if it was Alys again – she'd tried to follow him up when he'd been taken away after the court, but had been denied access. Sir Roger had ridden off somewhere on his own again, otherwise he might have intervened; Edwin would try to get a message to him later, somehow. Surely even a condemned man should be allowed to see his lawful wife.

But the rasping 'I'm telling you now, boy, get out of my way or you'll regret it' gave away the identity of the visitor before the door even opened.

William Steward dragged himself in, barked 'Shut the door and leave us in peace' at the guard, and waited until he was obeyed before he sat down heavily on the edge of the bed.

'Well. Here we are.'

There was a moment of silence.

'Edwin –'

'William, I –'

Edwin gestured for the older man to speak first.

'I'm not going to let this happen, Edwin, I swear.'

'I don't think there's much you can do about it.'

'Dammit, I was a soldier once, before most of these striplings were born. If I have to take up my sword again –'

Edwin was alarmed. 'Don't do anything like that! The last thing we need is you getting arrested as well.'

William let out a strangled cry of frustration and thumped his hand down on the bed frame. 'But it's not right!'

Strangely, his uncle's anger made Edwin feel calmer. 'There is still some time. But violence is not the way. I was just thinking that I wished Martin were here, but actually that wouldn't help – the forces of justice are against us. I've been found guilty by the jury, so any attempt to start a fight about it will put you on the wrong side of the law as well. We must think. The only thing that will save me is finding the real culprit, and the answer must be here somewhere.'

William sat for a moment, cleared his throat, looked as though he would start to speak, stopped, and then began again. 'There is another way you could save yourself.'

Edwin looked at him sharply.

'You could …'

Edwin started shaking his head, but William wanted to continue now that he'd started. 'All you have to do is tell them that the mason did it. The men in the village are angry with you because you didn't side with them when they blamed him. If you agree with them now they'll surely overturn their verdict. And the sheriff won't mind as long as he's presented with a culprit.'

Edwin looked at him for a long moment before trusting himself to speak. 'And this is really what you think of me? You think I'd condemn an innocent man to death so I can save my own life? What would I be worth then, in the eyes of my fellow men, my family? In the eyes of God?'

William had been staring at the floor during this, no doubt aware that Edwin was speaking the truth, and ashamed of himself for bringing it up, but now he raised his head again and spoke with anger. 'Of course I don't want you to do that, not if there's another way! But dammit, boy, they're going to hang you. Probably the day after tomorrow. And I will do anything – *anything* – to stop that, you hear?'

'I can't –'

But William was in full flow, tears in his eyes and rolling down his scarred face. 'I remember the day you were born! How happy your parents were, and Cecily, after we – I've watched you learn to walk, to talk, to think. You're the living image of your father, God rest him, and thank the Lord he's not here to see this. I can't stand by and let this happen to you. I won't.' He thumped the bed frame again.

'Stop that.' Edwin spoke rather more sharply than he had intended, and William was surprised enough to break off. 'You'll only hurt your hand, and that's the last thing you need on top of everything else.' He tried to gather his wits. 'Two days. Well, a day and a half. Maybe more if we can talk the sheriff round, but I wouldn't count on that.' He stood and began to pace up and down the chamber. 'I've got all that time to sit here and think, which is good, but I won't be able to get out and ask questions, which isn't.'

William was looking at him with dawning hope in his eyes. 'I can do that, or some of it, anyway. And I can get some eyes and ears around the place.'

'I'll also need to talk to Alys, if we can manage that. We've tried already, but they wouldn't let her in. Sir Roger could overrule them, but he's gone again – and where *does* he keep riding off to, on his own?'

Edwin stopped his pacing and took a deep breath. He didn't feel sick any more. 'First things first. Listen. Please, whatever you do, don't put yourself in any danger, because there is a killer out there somewhere. But if you can sound out who in the village was most in favour of convicting me, and who might have been less keen, that would be a help.'

William nodded and hauled himself to his feet. 'Consider it done. At the moment you can trust me and Crispin, and that's about it. And Father Ignatius. I'll get him to come as soon as I can – they can't stop you seeing a priest.'

'Good.'

William made his way to the door, then hesitated. 'I know what you said. About the mason. And I admire you for it. But this is your *life*, Edwin – I'd rather have you perjured and alive than honest and dead, and so would Alys and your mother.'

Edwin shook his head. 'I won't. I can't. I will not send a man to hang when I know he's innocent.'

'Even if it kills you?'

Edwin hoped his courage would last a little longer. 'Even if it kills me.'

———

The walls were still there. They had faded into darkness as the crack of light around the window shutter disappeared, but they were still there, confining him. Pressing in on him. There was a tallow rushlight in the chamber, but he had not yet asked for it to be lit. It would last maybe an hour, so he'd save it for later in case demons came out of the dark.

He'd been given a bowl of vegetable pottage and some bread from the castle's evening meal. Eating was the last thing he felt like doing, but if he was going to stay alert through the night and tomorrow, hunger would not be his friend. So he had forced it down. He'd been about halfway through when it occurred to him to wonder whether he should be suspicious of poison, but it was too late by then, and anyway, what would be the point? He would be dead in two days anyway. And besides, the danger came not from the castle but the village.

All his life he'd been a villager, aware of the castle looming above him and proud that his father was admitted to it as part of his duties. But both he and Father had been one of 'us', not one of 'them'. Now Edwin saw that it was the other way round; he might think he still belonged in the village, either because he slept there or through some kind of residual memory, but now he was one of 'them', and he needed to start thinking of the inhabitants of the castle, of the earl's household, as 'us'. It had become clearer over the last few days – indeed, he should have seen it earlier. He could come and go in the castle at will, with no challenge to his right to be here or his implied authority.

Authority. That was what was currently missing from the situation. All of this would not have happened if the earl had been present, or even Sir Geoffrey. But Sir Roger was battling demons of his own and could not control the situation; and with no bailiff either, there was nobody to turn to. Which was why he, Edwin, had been asked to step in to resolve disputes recently. He was the earl's only senior representative here.

Wait.

Had he been accused and locked up to stop him asking questions? If so, then the culprit had succeeded – he couldn't do anything from here. But that meant that anyone else asking questions would also be in danger. And to accuse a third person of murder was impractical, so if the killer felt someone was getting too close then he might simply …

Oh, Lord.

A moment later, Edwin was up and banging hard on the door. 'Hey! Let me out! It's important!'

There was no reply other than 'Of course it is. Now shut up before I come in there and shut you up myself.'

Edwin thumped harder on the door. 'You don't understand – you have to let me out! Now!'

———

Alys opened her eyes. The bed was cold and uncomfortable this morning. She turned over to see if Edwin was awake.

She wasn't in her bed. She was lying on a straw palliasse in William and Cecily's cottage. The tiny moment of half-awake comfort disappeared as it all came crashing down on her, and she felt heavy, nailed to the floor, unable to rise and face the day.

A sound came from the bedchamber at the end of the cottage, and the door opened.

It was Cecily. 'Is William out here?'

Alys managed to sit up. 'No.' The room was empty, and there was no indication that William had already gone out. Besides, his awkward, dragging gait so close to her would surely have woken her up.

Cecily moved forward to coax the fire into life. 'He said he would be busy until after nightfall yesterday, so he probably decided to sleep at the castle rather than trying to make his way back in the dark. I'm going to see Alban first thing, so I'll go up into the ward afterwards and ask for William.' A tiny flame sprang up on the hearth, and she fed it some twigs. 'I hope he hasn't slept on the hall floor, or he'll be so stiff he can hardly move today.'

The fire now well alight, she turned to Alys. 'And we will consult him on what we can best do for Edwin. If I know William, he'll be halfway to tearing the walls down by now.' She put her hands on Alys's shoulders. 'Have courage. All is not yet lost.'

Alys didn't want to be left in the cottage on her own, so she agreed to accompany Cecily to the masons' camp. Then she too would go up to the castle, and make as much fuss as she could about being allowed to see Edwin. If she could only talk to him, touch him, know that he was still real and living, she could perhaps persuade herself that there was still hope.

Before long, they were on their way up the village street in the pre-dawn light. Others were about their business: men on their way to the fields, women starting the day's chores, and Gyrth collecting the first of his charges to take to the woods. But no greetings came Alys's way, no friendly looks or waves. Indeed, as they came level with the carpenter's workshop where it stood on the other side of the green, Young Robin stopped what he was doing in order to fold his arms and glare at her with such ferocity that she shivered. And there was not just anger in the expression on his battered face; there was a sort of anticipation, as though he were a wolf looking at its prey. Alys hurried on, trying not to think of what might happen to her if Edwin did not return.

They reached the path that wound its way up to the castle, and then turned off to the side towards the camp. But something caught Alys's eye and she stopped. 'What's that?' She pointed to one of the water-filled holes that rutted the path, a deep one. Something bulky was sticking out of it, but it was difficult to see with the sun not properly up.

She took a few steps towards it and then stopped as she felt every hair on her neck rising. She turned and spread her arms to prevent Cecily from approaching. 'Don't look.'

Cecily caught something in the tone of her voice. 'What is it?' Alys tried to stop her, but Cecily's increasing panic made her strong and heedless, and she pushed Alys's hands away. She walked one or two paces and then broke into a run. 'No! Oh no!'

There was nothing to do but follow her – follow her to the crater where the body of William Steward lay face down with his head under the water.

Cecily's piercing screams and howls of anguish brought people running from all directions: men came down from the castle and up from the camp and the road to the fields; women streamed out of the village. Locked in the horror of the moment, Alys sought only to hold

Cecily, to stop her from injuring herself as the first, overwhelming grief struck her.

More screams sounded as the village women saw the body. There was a clamour of people, nobody saying anything worthwhile or helpful, and then a man shouldered his way through the crowd. It was the castle sergeant-at-arms.

'Stay back! All of you.'

He knelt by the side of the hole and put out a hand to William, but it was clear to all of them that nothing could be done – he was dead and stiff.

The sergeant stood up and turned to Cecily. His voice was gentle. 'I'm sorry, mistress, but he's gone. He must have tripped and fallen in the dark last night.'

He crossed himself and then began issuing orders to his men to move the body.

'Stop.'

Alys hadn't meant to sound so authoritative, and the sergeant was so surprised by the tone that he paused mid-word and turned to her. 'Mistress?'

There were murmurs and faint sounds of derision from the villagers – 'Who does she think she is?' and 'Thinks she's Edwin now, does she?', but she ignored them.

'If you please,' she said, concentrating only on the sergeant, 'he didn't just trip.'

'How can you know that? Did you see something?'

There was a sudden hush.

'I didn't see what happened to him, but I can see him now.' She pointed. 'And there is a footprint on his hood, there, on the back of his neck.'

The crowd surged forward, and it took a few moments for order to be regained. Alys was still holding Cecily, who had stopped screaming but was now making a dreadful keening noise, and she kept her arms about her as she addressed the sergeant once more. 'Well?'

He nodded. 'You're right. Whether or not he fell or whether he was pushed, after that someone pressed his foot down on him to hold his head under the water.' He raised his voice so all could hear. 'The steward has been murdered.'

'What?'

All turned at the sound of the voice to see Sir Roger striding down the hill. The crowd parted to let him through and he came to stand next to Alys and Cecily. He stared down at William's body, standing in silence for so long that Alys wondered what he could possibly be thinking. Then she became aware that he was starting to shake. But he was a knight – surely he couldn't be that shocked or upset at the sight of a body?

But she had misinterpreted: it was not shock, it was anger.

When he finally did speak, there was such fury in his voice, rage so barely suppressed, that those nearest to him had to step back to avoid being blown away by the force of it.

'This is your doing,' he almost spat at the villagers. 'Murder. A murder in the dark, of a defenceless cripple, a man who has served the lord earl loyally all his life, a man who suffered terrible injuries in defence of the old earl and who has lived with the consequences ever since.'

His eyes raked them all. 'And more than this – he is dead because you were happy to convict the wrong men of murder. Denis the mason has been locked up all night and cannot have done this. Edwin Weaver has been locked up all night and cannot have done this. So unless you want to try and tell me that we have a *third* killer on our hands' – he paused, as if daring anyone to say so, but there was silence – 'then you have wilfully let the culprit walk free so you could blame others for your own purposes.'

He allowed his voice to rise a little, and he put his hand on the hilt of his sword, although he did not draw it. 'I have been too lenient. By all the saints, I have let you get away with too much, in the name of the law. And this is the result.' He pointed at William's body. 'Look at him. Look at him, all of you! See what you have done.'

Alys felt Cecily dissolve into sobs once more, but Sir Roger was continuing, oblivious. 'So this is what we are going to do. There is only one man who can get to the bottom of this before tomorrow, and you all know who he is. He has been convicted, yes, so we will stay within the letter of the law – Everard shall stay by his side from the moment he steps out of his chamber until the moment he is locked back in it, so he remains in custody.'

Sir Roger pointed a finger at all of them. 'And he will walk among you. He will talk, he will question you. You will answer to him, or face me. And if *one hair* of his head is harmed, I swear by all the saints that I will hang every man who sits on the jury.'

A final deep breath. 'Is. That. Clear?'

Even the more bellicose among the villagers didn't dare speak, or even raise their eyes. They stared at the floor, nodded, murmured, and melted away.

Sir Roger closed his eyes and turned his face to the heavens for a moment. Then he opened them, knelt in the mud, and began to say the prayer for the dead. He was joined by Father Ignatius, who had appeared belatedly – he would have been saying his morning service, thought Alys, inconsequentially, when Cecily screamed, but he did not allow it to disturb him.

Once they had finished, the two men crossed themselves and stood up. Sir Roger's eyes were sunk even deeper into the hollows of his face, and his voice was agitated as he gave his orders, telling the sergeant to go and let Edwin out, the other men to take the body to the church, and the masons to get back to work.

Philippe, the master mason, hovered. 'Sir ...'

Sir Roger indicated that he should speak. Philippe said something; he spoke in French, but Alys could make out that it was a question about Denis.

Sir Roger replied in the same language, his tone conciliatory but with a shrug that seemed to indicate helplessness. Then he addressed the men who were watching their comrades lift and turn William's body. 'Have Denis taken out of that cell and put in a room in the household quarters. Keep him there, but make sure he's warm and gets something to eat.' And then something to Philippe again.

Philippe bowed his thanks, and then said something that definitely contained the word 'Edwin'. Sir Roger replied, and the mason bowed again before leaving.

Sir Roger turned to Cecily. 'Mistress, I am so sorry. Your husband was a fine man.'

The body was now out of the water and lying on its back. Alys had to avert her eyes from the poor face, bloated now as well as scarred, but Cecily knelt to push back the wet hair with a gentle hand.

Sir Roger now addressed Alys. 'Please, take her home. I'll find a man to go with you.' He ran his eye over those of the castle garrison who were still unoccupied, but they were shoved to one side by the smith. 'I'll go, my lord, if you don't mind your horseshoe waiting an hour.'

'Good. She knows you, so that will be better than a stranger. And, of your goodness, ask your mother to attend to the laying out. I'll see she's paid a fee.'

Crispin inclined his head. 'Such an old friend.' He almost choked. 'And I'll see Mistress Cecily home safe.' Alys was taken aback that such a huge man could display such emotion – his expression was agonised. Of course, he must have known William a long time.

Sir Roger turned to Alys again. 'This is a mess,' he admitted, with raw honesty. 'We all know Edwin had nothing to do with it, but he's still in danger. All we can do is pray that he can find out what happened before the sheriff gets here. I'll go and talk to him now.'

Alys watched him go. She was in such a jumble of mixed emotions – William was dead, but she would soon see Edwin and he might yet be reprieved – that she hardly knew how to feel. But one thing was certain: she would do a lot more than pray in order to save her husband's life.

Edwin's eyes swam with tears as Sir Roger appeared in the open doorway. He should stand, but he couldn't; his legs wouldn't hold him. He was shaking all over. William. His uncle, who had been a permanent fixture in his life, was gone. No more would Edwin sit with him to help with the accounts, surrounded by the comforting aroma of spices; no more would they laugh around the fire during the winter evenings.

And he could have stopped it. If he'd fought harder to get out of the chamber last night; if he'd *thought* harder about what he was doing before he asked William to help. How in the Lord's name was he going to face Cecily? And Mother and Sir Geoffrey, come to that, if he lived long enough to see them again.

'You've heard the news, then.' Sir Roger came towards him, hesitated a moment, and then sat next to him on the edge of the bed. He put one hand on Edwin's shoulder. 'I'm sorry for your loss.'

Edwin nodded, not trusting himself to speak, and scrubbed the sleeve of his tunic across his eyes.

'Did they also tell you that you're free to leave the chamber, as long as Everard is with you, so you can find out what happened?'

Edwin nodded again. He tried to take a deep, calming breath but succeeded only in producing ragged gasps.

Then, rather to his surprise, Sir Roger's own shoulders were heaving, and he dropped his head into his hands. 'It's all gone wrong, Edwin, so wrong!' His voice was muffled. 'After what happened before ... and now my first command, and look what's happened! Truly I'm being punished by God, and I don't know how to make it right. Only you can help straighten the path.'

Edwin could perhaps have responded that Sir Roger wasn't the one facing an imminent sentence of death, but that wasn't fair. If Edwin were executed then Sir Roger would carry the crippling grief and guilt all his life, and to him even being dead would be better than that. This was a man in crisis, a man on the edge: among the other communications Edwin had received when the guard came to open his door was the news of Sir Roger's threat to hang the whole jury. The world had gone mad; or, at least, Conisbrough had.

He needed to pull himself together. He would – he swore it in the Lord's name – find out who had killed William. He'd wanted to find Ivo's murderer, of course, but that was simply out of a desire to see justice done. But this? This was different.

Sir Roger had lifted his face; his chin was resting on his hands as he leaned forward, staring with a gaze that could pierce the wall and see a thousand miles.

Edwin cleared his throat. 'I may question anyone that I like?'

Sir Roger's mind was still far away. 'Yes.'

'Then I'd like to start with you.'

That surprised the knight enough to capture his attention. 'Me?'

'Yes.'

'Very well then. Go ahead.'

Edwin looked meaningfully at the open door; he couldn't see anyone from where he was sitting, but there was no doubt someone within earshot.

Sir Roger got up to shut it and then turned, standing with his back to it to face Edwin in the sudden gloom. 'Go on.'

'Did you kill Ivo and William?'

'Of course not! How could you –'

Edwin waved him into silence. 'I didn't think that you did, but I had to hear you say it out loud. So, here is my second question: where have you been riding off to on your own?'

Sir Roger's face was a mask of indecision. 'I can't tell you. At least, not yet.'

'If not now, then when?'

'I can't tell you that, either.'

Edwin wanted to shake him. Here he was, in danger of his life, and the one person in the castle he might have thought he could rely on was standing there being cryptic and unhelpful.

'William is dead,' he said, brutally. 'Do you want me to be next?'

'How can you possibly say that?'

'Then tell me.' This was as close to insubordination as Edwin had ever come to a man of rank, but the stakes were getting higher by the moment. 'Why won't you help me? Why can't you just …?' He made a helpless gesture, unsure of what he even wanted the knight to do. Make it all better? Make it all go away? Work a miracle?

Sir Roger sat back down on the edge of the bed. 'I've failed here, Edwin. I've failed in my first command. The men don't respect me – they don't treat me the way they treat Sir Geoffrey.' He waved away Edwin's reply before he could even make it. 'Oh, of course I couldn't expect them to treat me exactly the same – I haven't yet earned that level of respect. But the problem is, there are many men here who have known me since I was seven years old. They don't see me as I am now – they see the little boy learning to ride and to fight, the one who got ducked in a rain barrel when he was cheeky to the senior squire.' He ran his hand through his hair. 'And the older ones tell the tales to the younger, and now nobody can see me for what I am today.' His expression was almost begging. 'Tell me what to do.'

'All right. I need you to keep the peace while I'm working. I'm going to upset some people, and everyone seems to be half-mad anyway. Men, patrols … whatever you need to do, but make sure there is no outbreak of violence.'

'I can do that.'

'And please don't hang anyone or threaten them with it until I've found the culprit.'

Sir Roger looked a little ashamed. 'I don't know what came over me. Like you said – a kind of madness. You know I wouldn't.'

Edwin thought for a moment. 'I know you wouldn't, but maybe others don't. So don't make a public announcement rescinding the threat just yet. It's not that I want people to be in fear of their lives – the Lord knows I know what that feels like – but if it helps people to keep their heads down and stay out of danger, then so much the better.'

'Very well. Now, as to you: as far as the law is concerned you're still in custody, so don't make any attempt to get away from

Everard – keep him by your side. And you'll have to come back here tonight, but as long as the daylight holds you may go about as you wish, and everyone knows that.' He put his hand on the door latch. 'Good luck.' And he was gone.

Edwin had barely stood and reached for his cloak when Everard appeared in the doorway. 'I've got my orders, Edwin, and I assume you have yours.'

'Find a murderer, within a day or a day and a half? When nobody has a clue what's going on? What could be simpler?' He fastened the clasp and walked out of the door.

Almost the first sight that met his eye was a puffy-faced Wulfric, standing dejectedly outside the chamber that William had been using as a temporary office. As he saw them approach he rubbed his knuckles into his eyes. 'I seen them taking him to the church.'

Edwin put a hand on his shoulder. 'I know.'

'I don't know what to do.'

Edwin didn't, either, but leaving the boy here to cry wasn't going to help anyone. 'Come with me for today, and I'll find you something to do. Best to keep busy.'

The fresh early morning air, cold as it was, helped to waken his mind, and as they left the castle and headed for the village he was already running through in his head some of the things he would need to do. But first things first – the grief must be faced and his guilt acknowledged.

As they neared William and Cecily's cottage he could see Crispin standing outside the door, glaring at any of the groups of gossiping onlookers who got too close or lingered too long. He shook his head as Edwin reached the door. 'Sad business.'

Edwin sighed. 'Yes. Sad – and evil, and avoidable. Cecily's inside, I take it?'

'Aye. And my mother, and your wife too.' He stepped aside. After a moment's hesitation he let Everard pass as well, but Wulfric took one look at the smith and decided to stay outside.

There was nobody in the cottage's main space, but Edwin could hear sounds from the bedchamber. He stopped just inside the door, barely over the threshold, not wanting to intrude on the women. 'Hello? It's me, Edwin. May I come in?'

'Edwin!' Alys flew out of the chamber and across to him. 'Sir Roger said he would – and I was – but Cecily is …' She stopped and looked at Everard.

'He has to stay with me, my love.'

Everard cleared his throat. 'Can't see there's another way you could get out of the cottage from the chamber, so I'll just stay here where I can watch both doors.' He set himself into the universal, immovable, patient stance of one who had been a castle guard for more years than he cared to remember, and seemed almost to fade into the background.

Edwin allowed Alys to lead him to the bedchamber. Cecily was lying down, her face streaked, and Agnes was stroking her hair and speaking soothing words.

'She's drunk it all,' Agnes said to Alys, 'so she should sleep a while.' She waved an empty cup at Edwin. 'Just a draught to help her stay calm. Nasty shock, finding him like that.'

Edwin felt Alys's hand squeeze his own, and he squeezed back. Then he knelt by the bed, trying to ignore the embarrassment of seeing his aunt with her hair loose. 'Cecily?'

She wasn't quite asleep yet. 'Edwin?' She turned her head. 'Edwin, something terrible has …'

He tried to keep his voice steady. 'I know. And I'm going to find out who did it, I promise.'

'But his soul – so sudden, he wasn't shriven.'

Dear Lord, Edwin hadn't thought of that. 'We'll have Masses said for his soul, Cecily. Lots of Masses. And if I can, I'll send word to Mother to come back as soon as she can.'

She murmured and nodded, her eyelids heavy, and then she drifted off.

'I need to get to the church,' said Agnes to Alys. 'Can you stay with her?'

Alys looked at Edwin.

'It's the best thing you could do just now. Stay with her in case she wakes, and keep safe inside. I'm going to the church too, so I won't be far away.'

'All right.' She looked wan as she subsided on to a low stool and took Cecily's hand, and Edwin was torn. He should stay here with her, should comfort his wife and his aunt in their hour of need, but he had to go – his duty lay elsewhere.

He, Agnes and Everard all left the cottage together. 'Any trouble?' Edwin asked Crispin.

'No. A few wanting to gawp, and some I think really sorry about William's passing. Robin came by to pay his respects, him being a friend of William's many years – real upset he was. And Young Robin says he can leave the other boys working and stand here to mind the door if I need to get back to the castle.' He looked at the sun; it was about halfway between dawn and noon.

'Good,' said Edwin, although something was niggling at the back of his mind that he didn't have time to explore. 'I'll be at the church if anyone needs me.'

'All right.' Crispin turned to the tiny wizened figure next to him. 'And you take care, Mother.'

Agnes gave a toothless laugh. 'Anyone tries to kill me, boy, they'll get what's coming to them.'

They set off on the short walk across to the church. Inside they found the body lying on a trestle table, the face covered, and Father Ignatius praying.

Edwin reached for the purse at his belt. 'There's not much in here, Father, as I don't carry it around with me, but this should be enough for Masses until we bury him, and I'll find more. He wasn't shriven.'

The priest broke off long enough to reply. 'I know. And I'm praying for his soul's passage through purgatory. He was a good man and we'll bury him with all the rites. Do you need me to wait, or shall I make the arrangements?'

Edwin crossed himself and gently removed the cloth. William's swollen face bore witness to the manner of his death, and a glance at the rest of him was all Edwin needed to reassure himself that there was no blood. 'I think we all know how he died, so there's nothing to be gained by keeping him above ground.' He cast an enquiring glance at Everard.

'Sir Roger didn't give any particular orders, so whatever you say.' The sergeant looked at the body and sighed. 'Played together when we were boys, so we did, and both got picked to go with the old earl to France. I was there when he got that.' He pointed to the scar that disfigured William's face even in death, and then placed a hand on his still, silent chest. 'Rest easy, old friend.'

He and Edwin moved away to leave Father Ignatius to continue his prayer in peace; Agnes reappeared from the sacristy with a bowl of water and some rags. As soon as the priest finished and stood, she set to work.

Edwin took one last look at the body. 'We have a lot of different cloth at home. I'm sure there's some linen – Alys will know. So he'll have a decent shroud.'

Agnes nodded but didn't speak, fully engaged now in her sad but necessary task.

'So, what do you want to do?' Everard was asking.

Edwin thought for a moment, chewing his lip. 'You probably don't want to go traipsing all over the fields, and besides, we'll waste half our time if we do that. I suggest we set up here and have people fetched to speak to us. We have Sir Roger's word, so they can't refuse. Besides,' looking back at Agnes, 'being in the presence of the dead might encourage them to speak the truth, finally.'

The church's main door opened, and both of them turned towards the ray of light that spread across the floor.

It was Osmund, who looked disconcerted to see them. 'Is the priest here?'

Edwin looked round. 'In the sacristy, I think.'

Osmund came in, skirting a nervous path so he wasn't too near either them or William's body. 'I just need a word with him.'

Edwin and Everard busied themselves moving the bench that normally stood against the side wall, and finding more trestles to set up, for Edwin wanted everything to look as formal as possible. In order to fetch the board to lay across the top he had to move nearer the entrance to the sacristy, and so he could not help hearing Osmund say, in an agonised tone, 'But Father, I need to confess.'

Chapter Eleven

The morning passed. Cecily slept, and Alys was not disturbed. She sat quietly by the bed, watching, spinning, thinking.

The scenes of the morning ran through her mind, but she tried to put her feelings of horror to one side and concentrate on what she had actually *seen*. Anything she could recall might be of use to Edwin. So, in the silence of the chamber, away from the world outside, she span and she sank into her thoughts.

Nobody had been near them on the path, and there was no question that they might have seen the culprit escaping, because William had been dead some time. Had he been killed before or after the castle gate was opened? That would either implicate or absolve those who lived inside the walls.

She cleared that from her mind. Edwin would think of that – it was obvious. What she needed to do was consider what she had witnessed, and what she could gather from the reactions of those who had been there. That was what Edwin could not do, for he had not seen.

Cecily had screamed. Those who were making their way to the fields had stopped in their tracks and turned. The nearest men had come running, with Hal's father and brother first among them. They had simply stood, aghast. Then others on their way to the fields. After that, men from the castle, who had only had to run down the hill; then people from the village, and finally the masons, who had been drawn by the increasing noise but – unsurprisingly – didn't want to get involved. They had hung back, in a little knot of themselves, until Sir Roger had spoken to the master mason.

She was getting ahead of herself. Sir Roger had arrived last. Crispin had been there somewhere, though she couldn't think whether he'd come from the castle or the village. The castle, surely? Who from the village had been there? Robin the carpenter had pushed his way through the crowd, looking distraught; he had been a close friend of William's. Some of his sons were with him, but not Young Robin – Alys would definitely have noticed him.

That was an interesting point. Who *hadn't* been there? Who might have stayed away from the scene of his own crime?

She closed her eyes. That was a much more difficult question, especially given that she didn't know everyone in the village. She tried to recall the faces around her, though she had been busy trying hopelessly to comfort Cecily. Aelfrith had not been there, but he wouldn't be in Conisbrough at dawn anyway. Gyrth, the swineherd – Alys hadn't seen him, and from what she knew of him, surely he would have been distressed enough at the scene to make his presence obvious. Father Ignatius had not arrived until later, and Agnes had only approached them as they were already on their way back down. But she was so old and moved so slowly that it would have been a surprise if she *had* arrived earlier.

This took Alys's thoughts on to the other women. Had Rosa been there? She couldn't recall at the moment. But the usual gaggle of good-wives, the chatterers from the well and the village oven, they had been there. Could William have been murdered by a woman? He was a grown man, to be sure, but a cripple, and if he had been pushed or tripped from behind while he was already unsteady on the hill, it would not have taken great strength to put him flat on his face. But could a woman then have done what must have been done next – put her foot on the back of his neck and hold down his struggling form until the last breath left his body? But how could *anyone*, man or woman, do such a thing?

Alys shuddered and came to herself in the room again. Cecily was still asleep, but she would no doubt wake soon, and it would be good to have some broth or pottage ready for when she did. She stood and tiptoed out of the chamber into the cottage's main space.

The fire had died down, so she took a little while to bring it back to life before hanging up the smaller of the two cooking pots. Some barley had been soaking overnight, so that went in; there were some leeks on the side table, picked from the garden yesterday, so she chopped up a couple of those, and then added a handful of peas. That would do; in an hour Cecily would have something soft to eat, easy to get down past the lump that would be in her throat.

But it needed more water, otherwise it would boil dry. Alys looked around, but the covered bucket was almost empty; they had left the cottage so early that morning that they hadn't filled it. Still, she needn't leave Cecily and go all the way to the well; after this much rain the butt in the garden should be full.

She opened the door and found herself face to face with Young Robin.

Her jerk of surprise caused her to drop the bucket, which fortunately had the effect of making him step away from her.

'How long have you been there?' was the best Alys could manage, as she sought to regain control of her suddenly wild heartbeat.

'Since Crispin went away. He had to get back to work.' He leaned in towards her, his bruised face uncomfortably close. 'Standing here, thinking about you being in there all alone.'

'Cecily is here.'

He smiled. 'And fast asleep, or so I hear. She wouldn't hear a thing.'

He put out a hand towards her and she smacked it away.

Immediately his smile vanished. 'I'd be careful if I were you. I –'

'You stop that!'

The voice came from the street, and Alys was surprised to find Robin the carpenter coming to her rescue.

He entered the gate and walked right up to his son. 'Have you no respect, boy? William dead only this morning and look at you! Now get back to work, or you'll feel the back of my hand.'

Young Robin was some inches taller than his father, but parental authority still held. 'Aye. Well, I've got plenty to do.' He murmured under his breath to Alys. 'And you're not going anywhere in the meantime.'

He strode off, and Robin turned to Alys. 'I'm sorry, mistress. He's not a bad boy, he just doesn't know how to behave himself around women. No mother, you see.' He paused. 'And …' His face twisted with emotion. 'How is Mistress Cecily? After …'

There was little comfort Alys could give him. 'She's sleeping, but she'll soon stir. She was in a terrible state earlier, and I've no reason to think she will be any different when she wakes.' She was amazed that her own voice was so steady, but she'd already cried herself out over the last few days; all she felt at this moment was an extreme weariness.

She belatedly realised that Robin was still there, standing in silence and looking at her with some sympathy. 'So,' she continued, 'I just came out to get some water for the cooking pot.'

Robin looked into the butt near the door. 'You don't want this – all that rain must have knocked some muck off the roof into it.'

The water was indeed murky. She'd have to empty the butt and clean it before it could collect any water that was usable, which at this moment seemed like a much bigger task than she could cope with.

'I'll get you some fresh.'

She ought to protest, but she couldn't summon the energy to fight against kindness, so she simply stood as he carried the bucket to the well, filled it and returned.

'I'll be back to work,' he said, as he handed it over, 'but I can send one of the girls round later if you need anything. Just shout.' Alys watched him go, without replying.

A knot of young women was nearby, no doubt ready to gossip about what they'd just seen, but she didn't care. She started to turn.

Rosa broke off from the others to hurry over. 'Are you … do you want some company?'

'I have to go back in.' But her hand was hesitating on the door. 'Actually … yes please, just for a moment.'

Alys didn't want to talk about Cecily, or about William, so she cast her mind about for a different subject. 'The carpenter,' she said, nodding towards the workshop he was just entering, and remembering something she'd heard. 'Did he have another daughter? Older than Avice?'

'Yes.'

The curt answer surprised Alys enough to continue. 'What happened to her?'

Rosa blushed. 'She got married and moved away.'

'And ...?'

Rosa looked about her, as if to make sure they weren't being overheard. 'It's only gossip. Well – at least, we all know it's true, but we're not supposed to talk about it.' She put her head close to Alys's and whispered. 'You know Robin's wife has been dead for years, and he hasn't got married again. So he ... well.'

Alys was obviously supposed to infer something from this, but she didn't know what. 'And?'

Rosa leaned even closer. 'Well, when Ida got married, to a fellow over near Wath, she was already with child.'

Alys wasn't shocked. 'It's awkward, but it does happen, surely?' Indeed, she could think of several young women in Lincoln who had married in haste because of just such a reason.

Rosa shook her head. 'It's more than that. It wasn't his, you see – and though she's got a fine little boy, we all know that he's her brother as well as her son.' She stepped back. 'I should go.'

It took Alys a moment for the enormity of that statement to sink in. That could only mean that ... she looked over at the carpenter's workshop and felt her cheeks redden. Then she went inside and shut the door.

The meal wasn't quite ready when Cecily woke, so Alys sat with her, ready to talk or to remain silent, as the older woman preferred. To start with, Cecily just stared into space, and then she reached out her hand for Alys to take.

'It was always likely that I would outlive him,' she began, still looking at the wall. 'He's older than me, and his injuries meant that he's been finding it harder every winter. But for this to happen ...' she tailed off, and Alys felt her hand being squeezed.

'Edwin will find out who did it.' Alys spoke with more confidence than she felt, for how could he, in such a short time and with everyone seemingly against him?

'Oh, I hope so,' said Cecily, turning her hollow eyes to Alys. 'And when he does, when he finds William's murderer, I will be there to watch that man hang.'

There was a knock at the door. They exchanged a glance, and then Alys got up. She opened it just a crack, but when she saw only the little boy who had run errands for William, his face grubby with wiped-away tears, she let him in.

'Who is it?' came Cecily's voice from the chamber.

'It's me, Mistress. Wulfric,' piped the boy. 'Come to fetch Mistress Alys to the church, as Edwin wants to speak to her.'

Alys was torn. She needed to help, but as to leaving Cecily …

But Cecily was already appearing in the doorway, pinning her wimple in place. She held out her arms to the boy and he ran to her, pushing his face into her apron.

'There, there.' She looked at Alys over Wulfric's head. 'I won't be the only one who misses him.' And then, in more like her usual tone, 'Now, Alys, if Edwin needs you, you must go. I'll be all right here.' She looked into the pot, and then down at Wulfric. 'There's plenty here and I expect you're hungry.'

She bustled about, ladling some into a bowl, and held it out to the boy. 'Here. Keep your strength up.'

By the time Alys had found her shawl and wrapped it about her, Wulfric had already finished, so he came out with her, slipping his hand into hers as they made their way to the church.

Edwin sat behind the table, forcing himself not to try and hear anything that might be coming from the sacristy. Dragging himself away had been one of the hardest things he'd ever done – what if the conversation there could save his life? But listening to another man's confession was a heinous sin, and if Edwin really was going to die within the next couple of days, he couldn't imperil his immortal soul. All he could do was hope and pray either that Osmund's confession was nothing to do with the situation at hand, or that, if it were, he would hear about it by other means.

At Edwin's request, Everard sent young Wulfric to fetch the reeve, and Edwin tried to compose himself for a long day of questioning and thinking.

The reeve arrived, and Edwin immediately sensed his hostility. Instead of standing before the table he sat down and folded his arms. 'Well?'

The best way to approach this was probably to go on the offensive. 'Do you think I'm a murderer? Truly?' he asked, while looking point-edly around him to remind the reeve that they were in a church.

'I can't see into other men's souls. You can't have killed William, I'll give you that, but you're too friendly with those foreigners, so who's to know you didn't help one of them? And now you're bothering us and keeping us from our work instead of doing your duty and standing up for us.'

'I am doing my duty, which is to find out who killed Ivo and William.'

The reeve made an angry gesture. 'You see? You're doing it again. We know who killed Ivo, he's up in a cell. And if it wasn't exactly him who did for William – God rest his soul – then it was one of the others. They're all strangers.'

Edwin felt like he was banging on a door that was locked and bolted from the other side. 'Have you genuinely no interest in finding out the truth? What if the murderer is someone from the village, and we let him get away with it, and he kills again?'

The reeve leaned forward. 'We're not killers. We're peaceful men, and we always have been. It's only since the likes of you have got above yourselves that this sort of thing has happened. Get rid of those foreigners, and everything will go back to normal. And for the love of God stop asking so many questions!'

Edwin paused, wondering why the man in front of him was so agitated. It could surely only be because he had something to hide. But what was it, and did it have anything to do with the murder?

'Have you finished with me now? Because I've got work to do.'

It was on the tip of Edwin's tongue to say 'so have I', but before the words could reach his lips, Osmund came out of the sacristy. He seemed about to hurry past them, his face averted.

Edwin let the reeve depart and called out. 'Osmund! We may as well speak to you next, seeing as you're already here.' He saw the man stop, then brace himself before he turned. Then he came to stand before the table. He looked upset. But how to get anything out of him without infringing on the sacrament of confession?

The silence lengthened as Edwin considered what best to say, but as it happened, this was enough on its own: Osmund could stand it no longer and fell to his knees, his hands grasping at the front edge of the table.

'Oh please, you have to forgive him – even if he did do it then he didn't mean to, he didn't know what he was doing!'

'He? Do you mean Gyrth?' Edwin's mind began to work, reaching several steps ahead before Osmund had even finished replying.

'Yes, oh yes. You see, it was that morning when Ivo's body was found. Gyrth, he had blood on his hands.'

Edwin held up a hand. 'But we've all seen him with blood on him. We all know it's because he doesn't like the slaughtering. What makes you think that day was different?'

'Because it was too early. It was hardly light, and they don't start with the slaughtering until the sun comes up. So how could he have blood on his hands? And then when I saw –' He broke off.

'Saw what?' That was Everard.

Osmund, still on his knees, looked straight at Edwin. 'I saw your wife helping him to wash it off.'

'What?' Edwin was half on his feet.

'Outside your house.'

Edwin pressed his hands together in front of his face, closing his eyes for a moment and trying to marshal his thoughts. This conversation hadn't taken the turn he was expecting. 'Just a moment.' He looked up, hoping his face was calm. 'And this is why you were so ready to believe that I had something to do with it.'

Osmund nodded.

'All right. That makes sense. Now, tell me again about that morning, and tell me exactly – I want to know what you saw, and it's important that it's all in the right order.'

'We woke before dawn, like usual. Gyrth took his bit of bread off the table and put it in his pouch to take with him.' He looked up at both of them. 'He's out all day, you know, and he's a growing lad.'

'Of course. Now, carry on – what happened next?'

'I was a little after him – takes me longer to get up in the mornings these days. My back gets stiffer every winter. I put on my boots, put some barley to soak in a bowl so we could eat it that evening. Then I went out.'

'Then what?'

'I saw Gyrth. He was coming the wrong way, back towards me, and he had this blood all over his hands. I started to go to him, but he went into your garden and in your sty. He hides sometimes when he knows he's done something wrong. I was on my way over when your wife came out and saw him, so I stayed back – I don't think she saw me. She helped Gyrth wash his hands, and spoke to him to calm him down. I didn't hear what she said.'

'But how did you –'

'So I looked up the street, and I seen Gyrth's stick lying on the ground outside the bailiff's new house, so I went up there to see what was what, and looked inside to see if anyone was there who might have scared him, and that's when I saw the body and I knew that Gyrth must have killed him.' He had tears in his eyes.

Edwin held up a hand to silence him while he tried to think his way through everything. He cast his mind back to the morning in question. He had left the house before Alys did, so Gyrth must actually have been in the sty as he walked past it. Which meant that …

'Fresh blood, or dried?'

Osmund was momentarily confused. 'I … I'm not sure. But does it matter? Please, the important thing is that he's not right in the head, he didn't know …'

Everard spoke, and Edwin heard both the sympathy and the relief in his tone. 'We'll see what we can do. Look, if Gyrth did it then at least we know Edwin is innocent, and so you've saved his life by speaking up. He'll put in a good word for the lad, I'm sure. And we all know what he's like – God must have made him like that for a reason.'

Edwin was still looking at Osmund, whose face contorted at these last few words. He nodded to himself. 'And that's what you wanted to confess,' he said, gently.

Osmund's face creased, and tears squeezed out of his eyes.

'What?' Everard hadn't kept up.

'When he went to see Father Ignatius, he said he wanted to confess. *He* wanted to confess. He thinks that Gyrth killed Ivo, which isn't his sin, so he must have wanted to admit to something for himself. And the only logical explanation is that he felt responsible for what Gyrth had done.'

Osmund was now twisting his cap in his hands. 'Everyone's always been so kind to him. But it's because they think the Lord made him that way. But it wasn't the Lord, it was me.' Tears coursed down his face, making tracks through the embedded grime. His voice became hoarse. 'I dropped him. On his head. When he was a baby.'

Edwin heard Everard take in a sharp breath as he understood the implication.

Osmund continued. 'I was playing with him, bouncing him up and down. I was young, and glad to have a son, and he smiled at me. But then he slipped.' His voice cracked. 'I don't know how, but he just slipped out my hand, and he fell head first down on to the stone round the hearth. He didn't even cry, or scream, or anything. He was just quiet.'

He began rocking back and forth. 'I thought I'd killed him. But he was breathing, and he looked normal apart from a lump on his head. And that went down eventually, so I never told anyone.'

'Not even your wife?'

'Well, her, of course. She noticed the lump as soon as she came back in. But she died not long after – you were only a tot at the time, you wouldn't remember – and then it was just him and me.

And he grew up … wrong. In his body he's fine, but his head just don't work properly.'

He wiped the back of his hand across his face, calming a little now that the worst was over. 'Couldn't afford to get married again, and who'd have me anyway, with Gyrth to look after? So it's just him and me. And every time I hear someone say "God made him like that" I sink a bit deeper and it gets harder to say what really happened. So I never have, until today.'

Osmund hauled himself to his feet. 'But if he's done wrong then we both have to face it, and I can't let you hang in our place. Your mother and father were always good to us, and it's not right.' He squared his shoulders. 'But the fault is mine, not Gyrth's. I made him the way he was.'

'Not necessarily.'

Edwin looked up in surprise. How long had Father Ignatius been standing there?

The priest turned from Osmund and addressed Edwin. 'I would not have revealed to you anything that Osmund said in confession, but he has chosen to tell you all this of his own free will.' He turned to Osmund. 'And this I say to you: do not take the Lord's actions unto yourself.' His voice took on an unusually stern note. 'How are you so sure? How do you *know*, deep in your heart, that you caused this, and that it was not the Lord's plan for Gyrth all along?'

Osmund was lost for words.

Edwin spoke calmly. 'Father Ignatius is right. You can't know that it was you. But you *can* rest safe in the knowledge that Gyrth did not kill Ivo.'

'But …'

'Osmund, listen. Gyrth had no blood on his hands when he left your cottage before dawn. And Ivo was already dead by then – I saw his body not long after you did, and he had been dead for hours. So Gyrth couldn't have murdered him.'

Osmund sagged, but he still seemed hardly able to believe. 'But the blood?'

Edwin rubbed his eyes. He was tired, and he still had much to do. But it was important that this man should know of his son's innocence. 'It would be difficult to get the whole story out of him. But what I think happened is this: he was on his way to get the first pigs, and he saw Barty coming out of Ivo's house with the hammer – a new toy to play with. Gyrth was curious enough to go inside, maybe to see if there was anything else. When he got inside, he saw the body. He touched Ivo's face, smearing the blood on to his own hands, and then panicked and ran away. I'd told Alys before that Gyrth gets upset at the sight of blood, so she helped him to wash and calm himself.' He sighed. 'But it never occurred to her that the day's slaughtering hadn't started yet, which is probably why she didn't mention it to me.'

Osmund's face was slowly gaining in hope. 'So ... my boy's innocent?'

'In both meanings of the word, yes. He's one of God's innocents, and he's done no wrong. He didn't kill Ivo, because Ivo was already dead by the time Gyrth went anywhere near him. And he certainly didn't kill William.'

'You mean ... I can go? And Gyrth won't have to appear before the court?'

Edwin looked at Everard and at Father Ignatius. 'I can't see any reason why he would need to. The only thing he could possibly be charged with is not raising the hue and cry when he saw the body, but given his childlike state, I'm not sure he'd be expected to anyway.' The other two nodded their agreement. 'So, yes, you may go. But if you hear anything that might help, come and tell me. Gyrth's innocence means that my own guilt still stands until we can find out different.'

Osmund stuttered out some thanks, and was gone.

Edwin allowed himself one moment only to pause before he turned to Wulfric, who had been sitting wide-eyed at Everard's feet all the while. 'Not a word of this, do you understand? Swear to it now, while you're in the church.'

'I swear.'

'Good. Now, fetch Philippe, the master mason, for me, there's a good lad.'

While he waited, Edwin tried to keep the panic stamped down within him. If he started to let it out … but no. He had to try and concentrate on the matter at hand. Think. Take stock. He did now have some new information – he had solved the mystery of the smeared blood on Ivo's head – and he had proved one more person innocent. But he didn't have time to eliminate every inno-cent one by one; he needed to find the guilty man, and that could still be anyone.

No, not anyone: the culprit must be someone from outside the castle. Both Ivo and William had been killed at a time when the castle gates were closed and everyone was safe within. The only person who had left after lock-up time had been Ivo himself, which meant that his killer must be someone from outside – a villager.

Or a mason.

Philippe arrived in due course, removing his hat as he stepped into the church.

'Some of my men wish to leave,' he began, without preamble. 'I've told them to wait until this is settled one way or the other, but after that I can't stop them.'

This was the last of Edwin's problems right now, but there might be something of importance in it. 'How many?' he asked. 'And who?'

'I can make you a list. But that's only those who want to leave now; if Denis hangs, they will all go, and the lord earl's hall will not be finished.'

Edwin sighed. 'I can't blame them. It's not as if they've been made to feel welcome while they've been here.'

'We don't expect to be greeted with open arms or treated like brothers. People have their homes and families, and we're strangers, so of course a level of distance is maintained. But being wrongfully accused of crimes and then having our camp burned to the ground – at the risk of our lives – is too much.'

'Where will they go?'

Philippe shrugged. 'Anywhere. There is always work for men who can work in stone – castles, churches. And even individual houses, now that more and more are being built out of it. Who knows – maybe one day all the buildings of the land will be in stone rather than wood.'

Edwin thought that was hardly likely, but it was true that churches and castles would always need repair. But this was getting him nowhere. 'I need to know if any of your men might have been out and away from your camp before dawn this morning.'

Philippe spread his arms. 'I'm their employer, not their mother. Nobody would have been working at that time of day – you need good light to carve stone – and nobody would have been on his way to the castle, because the gates would have been shut. But I can't say that nobody creeps out in the night to meet a girl.'

Edwin suddenly felt that all he wanted to do was sit down and cry. It was so hopeless.

Philippe was continuing. 'But I am certain that none of my men would have harmed monsieur the steward. He was good to us – payments made on time, good food supplied – and we respected him.' He paused to bow towards the shrouded corpse and cross himself. 'Monsieur the bailiff, yes, we might have argued with him – though we did not kill him, certainly – but we had no quarrel with Guillaume.'

Edwin said nothing as he tried to keep the tears in.

'Of course,' Philippe continued, more gently, 'he was your kinsman, yes? This is a bad business for you.'

You can say that again, thought Edwin, but he didn't voice the sentiment. 'Yes. And I will find who did this, so that William – and Ivo – can have justice, and also so that Denis can go free. Because there's no justice in that, either.'

Philippe leaned forward to shake his hand. 'I am with you. Any way I can help, just tell me.'

'Thank you. Can you check with all your men – check thoroughly – who might have been out of the camp last night or before dawn this morning? Even if it was only to meet a girl, I want to know, because someone might have seen something.'

'I will. I will send word to you as soon as I know.' He bowed and was gone.

Edwin tried not to allow himself any time to think. He turned to Wulfric. 'And now, if you please, fetch my wife.'

———⊷⋅⊶———

Alys felt Wulfric's hand clutching hers as they made their way to the church. She realised how little she knew about him; he was just the boy who ran messages for William, and who therefore faded into the background. But his evident distress, and Cecily's sympathy for him, seemed to make him a real person.

'Do you live up at the castle?' she asked, as a way to open a conversation.

'No. I live here with my family and just go up there every day. Get my dinner there, though, which is better than anything at home.'

'Oh, you have family here? But you don't work for your father? They send you out?'

'There's too many there already, and not enough work.' He pointed towards the carpenter's workshop. 'And besides,' he drew himself up and spoke proudly, 'Mistress Cecily says I'm the most *presentable*, and she says Master William couldn't manage without me.'

He fell silent, and Alys looked down to see that his lip was wobbling. 'I'm sure you did him good service,' she said. That didn't help – she needed to distract his attention. 'And now, with all the experience you have, I'm sure you'll find another job.'

'Really?'

'Yes, really,' she said, hoping she wasn't raising false hopes and making the situation worse. 'Because there will have to be a new steward, and surely he'll need a boy who knows his way around.'

The hand in hers relaxed a little, but then tensed again as they neared the carpenter's workshop. Robin was nowhere to be seen, but

Young Robin was there, looking daggers at both of them. He took half a step forward, and Alys wasn't sure which of her and Wulfric was trying hardest not to hide behind the other one.

'Your brother?'

'Free with his fists, he is. Thinks he's so clever, just 'cos he's the oldest,' muttered Wulfric, careful not to let his words carry as far as the workshop.

'He hits you?'

'Course he does. Even more than Pa does. But we'll be as big as him one day, me and Barty, and then we'll see,' he added, darkly.

'Oh, you and Barty are going to set up on your own, are you?' Alys tried to speak lightly.

'Yep. Me and him, we'll have a nice house, and Joanie and Ada can live there with us, and we'll all be fine.'

'And what will you all do? Will you have fields to work in?'

'Barty doesn't know what he's going to do yet, but that's all right 'cos he's only little. But I'm going to be a steward, and have a nice house like what Master William's got.'

Alys had to admire his ambition.

But his face had fallen again. 'I mean, like what Master William had. Before …' He tailed off.

They had reached the church. Alys gave his hand a final squeeze. 'Try not to worry too much, Wulfric. I'm sure everything will be fine.'

He was unsure. 'You think so?'

'Yes.'

She tried to give him a reassuring smile. She wasn't sure it came out right.

'Mistress?'

'Yes?'

'What does "presentable" mean?'

Now she smiled properly. He ran in ahead of her, and then she was, without warning, struck by a burst of feeling for her own little brothers. How she missed them! Wulfric would be about the same age as Randal, she supposed. How were they faring without her back in Lincoln? But that was a worry for another day.

She took a moment to adjust her eyes as she entered, but the day outside was so dull, and the church lit by candles, that there was hardly any difference.

Edwin came forward to greet her, taking both her hands in his. He looked weak and shaky.

There was a table set up, but he led her away from it so they could sit together on the bench at the side.

'I wanted to get William to sit on this bench, you know,' she said, noticing and then averting her eyes from the shrouded figure.

'Did you?'

'Yes. When we were at Mass on Sunday. He looked unsteady on his feet, but I knew he wouldn't move to sit with the old folk.'

'No, he wouldn't. He'd never admit to such weakness.'

They sat in silence for a few moments before Alys spoke. 'Would it help if I told you what happened this morning? When we ... found him?'

'Yes. But wait, I have something to tell you first.'

He related what he had learned about Gyrth. She was struck by how stupid she'd been, both in not realising that the blood on his hands couldn't have come from the pig-slaughtering, and in not telling Edwin about the episode sooner.

He waved away her apologies. 'It's fine. But as to this morning: tell me everything you can remember.'

She ran through all that she had thought of, from the moment of her waking, to them finding the body, and all that she could remember of who had been there and who hadn't.

'But you're not sure whether Crispin was there or not?'

She shook her head. 'I've been trying and trying to recall when I first saw him, and all I can say is I didn't notice him until he spoke, but I can't swear to whether he was there before that or not.'

He paused before speaking. 'But he does sometimes come and go from the castle at odd hours, to see his mother.' He looked over his shoulder, but Agnes was nowhere to be seen; the only other living creatures in the church were Wulfric and the sergeant-at-arms, who was doing his best not to eavesdrop.

Alys was shocked. 'But Crispin wouldn't … I mean, he's been protecting us! And he seems to think very highly of Cecily.'

Edwin put the heel of his hand to his forehead, the way he did when he had a headache. 'This is what it does to you.'

'What?'

'The constant … suspicion. For months I've been trying to find criminals and murderers, and it makes you lose your trust in everyone. Why in the Lord's name should I suspect Crispin of anything, when he's always been so friendly, so good to me? But others have been friendly and then turned out to be … I'm not sure I can stand it any longer.'

There was another silence, but he had his thinking face on, so this time Alys didn't interrupt.

'You believe I should talk to Young Robin, don't you?' he asked with a suddenness that made her jump.

'How did you – I mean, what?'

'I'm not blind, Alys, and nor am I stupid. I've known him since we were boys, and I know what he's like. I've got a fair idea of what must have happened the other day, and I'm only upset that you didn't think to tell me about it.'

She didn't know what to say. But one thing had to be made clear. 'Edwin, he didn't – I mean, I got away before he could –'

'I know. Otherwise, do you think he'd still be walking around? But I'm so sorry I wasn't there to look after you.' He traced his finger over the scrape on her knuckle. 'Still, it looks like you can look after yourself.'

'I don't think he's ever met a girl who was brought up in a big city.' She remembered his hands on her, and then – with some satisfaction that she couldn't quite overcome – the feel of his nose crunching under her hand. 'But I didn't get this from hitting him. It's on the wrong hand, and the wrong place.'

He looked confused.

'What I mean is, I – or any woman – couldn't punch a man hard enough to keep him away. And I certainly wouldn't do it with my left hand. Instead, what I was always taught to do was to shoot the heel of my hand forward to hit him hard on the nose.' She demonstrated with her right hand. 'Even if you don't break it, it gives him enough of a shock that he's off his guard, so you can run. Or,' – again the hint of gloating, which wasn't becoming, she knew – 'so you can use your knee to teach him a lesson, and *then* run.'

She almost laughed as she saw the way her husband was looking at her. 'As you say, I can look after myself. And as to this,' she held up her injured hand, 'this was just from hitting it on the side of a tree as I ran away.'

'Oh, I do love you.'

She felt the tears spring to her eyes. 'And I you.'

'And I will talk to him. About the murders, I mean.'

'Good.'

'But I will try my hardest not to pin blame on him if he didn't do it. It's tempting, after what he tried to do to you –'

'And what he's no doubt done to other girls.'

'– and what he's no doubt done to other girls, but hanging him for a crime he didn't commit would be murder, just as someone wants to do to Denis.'

She didn't say it. She couldn't say it.

But he did. 'And it's what someone wants to do to me.'

Chapter Twelve

Wulfric came back with Young Robin, pointing him forward before running outside again.

'He's off to fetch Father – he's up at the masons' camp. Because *some* of us have got work to do.'

Edwin knew he was going to get angry during the course of the forthcoming conversation, and he was glad that Alys had left before it started.

He folded his arms. 'We'll wait.'

The silence lengthened.

Everard, who had evidently done a good job of not overhearing Edwin's conversation with Alys, and who no doubt felt that this was just going to be another chat about what Young Robin might have seen, decided to break the ice.

'What happened to your face?'

'Nothing. Just a work accident.'

He met Everard's eye as he spoke, but Edwin observed his fingers twitching slightly, and wondered if they did that every time he told a lie.

Young Robin didn't add anything, and Everard had run out of conversational gambits. They waited in a strained silence until sounds were heard outside.

'Don't tell me what to do, boy, or you'll know about it,' growled Robin as he came in. 'Don't care who you think you're working for, you're still my …' He stopped as he saw Edwin and Everard facing him from behind the table. He already had his hat in his hand – the automatic reaction of one who had been entering the same church all his life – and Edwin saw him clench it as he also noticed William's shrouded body.

'Tell me where you were on the night Ivo died, both of you.' He might as well go on the offensive while Robin was still off his guard.

But it was Young Robin who answered. 'At home. Where else would we be?'

Edwin looked enquiringly at Robin.

'Like we are every night, Father,' continued Young Robin, with a little too much emphasis. 'I was at home all night, wasn't I, and you saw me there?'

Robin recovered. 'Yes, of course he was. And I – I've got children to watch over, haven't I?'

Edwin had seen Young Robin's fingers give that same little twitch, but that wasn't proof positive that he was lying, so he left it for now.

'And you didn't see or hear anything unusual?'

Young Robin's pause was enough to make Edwin react this time. 'You did?'

He shrugged. 'Went out to have a piss, didn't I? Only for as long as it took.' A crafty look came over his face. 'Did see someone out and about who shouldn't have been, though.'

'Why in God's name did you not say anything before?' That was Everard, jumping in before Edwin could open his mouth. 'At the court? Or afterwards?'

Young Robin shrugged. 'Because the mason did it. Or Edwin, or both of them. What difference would it make, knowing that Aelfrith was in the village?'

Edwin sat up straight. 'Aelfrith?'

It wasn't exactly a moment of triumph – he could get in trouble for concealing information – but Young Robin seemed to be enjoying the surprise he'd created. Under the bruising on his face, his expression was smug.

'Well, all the girls reckon he's good-looking, don't they? Can't see it myself. But if he'd come in to get away from that Godawful mother of his and have some fun, who am I to rat on him?'

This didn't make any sense to Edwin. Why hadn't he … 'How do you know it was Aelfrith? If it was dark?'

'There was enough of a moon to make out who it was. Besides, I heard him talking to someone.'

And you couldn't possibly mistake Aelfrith's voice for anyone else's, thought Edwin. Damn. 'Who was he talking to?'

'Don't know.' Young Robin leaned forward with a smirk. 'Do you know where your wife was all night that night?'

Edwin leapt to his feet, and Everard held out a restraining arm. 'Now then.' He turned to Young Robin. 'Slandering the name of a virtuous woman is a serious business. If you don't have good proof, then I suggest you take that back.'

The elder Robin interjected. 'You do as you're told and shut up.'

Young Robin adopted an insouciant tone. 'I take it back. Aelfrith can take his pick, though I don't know if he prefers married girls to virgins.' And then, after a pause, 'Still, your wife will be a widow before long. She'll need a man to look after her.'

The rage rose in Edwin's head, and he would have thrown himself over the table if Everard hadn't stopped him. Young Robin found it all hilarious, but his father didn't. 'Stop it, please, stop it!' he had tears in his eyes. 'William's dead, and there's more death to come, and you're making jokes!'

Everard moved around the table and ushered the two Robins firmly towards the door. 'That's enough for now. You should take a harder line with the boy, Robin – if he was my son he'd get a thrashing for disrespect like that. And as for you, lad – you should be ashamed of yourself. Get out, and think on your shame.'

He pushed them outside. 'I've always thought there was something particularly dislikeable about that boy.' He collected himself. 'But try to put it all out of your mind. You too,' – this to Wulfric – 'and make sure you don't grow up like your brother.'

'No chance,' said the boy, with such a thunderous face that Edwin noticed it even in the midst of his own thoughts.

He sat down and beckoned. 'Can you tell me anything about what your father and brother said? Can you tell me if it's true or not?' He didn't want to turn a family on itself, not really, but this was important.

It didn't matter anyway, because Wulfric couldn't help. 'I get tired, and I sleep all night. Avice tells us younger ones to get to bed, and then I don't wake up until she calls me in the morning. Sorry.'

'Don't worry. It's no matter – it was just a thought, that's all.' Edwin turned to face Everard. 'I think I need to talk to Aelfrith. It would take a long time to get a message to him and bring him here, though – can we go out to his farm?'

Everard walked to the door and looked out. 'Not now, no. We've been in here longer than I thought – it's not far off sunset, and we wouldn't even get there before dark, never mind get back. Besides, it's pouring again and the road won't be good. We'll have to wait until the morning.'

Edwin chafed at the loss of time. The sheriff would be here tomorrow – and even that was if he hadn't already arrived while they'd been in the church. But he wouldn't solve the murder by breaking his neck on the road, and he supposed that Everard would be loath to take him out of Conisbrough in the dark for the additional reason that he might try to escape.

He sighed. 'So, what now then?'

'I'll take you back up to the castle. Those were my orders.' He picked up his hat. 'You go home, son – if we need a messenger in the morning, I'll find you.'

Wulfric nodded and slipped out, although he didn't look particularly enthusiastic, and Edwin didn't blame him. His eldest brother was a bully who would probably take out his anger and resentment on his siblings.

Edwin considered the carpenter and his family as they made their way up the hill to the castle. Young Robin was a liar, that much was obvious, but what exactly was he lying about, and what was his purpose in doing so?

They reached the inner ward. Edwin expected to be taken straight back to his room, but instead Everard motioned him towards the communal table, where the braziers were just being lit. 'There's a guard on the gate, and no other way for you to get out unless you can fly off the walls, so you may as well eat with us. You've got friends here, you know.'

Indeed, as Edwin neared the table, men were greeting him and making room for him. One or two of them had been in the earl's company at the recent battle on the south coast, and word had somehow got round that Edwin had acquitted himself well. They'd always thought him harmless, at the least, with no reason to dislike him, but talk of how he'd held his courage in the heat of battle had raised him in their estimation.

He was slapped on the back. 'Here. Sit down. Have you got yourself out of this mess yet?'

Edwin tried to reflect the mood. 'Not yet. But I'm working on it.'

Several of them chipped in. 'Good for you. We've got your back if you need it – not that you should.' 'You know Richard Cook threatened to starve any man who spoke against you – don't think young Jack will be eating for a while!' And a darker 'None of this would be happening if Sir Geoffrey was here.'

'You shut that now, Tom,' said Everard. 'I won't have disrespect for our betters here.'

'Yes, sir. Sorry, sir.'

'That's better. Now, here's the meal – you get yours last.'

Edwin hadn't eaten since dawn, and now, to his surprise, he found that the meat and offal pie brought water to his mouth. He reached for his eating knife and was momentarily confused at its absence before remembering that he'd had to give it up earlier. He still had his spoon in his belt pouch, though, so he made the best of it.

He had not long finished his meal when he was elbowed from one side. 'Over there.'

Edwin turned to peer into the dark. Just by the torchlit gatehouse he discerned Alys, standing uncertainly and carrying something. He waved.

She spotted him and came over, a little hesitant in the presence of so many men, but the one sitting next to Edwin stood up and gestured to the empty place.

A little embarrassed at having to speak to her in front of so many others, Edwin took her hand. 'How are you?'

'I'm all right. I – I wasn't sure if you'd get anything to eat, so I've brought you the rest of the cinnamon bread.'

'Course we'd feed him,' came a voice from over the table. 'He's one of us, in't he?'

Edwin felt nothing but gratitude, to all of those around him. 'That's kind. Given that I've had some pie already, maybe you won't mind if I share it?' The food served at the castle was hearty, but spices only usually found their way to the top table, so the cinnamon would be a treat.

Alys agreed, so Edwin broke it up and passed it around. There wasn't very much of it, but most of those around him got a taste, and they all remembered to thank her.

Everard stood. 'Can't leave you completely alone, but I'll be over here. And the rest of you, shift. Wall duty or tidying the armoury, sort yourselves out.'

There was a little grumbling, but not much, as the benches gradually emptied.

'Did you discover anything after I left?' Alys kept her voice low.

'A little, but I'm not sure how relevant it is.' He told her of his conversations with the two Robins – leaving out the parts that related to herself, obviously – and of what had been said about Aelfrith.

She gasped. 'Really? He was really in the village that night?'

'I don't know – I only have Young Robin's word for it, and he's not exactly trustworthy. But I'll go out to his farm tomorrow and talk to him face to face.' He paused. 'How is Cecily?'

She grimaced. 'She's trying to be brave.'

Edwin put his face in his hands for a moment.

'But I forgot – I have something else to tell you, something I forgot to mention when I came to the church earlier.'

He raised his head. 'What?' To start with, he couldn't work out why she was telling him some garbled story about Robin's eldest daughter, whom he remembered from earlier years. She'd got married and moved away, which wasn't all that unusual. But his interest was piqued by some aspects.

'Now, let me finish by asking you a question,' she said.

'Yes?'

'Was everyone you spoke to today a man?'

'Apart from you, yes.'

'You've missed out, then.'

'But –'

'No, listen, please. The jury might be all men, but the village isn't. The women know a lot that just passes their menfolk by. You call it gossiping, but sometimes it's important.'

'Such as?'

'You spoke to Robin. You asked him where his son was on the night Ivo was killed. If you speak to him again, ask him what his *daughter* was doing.'

———◆———

Edwin woke up, and had a pleasant half-moment of warm sleepiness before it all hit him, and he felt sick, a stone settling in the pit of his stomach. Today was the day. He'd been lucky that the sheriff hadn't arrived yesterday, but he could count on no further delay, so he needed to sharpen his wits and get everything straight *now* – before noon, preferably – so he had the real culprit ready to present.

He had agreed with Everard that they would ride over to Aelfrith's farm, so as not to waste any time, and he had subsequently amended his request, after Alys had left him the previous evening, to ask that they might call in on Robin again before they set off.

They found the carpenter already in his workshop with several of his younger sons.

'I need to speak with you again.' Edwin knew that Robin wasn't going to like it, but he didn't have time for niceties.

'Speak, then,' he replied, not looking up from his work.

Edwin hesitated as he looked at the youngsters. 'Can we go inside?'

'No.'

'I really think that you'd prefer it if we did, given what I've got to say.'

Robin dropped the chisel he had in his hand, and then fumbled as he bent to pick it up. 'You lot get on with shaping that beam. I'll be checking it when I get back, mind.'

He led the way inside, and Edwin followed, leaving Everard to tie up the horses.

The cottage was dingy and not terribly clean. Blankets were piled haphazardly everywhere, and Edwin wondered how so many of them even managed to find the space to sleep. It was otherwise empty; the boys were all out at work, and Avice presumably about her morning tasks with the younger girls in tow. Edwin was quite glad that she was absent, for if he was wrong then he was about to slander her dreadfully.

'What's he done now, then?' asked Robin, a little nervously.

Edwin had Avice at the forefront of his mind, and it took him a moment to realise that the question was about Young Robin.

'Nothing – or at least, not as far as I'm aware. No, I came to talk to you about Avice.'

'Avice? Why?'

'To put it bluntly, what was she doing the night Ivo died?'

'At home with the rest of us, of course.'

Edwin shook his head. 'I have a witness who says otherwise.' That was untrue, and he'd need to confess to a lie when he got the chance, but it was the only way he could think of to goad Robin into the confession.

Robin looked about him, as though an answer or an escape might appear out of nowhere. Then he sat down, heavily. 'Oh, *all right.*'

'All right what?'

'Short of money, aren't I, with all these mouths to feed? At least the boys can get out there and earn a few coins, but what use is she?'

Edwin reflected on the sole responsibility of cooking and cleaning for a family of fourteen, but he didn't want to distract the carpenter now he seemed disposed to talk. 'And?'

'You can't be that innocent, surely? There is one way a girl like her can make some money. She's my daughter and I can hire her out to whoever I like. There's a few regulars in the garrison, and even Ivo was tempted when I offered. You wouldn't think he had an eye for village girls, but he did. She's not worth much – less as we go on – but it all helps and the others aren't old enough.'

Good Lord, but Alys had been right. 'And that's why Ivo was in the village that night?'

'Yes. But I didn't kill him, I swear. Met him at his house – it's not finished, but it's quieter there than our place, and it was raining so he'd have wanted somewhere with a bit of shelter at least. There's half a roof and all that straw. I took the money, waited outside, then collected Avice and took her home. And he was hale and hearty when we left.' He folded his arms. 'My daughter is my property, and it's no crime.'

Edwin wasn't quite so sure about that, but he'd have to check, and that could wait. 'And you didn't see anyone else while you were out?'

'No.'

Edwin was struck by another thought. 'So how do you know that Young Robin was asleep at home all night?'

Robin shrugged. 'He was asleep when I left and asleep in the same place when I got back. Stands to reason, doesn't it? Besides, like I told you, it was that mason what done it. Why can't you see that? We'd all be better off if the lot of them just upped and left.'

'Where is he now?'

'Rotting in a cell with a noose hanging over him, I hope.'

'I meant your son.'

'Oh. Up in the woods, looking out more timber.'

Edwin addressed Everard, who was just coming in. 'Can you send some men out to find Young Robin?'

'Yes. Why, is he your man?'

'I'm not sure. But he's lied to me more than once, so I'll need to talk to him again. But we can't wait to do it now – we need to get to Aelfrith's. If you can have him brought back to the village, we can see him when we get back – hopefully there might be just about time before the sheriff gets here.'

'I'll see to it.'

Edwin watched him go, heard him calling to someone outside, and then followed him through the door and into the drizzle. He was halfway to his horse when he realised that Robin had made no protest about the prospect of his son being arrested.

———•◦•———

Alys was once again loitering in the outer ward when the sheriff arrived. It was mid-morning and a pale sun was struggling to break through the clouds and drizzle as he rode in with a troop of a dozen men.

He'd been seen from a distance and men were standing ready. She had hardly started to think whether – or how – she might approach him when Sir Roger appeared. Along with a few other curious onlookers, she sidled closer to see if she could hear anything useful.

'Geoffrey de Neville, Sheriff of Yorkshire.' He made a slight inclination of the head, but did not either bow or take Sir Roger's proffered hand. 'And you are …?'

Alys was, of course, predisposed not to like the sheriff, nor to welcome his arrival, but any hopes she might have had of a fair hearing for Edwin disappeared rapidly. It was quite obvious that Sir Roger was the ranking man at the castle, and here was the newcomer looking at him as though he were a jumped-up stable boy. She recalled murmurs from those of the garrison who interested themselves in such things that the sheriff and the earl were not on good terms. And if it was as bad as it looked like it was going to be, Edwin's obvious innocence wouldn't save him.

She swallowed a sob as she forced herself to concentrate and risked taking another step forward. Maybe one of them would say something – anything – that might help.

Sir Roger was, with some effort, remaining courteous, offering Neville rest and refreshment. 'And perhaps that would give you the opportunity to review all the evidence at your leisure.'

Yes, thought Alys. Take as long as you possibly can.

But the sheriff was having none of it. 'There is no need. You have the guilty party in custody already, I believe? A Frenchman? And another, if the additional news that caught up with me on the way here is correct?'

'Yes, but –'

Neville waved his hand. 'Never mind "but". I'm a busy man. You're obviously …' – he looked the knight up and down, taking in his youthful features – '… *new* to your position, or you would know not to hold me up in the carrying out of my duties.'

He made as if to walk off, but Sir Roger stood his ground. 'You also are new to your position, I believe? Indeed, the sixth sheriff of Yorkshire in five years? Otherwise you might know that finding the truth of the matter is of the utmost importance.'

Alys could see that Neville was riled by this, though he fought to keep his expression under control. But even if he had not been prejudiced against Edwin and Denis before, he would be now. What in the Lord's name was Sir Roger doing?

The sheriff's voice grew colder. 'I will accept your youth and inexperience as an excuse for such incivility – this time. Now, have both the convicted men brought here.'

A faint smile touched Sir Roger's lips so briefly that Alys wasn't sure anyone else had seen it except her. 'One is in the cell here. The other is out on the estate, about his duties.'

'What?' Neville was so shocked that he was momentarily lost for words. But then one of the castle men behind Alys sniggered, which made him find his voice again. 'You have let a condemned man roam free?'

'He is not yet condemned – the manor court has no such authority. And not free, either; my sergeant-at-arms will be by his side at all times.'

Alys watched as the sheriff considered, tapping his fingers on his folded arms. It was just possible that Sir Roger had pulled off something brilliant, diverting so much of Neville's ire towards himself that there might be less for Edwin. Or, on the other hand …

Neville had reached a decision. 'Well, I have the authority, even if they don't. I hereby condemn – what are their names?' – this to one of his own men, a clerk, hovering at his side – 'Edwin of Conisbrough and Denis, a French stonemason, to death for the crime of murder.'

Alys felt her knees giving way as everything started to spin.

Sir Roger, too late, realised his miscalculation. 'But …'

'Silence!' snapped Neville. 'I will accept your offer of rest and refreshment, while you send out men to fetch this missing fellow back here. I will wait attended only by my clerk while the rest of my men, and yours, find a suitable place for the hanging.' He turned to his sergeant. 'No need to bother erecting a gallows – just find a decent tree. There was one near the bridge, so check to see if that will do.'

'So you're going to hang the both of them, without even hearing more about the murder, at tomorrow's dawn?' Sir Roger sounded outraged.

'No.'

Neville's reply took all the onlookers by surprise. Enjoying the moment, he continued. 'As I said, I'm a busy man. I don't want to have to stay here overnight – if we have the hanging this afternoon I can get back to Sprotborough before nightfall and stay the night there on my way back to York.' He looked about him. 'We'll get on with it as soon as this man gets back, and as soon as we've got a noose ready for him.'

Alys couldn't hold on any longer. Everything stopped spinning and went black.

———

Edwin could see smoke rising from the farm cottage as they approached. 'Someone's there, anyway.'

'The fearsome mother, I expect,' was Everard's response. 'Look – the door's opening.'

An elderly woman appeared, wrapping a shawl around her and squinting towards them. 'Who's coming there?'

They reined in and Everard called out their names, and that they were here to see Aelfrith on a matter of importance.

'Everard? Haven't seen you for years. And you, boy – are you Godric's son?'

Edwin dismounted with an ease that would have surprised him a few months ago. 'Yes, yes I am. Is Aelfrith here?'

'He's out in the fields, but I can fetch him back.' Edwin wondered how she was going to manage that, and was on the verge of saying he'd go out after Aelfrith himself, when she took up a stick and used it to beat a short length of metal pipe that was hanging from the cottage eaves. She was vigorous in her attack on it, and the noise was tremendous – it must have been audible for miles around.

'That'll fetch him back,' said the woman. 'Now, come on in and make yourselves comfortable – it's not often I have company.' She disappeared inside.

Edwin and Everard exchanged a puzzled glance. 'I suppose that *is* his mother, and not someone else?' ventured Edwin.

'It's her all right.' Everard took both sets of reins and tied them firmly to the branch of a tree. 'But now I'm thinking of it, although I've heard a lot about her in recent years, I can't remember the last time I actually saw her.'

Edwin tried to recall whether he'd ever, in fact, met Aelfrith's mother, or whether his own knowledge was entirely based on hearsay. To his shame he thought that the latter was more likely. But her bad temper – and her supposed ill-health – were both legendary in the village. How had such rumours come into being?

The unexpectedly welcoming atmosphere was even more evident when they entered the cottage; Aelfrith's mother fussed around, making sure they were comfortable near the fire and fetching them cups of an ale that turned out to be very tasty. Then she quizzed Everard about some former acquaintances in the village, asking for her good wishes to be passed on to those of them who turned out to be still alive.

Edwin was still trying to come up with an explanation for all this when a sound from the door caught his attention and he turned to see Aelfrith standing on the threshold, aghast at the scene before him. He looked so taken aback that Edwin wondered if he might turn and run, and was half off his stool in anticipation, but Aelfrith stepped forward, composing his face into an expression that Edwin recognised as being 'I've been caught in the act so I may as well confess'. But confess to what?

Aelfrith started with some false cheer. 'So glad to see you have guests, Mother – I hope you're making them comfortable?'

She smiled at him. 'Of course. I just think it's a shame you don't invite visitors here more often.' She turned to Everard. 'I'm always telling him, you know, he should ask some friends to come and eat with us once in a while, and far past time he should be bringing home a wife to keep me company.'

'Now, that's enough of that, Mother – I'll marry when I'm good and ready, and not before. But I'm sure that's not what they've come to talk about.' He made an effort to keep his voice level as he addressed Edwin. 'So what can I do for you?'

Edwin gave what he hoped was a significant glance at the old woman, and Aelfrith took the hint. 'Men's talk, Mother – we won't bother you with it.' He sat down.

She grumbled good-humouredly about being deprived of precious company, but stood and moved off into a back room. 'I'll be about the bread dough if you need me.'

They waited until they could hear her about her task before Aelfrith spoke again. 'Well then.'

Edwin's mind was working. 'This isn't what we came to talk about, but I think I can see how it's connected. The only way that rumours can have spread through the village about your mother being a bad-tempered crone – excuse my language, but that's what the word is – is if you started them yourself, or at least if you made no attempt to stop them.'

Aelfrith had the grace to look ashamed, but he didn't say anything.

'But why?' continued Edwin. 'No, wait. It's because you want to put people off coming here – that's why you looked so shocked when you saw us.'

Aelfrith gestured his agreement but still didn't speak.

'So again, why? And what does this have to do with you being seen in the village on the night Ivo died?'

'What?' That shook the other out of his silence and almost to his feet. 'Who saw me? Where?'

Everard stood. 'Calmly, now.' He moved to place himself between Aelfrith and the door. 'You tell us everything.'

Aelfrith looked from one to the other. Beads of sweat appeared on his brow. 'I was in the village. But I was just meeting someone – it had nothing to do with Ivo, and I didn't even see him.'

Edwin gazed at him but remained silent, waiting to see if this would prompt further information.

Aelfrith pulled at the neck of his tunic. 'Honest, I tell you – I'll swear to it that I never saw him, nor heard anything.'

'Who were you meeting?'

'That I can't tell you.'

'For God's sake, boy' – that was Everard – 'you do realise how serious this is? Edwin's in danger of being punished for a crime he didn't commit, we're looking for a murderer, time's running out and you're holding us up because you're squeamish about giving us the name of some girl you're courting?'

Edwin was watching Aelfrith's face as Everard spoke, and things started to fall into place. 'I see it now.' And Aelfrith's expression of terror confirmed it. 'You don't want to get married, do you? That's why you let the rumours fly that keep everyone away. The only person in the village who sees your mother, apart from you, is Father Ignatius.' He could see that he was heading along the right path. 'And he always comes back saying that she is a nice person and thanking the Lord that she is still in health. But nobody believes him because they all think he's just being his usual charitable self, and it suits them better to listen to the gossip.'

Everard was confused. 'But what has this to do with anything else?'

'Do you want to tell him, or shall I?' Edwin asked.

'You're doing well so far,' came the bitter reply. 'You may as well carry on.'

'If people from the village came here more often, they would see a prosperous farm run by a handsome man with a pleasant and welcoming mother. How many girls – and how many of their fathers – do you think would be queueing up?'

'But why is that a problem?' Everard hadn't got it yet.

Edwin kept his eyes on Aelfrith. 'Because he doesn't want to get married, because *he doesn't want a wife*. And he won't tell us who he was meeting in the village because it wasn't a girl.'

He paused for a moment and then risked a glance at Everard, whose face now carried a mingled expression of loathing and contempt.

'Oh, stop it,' said Edwin. 'Knights have close friendships between men all the time, and if Father Ignatius doesn't condemn him then who are you to do so?'

'But –'

'Keep your voice down!' hissed Aelfrith, with a glance towards the back room. 'If she knew, it would kill her. Have mercy on her, at least.' He faced Edwin and squared his shoulders. 'If you need me to swear to all this to save you then I will, but nothing you can do to me will make me give you anyone else's name.'

'It's all right,' replied Edwin absently as he got to his feet, mind already back to the murder now he was sure Aelfrith had nothing to do with it. 'I know who it is. But I won't say anything.'

They left the farm and rode back towards Conisbrough in silence.

After a while, Edwin began to sense that they were not alone. He looked at Everard to see if he thought the same, and the sergeant nodded and drew his sword. They continued on with caution, Edwin breathing a sigh of relief as he could see the forest thinning ahead; they were nearly home.

'Come out from there!' barked Everard, suddenly.

'Don't hurt me!' squeaked a voice, and to Edwin's surprise Hal appeared on the path in front of them.

Everard lowered his sword. 'You stupid boy. What possessed you to –'

But Hal had eyes only for Edwin. 'Don't go back, Master Edwin. Just turn around.'

'What are you –' began Everard, but Edwin waved him to silence. They were near enough to the village for him to see what Hal was warning him against.

A group of men he didn't recognise were slinging ropes over a broad bough of the great oak that stood near the bridge. Ropes that had nooses at the end.

Everard swore, loudly. 'Get home, boy,' he said to Hal, 'before you get in trouble for warning us. Quickly now.' He waited until Hal was out of earshot before turning to Edwin.

'God forgive me, and I've never said this to anyone before, but if you want to run then I won't stop you. Just ride away, right now. They don't know who you are, not yet. I'll make a show of following you and then make sure I fall off, or pull my horse up lame, or something. You could be miles away before anyone else noticed.'

The urge to flee was so strong that Edwin actually tensed, ready to put his heels to the horse's flank, and it started to dance in anticipation. But what would be the point?

'And become an outlaw? Starving in the forest and liable to be killed on sight?' He shook his head. 'And, more to the point, it would be seen as proof of my guilt. My father's name would be shamed for ever, and as for Alys … no.'

Everard was looking at him with sympathy. 'But …'

'Yes, I know. They'll hang me – tomorrow morning at dawn, I expect. Which still gives me a few hours. And besides, even if the worst comes to the worst, I can go to my death proclaiming my innocence, which might convince a few people, and it might help Alys a little.'

He calmed the horse. 'My conscience is clear, and I will stand before the Almighty able to say truthfully that I had no part in Ivo's death – or William's. God will judge.' He paused. 'Now, let's ride on and face it before I lose my courage.'

Everard nodded. 'You're a good man, and a brave one. Your father would be proud.'

And what will Mother think, wondered Edwin, when she comes back from her honeymoon to find her son's lifeless body hanging from a tree? He would get the chance to say his farewells to Alys, but not to her – even allowing for the message that had been sent off to her following William's death, he couldn't hope that she would arrive back so soon. But she at least would have Sir Geoffrey to protect her. All he could do was to entrust Alys with a message to her, and then to trust that, in turn, Sir Geoffrey would extend his protection to Alys. The widow who had been his good-daughter for only a matter of weeks.

And what of him, Edwin? He wasn't going to be able to solve this before the sands of time ran out, so death – painful, shameful, public execution – was the only future that beckoned. He remembered the day, back in May – had it only been half a year ago? – when his best friend had gone willingly to meet his own end. He only hoped he could last out long enough to die before he broke down and dishonoured his name.

They rode across the bridge, now only inches above the churning water, and Edwin concentrated on that in order to keep his eyes and his mind away from the men at their work by the tree.

Someone must have been looking out for them: they had barely entered the castle's outer ward when they were surrounded by a crowd of yelling, gesticulating men. Edwin was pulled from his horse before he could dismount, and found himself grabbed, buffeted this way and that.

'Stand fast there!' A voice Edwin didn't recognise came from somewhere past the crowd. The pushing and pulling slowed down and then stopped, various groups moving apart. Edwin found himself surrounded by a close knot of men from the castle, who were looking warily at a wider circle of men dressed in what was presumably the livery of the sheriff. No weapons had been drawn – yet – but the threat of sudden violence was certainly in the air. Edwin had been around it enough recently to be able to smell it.

Sir Roger pushed his way through. He was wearing his armour, which was surely not a good sign. 'Edwin, I …'

'I said stand fast there!'

On being addressed in such a manner, Sir Roger's hand went to his sword hilt, his face rigid with anger. He turned.

A finely dressed, albeit travel-stained, man approached, others clearing a path for him. He looked Edwin up and down, and then addressed Sir Roger. 'This is him? You identify him?'

'This is Edwin, yes. A member of my lord earl's personal household.'

'And one who has, by due process, been found guilty of murder. Or are you suggesting that your lord is above the law?'

There was complete silence. Every single man there – the garrison, the sheriff's party, and all those who worked in the castle ward, who had also gathered when they heard the fracas, watched Sir Roger. Edwin could hear them all breathing. He could hear them *waiting*. Sir Roger's next move would be crucial.

Sir Roger looked at the floor, and then directly at Edwin. Those blue, blue eyes, so hollow now, were filled with sadness. 'I'm sorry.' Slowly he unclenched his hand from the sword hilt, held his arms out from his sides in a gesture of peace, and stepped back.

The garrison could do nothing but hold off as the sheriff's men came forward, seizing Edwin's hands and binding them before him. He felt the rope burn around his wrists as they pulled it tight. But why was this necessary? Was he going to have to stay like this all night?

The sheriff was speaking to one of his men. 'The priest is with the other, is he not? Take this one to the cell so he can confess as well. Never let it be said that I don't let men make their peace with God.

And while you're waiting, round up everyone in the castle and the village. They all need to see justice being done.'

Edwin felt himself being pulled away, his arms jerking forward uncomfortably, but he still didn't understand what was going on.

The sheriff saw his bewilderment and smiled. 'You're a murderer – what did you think was going to happen to you? We're going to hang you.'

It was getting noisy again, and Edwin was so confused and frightened and panicked and *terrified* that he almost didn't hear the last word of the sheriff's sentence.

'Now.'

Chapter Thirteen

Alys had awoken to find herself in a strange bed. She sat up in a panic and was rewarded with a return of the dizziness that sent her reeling.

But then she heard Cecily's voice, and she fell back as she realised where she was.

'I'm supposed to be looking after *you*,' she said, weakly.

Cecily stroked her head. She seemed to have aged ten years in a day. 'Just lie still until you feel like yourself again.'

After a few moments Alys tried sitting up, more slowly this time. She managed. 'But what …?' And then the panic hit her. 'Edwin!'

'He's not back yet. And I hope to God he never will be.'

Alys felt like her head was full of wool. 'What?'

'We've done what we can. We couldn't exactly disobey the sheriff's orders, but we've found a few boys and sent them out into the woods to look for Edwin. If they see him, they'll tell him what's going to happen, and if he's got any sense he'll turn around and ride away.'

Alys put her fingers to her forehead. 'We?'

Cecily looked towards the chamber door. 'She's awake – you can come in.'

Old Agnes entered, followed by Crispin and Father Ignatius.

The priest came to kneel by the bed. 'Let us pray for a miracle.'

'But …' Alys's wits were returning, albeit slowly. 'But, Father, you can't go against the law, surely?'

'There is man's law, my child, and there is God's law.' He sounded sterner than she had ever heard him.

They all prayed for a few moments, and then Father Ignatius got to his feet. 'I must go up to the castle. Regardless of what happens to

Edwin, Denis is under sentence of death, and I must hear his confession.' He stopped to rub his back with a grimace. 'Trust in God.'

They heard him leave the house. 'Trust in God, aye.' Crispin tapped the hammer at his belt. 'But not only in God.' He looked at Cecily. 'I'll see if there's any more news.' He, too, left, and the three women were alone.

Alys swung her legs over the side of the bed. 'How did I get here? The last thing I remember was …' she swallowed.

'Crispin brought you here,' said Agnes. 'I was keeping an eye on Cecily, and next thing I know he's kicking at the door, carrying you and saying he'd seen you fall up in the ward.'

'And then he told us what had happened up there,' added Cecily.

Alys stood up. Would her legs hold her? They did. 'There must be something else we can do.'

The other two exchanged a glance that didn't look hopeful, but Alys could feel energy and rage pouring back into her. If Edwin was going to die, she would die trying to save him, and then at least they could be together. Or she would kill anyone and everyone who meant him harm. She looked around for anything that might be used as a weapon.

They all heard the commotion from outside, but it was Alys who first distinguished the name 'Edwin' being cried aloud.

She was halfway to the cottage door when Crispin's head appeared round it. 'He's back. Come quick.'

They ran out. Had the message not reached him? Versions of it were being shouted in the streets as he rode by with the sergeant alongside him. How could he not hear?

But then she caught a glimpse of his face, and the expression on it.

'He knows,' she said to Cecily. 'He knows, and he's made a decision.'

She watched his beloved figure as he passed, looking neither to the right nor the left, and then she let herself be carried along in the current of the shouting crowd.

But they had hardly reached the outer gates of the castle when they were almost ridden down by the sheriff's men, who herded them all back to the village. Alys now saw what she hadn't noticed on the way up: the two nooses hanging from the bough of the oak next to the bridge.

This time she was not going to faint. The world was not turning black, but red. She pushed her way through the crowd and strode up to the swinging ropes. Before anyone realised what she was doing, she had taken out her eating knife and was beginning to saw through one of them.

One of the sheriff's men shouted, 'Hey! Stop that!', and before she had been able to do any significant damage she felt herself being pulled away, hands dragging her backwards and pinning her arms. Then there was more shouting and pulling as others got involved, and a shrieking which she eventually realised was coming from her own mouth.

One man was wrestled away from her, but a shout of 'Don't hit any of them!' from Agnes stopped Crispin in the very act of raising his fist. One blow and they would hang him too.

Voices of authority were now sounding, and people were stepping back and away. Alys found herself in the centre of a space, and she turned to see a procession of men approaching: the sheriff, Sir Roger, Father Ignatius, Denis – being held by two of the sheriff's men – and behind them all, Edwin.

Her heart was pounding so loudly it would soon force its way out of her chest. Her head was in a whirl, but through it all was the running question, *How can I stop this?*

One urge was to throw herself at Edwin for one last embrace, but that would be self-indulgent. No, she had to *prevent* this, not give in to it. Begging the sheriff would be no good, and would only serve to amuse him further. There was only one chance.

Alys ran to Sir Roger and dropped to her knees before him. 'Please, Sir Roger. Please, do something!'

The agonised expression on his face was her only hope. She clutched her arms around his legs so he could not move without kicking her off, which he would never do. She pressed her face against the mail links of his hauberk and prayed.

'Mistress, please …'

She looked up at his face. 'You can't let this happen.'

He was torn. 'But the law ...'

Behind them, the sheriff was ordering his men to make ready. Alys knew that if she turned, she would see the noose being put around Edwin's neck.

She stared deep into the knight's eyes.

'Coward.'

She hadn't said it loudly, but there was force and feeling behind it, and she felt the shock jolt through him.

This was her last chance. 'The law. What is the law? Man's law, or God's? Is this *right*?' She unclasped her arms from around him and stood. He was taller, but she took handfuls of his surcoat in her clenched fists and looked into the blue depths of his soul. 'Tell me, *is this what God wants you to do?*'

⸺•⸺

Edwin had no time to think as he was surrounded, pulled out of the castle gates and down the hill, his hands still bound in front of him. Everything was loud, blurred, overwhelming.

Alys was there. He saw her encircled by hostile men and started struggling against his captors, but it was no good. But then she was released and he saw her turn. If he could have held out his arms to her, he would have done, but instead he was pulled past.

He was brought to a halt under the tree, with Denis beside him. There was a brief pause while Edwin, and maybe everyone else as well, tried to decide if what was happening was really true. He exchanged a long look with Denis, and then nodded. It was all over.

Alys was facing away from him, kneeling in front of Sir Roger and presumably begging for his life. It's too late. It's over. *Please turn around and look at me so the last thing I see is your face.*

The rope was being put about his neck. The knot was to the back, and he knew what that meant. Surely he should be praying, but he couldn't.

And then, everything seemed to slow down, and he could see about him with perfect clarity. The horror and the hate, the terror and the sympathy. Every face, every movement. Everard and the garrison, unsure and looking to Sir Roger for the leadership he was not providing. Crispin, tense, one hand hovering over the hammer in his belt while his other arm was holding his mother in a protective embrace. Osmund – but not Gyrth, poor lad; at least he would be spared. Alwin, with his sons and daughter, Hal crying and looking sick. The reeve, hands clenched. Wulfric and Barty, hiding their faces in Avice's gown so as not to have to watch. Young Robin, his bruised face carrying a smirk. Robin, cuffing one of his other sons with the back of his hand as he sought to keep them in check. Cecily, tears streaming. Father Ignatius, his lips moving in prayer but his face a mask of rage.

Faces, faces. The only one he couldn't see was Alys's. She was now standing, but still with her back to him. But then she turned in disgust from Sir Roger and strode forward, and to Edwin it was like an angel come to welcome him home. She could not get near enough to touch him – the sheriff's men had weapons drawn to keep everyone back – but she stood proud and locked her gaze on to him.

Faces, movements. What had he just seen? He'd just seen something important. Something that meant –

At the sheriff's order, Denis was hauled up, kicking and thrashing.

In his last, desperate, splintered look at the world, Edwin kept his eyes on Alys, but his mind was still working. That was it. He knew, now, what had happened. He knew who the murderer was.

But it was too late.

'Pull!'

And then he was choking, and nothing else mattered.

Chapter Fourteen

And then he wasn't.

He was lying on the ground – he could feel the cool, solid wetness against his body and the side of his face. The rope was still tight around his neck but the awful, choking pressure had ceased. He could breathe a little, enough to force in some air that gave him the strength to move his hands. They were still bound together but he managed to squeeze his fingers inside the rope and loosen it. He took in a huge gulp of blessed air, but it was too much and the pain in his throat overwhelmed him for a few moments.

He became aware of two pairs of boots. One was standing on the ground in front of him; the other was kicking in the air. Denis!

Somehow he managed to get to his hands and knees and crawl half a yard so he was under the hanging mason. He felt Denis's feet plant on his back and the kicking ceased. From somewhere above him a rasping, choking wheeze sounded.

The other boots were attached to mailed legs, supporting a figure wearing a hauberk … Sir Roger. How had this happened? He didn't know. He didn't care. He concentrated on staying as still as possible and breathing as shallowly and evenly as he could while he came to terms with the fact that he was, somehow, still alive.

Belatedly, he began to hear, to make out words that were being spoken.

'You will pay for this.' The sheriff's voice, cold fury.

'No doubt I will, but only in this life. I would pay more if I let innocent men die and went to hell for it.' Calm. Had the real Sir Roger returned at last?

'Stand down, I tell you. Let the execution proceed and we will say no more about your … lapse.'

A woman's sob. Was it Alys? And pain in his throat, throbbing terror that the noose might be replaced.

'No. And I tell *you* to stand down, for you are outnumbered.'

'You wouldn't dare –'

'Oh, I would.' Edwin heard Sir Roger raise his voice. 'All of you. I say that what I am doing is right, but it goes against the law. Any of you who wish to depart, do so now. Any who wish to obey my orders, release those two men.'

Edwin felt tears running down his face as there was a surge towards him. Through the legs of the crowd he could see a few people slipping away, and others pushing children back towards the village, but he was being surrounded, the weight on his back was lifted, he was supported, and then the scent of flowers ... Alys was with him.

She cradled his head and he felt her tears dripping on to him. All he wanted to do was lie there, waiting for life to make sense again, but there was something important. Just before the rope had bitten – back in his previous life – he had been struck with insight.

He remembered. He opened his mouth to speak, before the culprit could get away, but all that came out was a croak. His throat was on fire.

He tried again. Alys bent her head to listen, and he managed to whisper a few words in her ear. She stiffened as she understood and then he heard her voice, calling for everyone to stop what they were doing. And then, after a pause, 'Edwin knows who the real killer is!'

There was silence. Edwin could see everyone turning to look at him. He tried to take another breath but it got caught and he couldn't speak. Instead, he pointed.

Alys had seen the change in Sir Roger's eyes, and she stepped back. Whatever he would do now she didn't know, but her own duty was clear. She placed herself as close as she could get to Edwin and looked into his eyes, willing him to know that she loved him and that she would be with him to the last. She heard the word 'pull' and saw Edwin being jerked off his feet as the noose tightened and the sheriff's men hauled him up. She screamed. She couldn't help it.

But then everything moved very quickly. Sir Roger drew his sword, stepped forward and sliced through the taut rope, which parted straight away to drop Edwin to the ground. He was alive – she could see him moving – but she couldn't get near to him, as the whole space under the tree was now a sea of sharp steel. She felt Cecily pulling her away from the danger.

Sir Roger, sword in hand, took up a position in front of Edwin. 'I will not let this happen.' Alys had expected him to shout, but he sounded unnaturally calm.

She watched the sheriff stride forward, his own sword drawn. Some of his men surrounded him; the others were still behind Edwin, off balance after the weight of the rope they were holding suddenly disappeared. She pointed them out silently to Crispin, who nodded and drew the hammer from his belt.

All was not yet over – she heard 'let the execution proceed' and Cecily's sob. But it was not to be; Sir Roger had prevented it, and now there was a rush of people, the sheriff's men were surrounded, she could move forward … she was with Edwin.

Why was she crying, when she was so happy? She didn't care. All that mattered was that he was here, he was alive, he was safe.

He was trying to tell her something. At first she made to shush him as he croaked, for surely nothing could be that important, but when he kept trying she put her ear next to his mouth.

'What?' He nodded to her; what little voice he had spent already. She looked wildly around her, unable to see … she had to do something.

'Stop!' She was little heeded. 'Stop, everyone! Stop what you're doing!' And then, when she had some attention, 'Edwin knows who the real killer is!'

And every single person there followed the line of Edwin's shaking hand as he pointed.

Robin the carpenter didn't even try to deny it. Once he saw Edwin indicating him as the culprit he just collapsed in a heap.

'I'm sorry, I'm sorry, I didn't mean to … but they were … and he was … and oh, William, I didn't want to hurt William …' He raised his hands to shield his face as he wept.

There was a stunned silence. It was broken by Young Robin, who grasped two handfuls of his father's tunic and hauled him to his feet. 'What are you saying?' Alys heard him hiss under his breath. 'Stop it right now, before –'

'But it was me,' he moaned. He turned his face from his son and shouted at them all in a kind of sobbing defiance. 'It was me, do you hear? I did it!'

Robin's other children were horrified, stupefied, unable to take in what they were hearing. But no, thought Alys to herself as she looked around. Not his children – his *sons*. Avice was looking at him with nothing more than contempt. And another glance told Alys that the little ones had, thankfully, disappeared somewhere.

She was still sitting on the ground holding Edwin, who was just starting to come back to himself, though he was in no condition to elaborate on his accusation.

The sheriff recovered more quickly. 'A confession. So we'll hang him instead and sort the rest of this out later.' He gestured to his men. 'Fashion another noose.'

'No!' This was from Young Robin. 'No, you can't!' He looked wildly around him. 'Stop them! Isn't anyone going to help?' He cast a begging look at Sir Roger. 'You were willing to save them – what about him?'

But the knight was shaking his head. 'They were innocent. He is guilty by his own confession.'

Young Robin addressed his father again, shaking him. 'Take it back! Tell them you didn't do it!'

'I did it for you,' was the weary, hopeless answer.

Young Robin lowered his voice. Alys caught his words, but Sir Roger and the sheriff, who were further off, probably didn't. 'Then run. Run now. If it's the last thing I can do for you.' With a sudden movement he dragged Robin a few paces and shoved him in the direction of the bridge. 'Now!' Then he barked at some of his younger brothers to help him.

'Oh no you don't!'

'After him!'

The orders had come from sheriff and knight simultaneously, and both sets of soldiers sprang into action. But as they moved forward to capture Robin, his sons formed a scuffling, punching, kicking, biting barrier that gave him just enough time to find some life in his legs. He ran for the bridge.

He'd only made it halfway across when, by ill luck (or divine providence, as Father Ignatius would say later) a rider appeared at the other end. Seeing his way blocked, Robin spent a few agonised moments wrenching his head this way and that, but he was trapped. With a despairing cry he took the only other way out, scrambling up on to the parapet and casting himself into the river.

The waters were high and swollen, and he was carried away from sight almost immediately, amid the cries and screams of his sons, some of whom were already racing to the bank calling out for him.

Alys had no idea whether Robin could swim or not, but surely no man could survive either that torrent or the cold for long. She buried her head in Edwin's shoulder.

Edwin clutched at Alys as he felt the life coming back into him. He couldn't see what had just happened, but from the reaction of those around him he could make a guess. All around him was uproar, the sheriff shouting, his men trying to catch hold of all Robin's sons, the villagers exclaiming, the masons shielding Denis from any further harm, Sir Roger trying to impose some sort of order on proceedings.

And then the sound of hoofbeats, and a voice that cracked through the air, reducing the scene to immediate silence.

'What in the name of God and all His saints is going on here?'

It was Sir Geoffrey. Suddenly everyone – Sir Roger and the sheriff included – looked like guilty schoolboys. The last of Edwin's fear and tension left him as he knew now that he would survive the day. But nothing else mattered except that his mother, who had been riding pillion behind Sir Geoffrey, was dismounting and running towards him and Alys. She knelt on his other side and put her arms around him. And soon Cecily was there as well, and Edwin was safe in the warm, comforting embrace of the women in his life.

After some moments they helped him to sit up. Edwin realised that his hands were still bound; he held them out to Alys, who produced from somewhere about her an unexpectedly large knife. He looked at her in surprise.

She tried to shrug it off. 'Cecily's cooking knife. I didn't know exactly what I might have to do.' It took her only a moment to slice through the rope, and he chafed his sore wrists and hands, feeling them sting as they regained some life.

And then he found he could just about get to his feet, and he could stagger the few paces to where Denis was still semi-prostrate, sur-rounded by his fellow masons. They parted to let Edwin through, and he crouched.

'You're alive, my friend,' he managed to whisper to the Frenchman.

Denis tried to reply, but after a painful croak he merely pointed to the deep weal around his crushed throat. He'd been hanging longer than Edwin, and was a heavier man – he was lucky to be alive.

Some messages could be conveyed without words; with the help of his comrades Denis got to his feet and held out his hand to Edwin.

And as Edwin took it he found himself engulfed in a rough embrace, and after that he was patted on the back by all the masons.

Father Ignatius was pushing his way through the crowd to them. He was a welcome sight, not only for the blessing he was already sketching in the air, but also for the skin of wine he was holding out.

Edwin gestured that he should pass it first to Denis, and he watched as the mason took a careful sip, choked, breathed in, took another swig, swallowed some of it, gasped, and ended up with the rest dripping from his chin. But he was smiling, and he caught Edwin in another tearful embrace that Edwin returned with overwhelming feeling.

Then Edwin stepped back in silence as Denis was borne away by his friends; Philippe stopped to shake his hand with fervent thanks, and then they were gone. They could hardly be blamed for not wanting to mingle with the villagers, after everything that had happened.

While all this had been going on, Sir Geoffrey had been snapping out orders. Everard and his men were strung out along the river bank looking for any sign of Robin, but none was to be seen. Young Robin and his brothers were bunched together with a couple of the garrison guarding them, but they were unhurt. The remaining villagers were still lingering, in little knots. Edwin spotted Hal, who half-raised a hand before putting it down again before his father could see. Edwin nodded at him firmly, hoping that the boy would understand his thanks and forgiveness.

Sir Geoffrey was addressing the sheriff. 'You will need to stay until we find him or his body. My men will accompany you back to the castle and see that you are comfortable.'

And to the surprise of any who didn't know Sir Geoffrey well, the sheriff – he who had seemed so powerful, so oppressive – simply gave a stiff nod and moved off.

Sir Geoffrey paused while he took stock of those around him. 'You' – this to Young Robin – 'I will not punish sons for the sins of their father, but we will hear the truth of this. Get back home and stay there until I say otherwise. I will look very seriously on any attempt to disobey, do you understand?'

They did.

Then he turned to the rest of the villagers. 'The Lady Anne' – he continued over the top of their murmurs of surprise at hearing Mother so described – 'will take her family back to the village, and I suggest you all do the same, or get about your normal work.' He paused. 'Needless to say, anyone who offers trouble or offence to my wife, or my stepson or daughter, will answer to me.'

He didn't need to say anything else. Edwin started to move off, hearing Sir Geoffrey address the only man left with him, Sir Roger. 'And you and I need to talk.'

Edwin might have a crushed throat and pain in his hands, and he might have only narrowly escaped death, but he was certain he would prefer that to being in Sir Roger's place just now.

It was later. Edwin wasn't sure how much later, because the first thing he'd done when he reached the cottage was fall on to the bed and into a deep sleep.

When he awoke he remained lying down, motionless. He was in his own bed, in his own home. The chamber door was shut, but he could hear female voices in the cottage's main space, and he smiled to himself as he listened to them and to the gentle sound of the rain pattering on the thatch.

After some time he heard a knock at the outside door and he forced himself to get up; he entered the main room from one end just as Sir Geoffrey came in at the other. The knight – Edwin still couldn't frame the word 'stepfather' even in his head, never mind out loud – was dripping, and the fire sizzled as he took off his cloak, spraying droplets.

Alys, Anne and Cecily had been sitting around the fire, tending something in the pot that predictably smelled delicious. Now

Sir Geoffrey moved the chair towards the warmth; to Edwin's surprise he didn't sit in it but gestured to him, while he pulled up another stool for himself and stretched out his legs. His boots began to steam.

'I've had the bones of it from Sir Roger already, so you needn't go through all that, or …' with a look at the wan Cecily '… too much detail about the deaths. But I do want to know who and how, and in the Lord's name *why*.'

Edwin opened his mouth and croaked.

Alys took up a jug that had been warming near the fire and poured some of the contents into a cup, which she passed to him. He sniffed.

'Warm ale with honey, and Cecily has put willow bark in it for the pain.'

He took a tiny sip and felt the soothing liquid pass down through his throat. He took another, and tried breathing in through his mouth. It was less painful than before.

It still wasn't exactly comfortable to talk, but he could at least form the words, and he tried to be as brief as possible in between taking more draughts.

'It was all because I was looking at it the wrong way round.' Sip.

They were confused, but Alys had a thought. 'Do you mean, because you were looking for someone who favoured his left hand? Like we thought to start with?'

Edwin nodded. 'Partly. But it was more than that. I was looking for the murderer of Ivo, and wondering why the masons should be blamed for it.'

He looked at them over the rim of the cup, realising he was going to have to explain in more detail. 'But it was the wrong way round, don't you see? I didn't either at first, but what I should have been asking myself was why someone wanted to pin a crime on the masons.'

They were still bemused, and his throat was hurting again. 'I'll explain more another day, but for now: Robin was terrified that he'd end up out of business as the masons did more and more – everyone kept joking to him that there would be no need for carpenters if everything was built of stone. And on top of that, they'd even started doing some of their own woodwork.'

Anne was shaking her head. 'Surely nobody would kill for that?'

Sir Geoffrey looked at her fondly. 'You'd think not, but men will kill for reasons that seem mad to anyone else. Trust me.' He nodded to Edwin. 'Carry on.'

'It does seem mad. But he's got all those children to feed, he's always desperate for money, and I think he just let it worry away at him. And as the worry grew, so did the thought that he could get rid of them in some way.'

Something caught in his throat; he held up a hand and made them wait until he could form more words. 'But there was no point getting rid of just one individual, and he could hardly kill them all, so instead he would have them blamed for something and hope they'd all get turned off.'

He took another sip as they all looked at him expectantly. 'But it would have to be murder, for they'd hardly get hanged or sent away for anything less – and he couldn't bring himself to murder anyone he knew well.'

Cecily buried her face in her apron and Edwin winced. 'I'm so sorry. Shall I stop?'

'No, no – carry on. I want to know.' She wiped her face and held Mother's hand more tightly.

'All right, but tell me if it gets too much. Then came Ivo's announcement that everyone in the village would have to pay to use a new bread oven.'

Sir Geoffrey interrupted with a derisive noise. 'Idiot man. That won't be happening, I can tell you.'

'So this threw him into more of a panic – how was he going to pay for enough bread for his family? – but it also gave him the opportunity. Ivo was already unpopular with the masons, and now everyone else hated him too. Who better to kill? Nobody would miss him. All he had to do was make it look like one of the masons did it.'

His throat was on fire, so he took a deep draught and motioned to Alys. 'You do the next bit.'

Alys looked surprised, but she took up the tale. 'Stop me if I get anything wrong. Robin saw Denis having an argument with Ivo, and so did many others. Then he got hold of Denis's hammer – I'm not sure whether it really was just lost or whether he stole it?'

Edwin saw her looking at him but he couldn't speak again just now so he gestured to her to carry on.

'But that's not important. He had the hammer. He made an agreement with Ivo for him to come down to the village at night to … ah …' she blushed, 'to see Avice, and then he lay in wait. He hit Ivo on the head with the hammer.'

She was about to move on when Edwin held up a finger. 'Don't forget.' He waved his left hand.

'Robin knew that Denis held his hammer in his left hand. So he had to make sure he did the same.'

'Ah.' Edwin had wondered whether anyone else would follow his line of reasoning. After all, it had only occurred to him just as the noose was tightening around his neck. He looked at Alys and smiled, willing her to work it out.

He saw realisation dawn. 'Oh, of course!' She held up her barked knuckle for all to see. 'That's why my hand reminded you of something.'

Sir Geoffrey intervened. 'This is all very interesting, but would you have the goodness to explain what in the Lord's name you're talking about?'

Edwin took another swig and gestured for Alys to continue. The cup was empty so he poured himself some more while she was talking.

'Robin didn't hold the hammer in his left hand. Maybe he didn't think he could hit hard enough like that. No – he held it in his right hand and struck it the other way' – she mimed a backhand swipe

– 'and that was a more familiar movement for him to make because *that's the way he hits his children.*' She sat back.

'Exactly,' Edwin managed. 'Then he made sure he dropped the hammer there. It was supposed to be found with the body, but he didn't know that two other people would go in the house before the hue and cry was raised.'

'Others?' Sir Geoffrey leaned forward. 'I knew of no others. Do I need to order more arrests?'

Edwin shook his head. 'No. Or at least, I don't think so. First was Barty, Robin's youngest son. He was up early and he just wandered over to look at the building work. He saw the body but he was more interested in the hammer, which he took to play with. So by the time was body was properly discovered, it wasn't there and Robin had his work cut out to blame the masons. And he panicked when we found out that Barty had it.'

'But nobody would blame such a small child for murder?' said Anne.

'No, of course not. Which was why I wondered why Robin's fear about it was so extreme – until I realised he was afraid for himself, not for Barty.'

He had to pause after such a long speech. But, equally, he had to keep going. 'Then came Gyrth – you know him, the swineherd?'

'The simpleton boy?'

'Yes. I don't know what made him go in there – maybe one of the pigs smelled the blood and ran away from him, or maybe he saw Barty coming out and wondered what was going on. But he saw the body. And you know what he's like around blood. He touched Ivo out of curiosity and then when he saw the blood on his hand he ran away.'

'And then,' picked up Alys, hearing Edwin's voice growing hoarse again, 'I saw him. I thought he'd just got blood on his hands from the slaughtering, so I helped him wash it off.' She looked at Edwin. 'Sorry. If I'd realised sooner I might have been more help.'

Sir Geoffrey nodded to himself as he took it all in.

'And so,' said Cecily, 'to William. It's all right,' she added, as Edwin began to shake his head, 'go on.'

Edwin glanced at his mother, who nodded. 'Very well. In short, William said he'd help me by talking to some of the men from the village. And where would he start except with his friend Robin? He would know all the gossip because people stop to talk at his work-shop. I'm sure William didn't really suspect him – he just wanted to ask him what he knew – but Robin panicked. He said he'd walk back to the castle with William, maybe to talk to me. William probably didn't want to go all the way back up, what with his pain, but he would never have said so, not to anyone except Cecily. He wouldn't even admit it to Alys in church the other day.'

'Stubborn old fool,' said Cecily, lovingly.

'And then when they passed that deep puddle, Robin tripped him up and held his head under until he drowned.'

The three women were in tears, and Edwin felt a burning in his own eyes at the thought of the awful last moments of the man who'd been his uncle and friend. 'You already know, don't you,' he said gently to Cecily, 'that it can't have been an accident? The footprint ...'

Cecily covered her face again as she nodded.

Edwin's voice really wasn't going to last much longer. 'And that's when Robin realised the enormity of what he'd done. It was after that that he started to get really nervous.'

Cecily jerked her head up in anger. 'Nervous? He should be. If he comes back alive then I'll hang him with my own hands.'

Edwin, too, found it impossible to forgive or to understand Robin. There were some very dark thoughts indeed in that man's head. He'd killed Ivo – a man nobody liked, but a man innocent of crime none-theless – for his own purposes. He'd murdered his friend of many years' standing in cold blood. He'd stood by while both Denis and then Edwin were sentenced to death – he'd even stood by while they were hanged. And an even worse idea started to worm its way in. Robin was a widower. Once he'd made Alys a widow, would he try to ... the idea made Edwin feel sick.

'But look,' said Sir Geoffrey. 'This is all plausible and convincing, but it's only conjecture. There's nobody who can confirm or deny any of it, unless by some chance Robin survived the river.'

'There is.' Edwin spoke with conviction.

'I don't think you're going to get much out of Young Robin, nor out of his other sons either. He'll be tight-lipped about his father, and he didn't seem to know much about it anyway.'

'Oh, you're right about that.' Edwin's eyes met Alys's. 'But Robin also has a daughter.'

Chapter Fifteen

Sir Geoffrey got up to leave. Edwin watched as his mother helped him on with his cloak, and then received a jolt as she said she would follow later. Of course; for her, 'home' was now either the castle or Sir Geoffrey's manor, not this cottage.

While she was busy fastening the clasp under his chin, Sir Geoffrey looked at Edwin and rolled his eyes towards the door.

'I'll walk with you,' croaked Edwin, taking the hint.

The earlier rain had subsided into a gentler drizzle, and as they made their way down the street Edwin pushed back his hood to feel the air and the drops on his face. He was alive. Carefully, he sucked in some of the evening air through his mouth, and was pleased to find that he could feel it reaching his chest; the crushing of his throat was not going to be permanent.

They said little as they took the path up to the castle. The afternoon was drawing in, but they could still easily see their way – and the deep puddle in its crater in the road. Edwin stopped, and Sir Geoffrey did likewise.

'Is this where it happened?'

Edwin nodded.

The knight crossed himself. '*Requiescat in pace*. He was a good man, and one I'd known a long time.'

They stood in silence for a moment until Sir Geoffrey spoke again. 'Roger should have sorted this out.'

'What, the hole in the road?'

'No – I mean – well, yes, that too. If he'd been paying proper attention he'd have sent a working party to fill it in before it got to that state – it doesn't reflect well on the lord earl to have his road in disrepair. But I meant …' he made a wide gesture. 'Everything. And word flies about, you know – I'd already heard something of it last week, which is why we cut short our stay. We were already on the way back when your messenger reached us with word of William's death.'

That would explain how they were able to arrive with such miraculous timing, at least. Edwin had thought that he was being protected by the lord, but in fact it was, ironically, down to Sir Roger's problems. 'He's been …' Edwin didn't know how much to say, or indeed how much he would be able to say. 'He's been different since he's been here this time. Since we were on the south coast, I suppose.'

Sir Geoffrey scratched his beard. 'I see that now. And I should have seen it before, but there was little time between him getting here and me leaving.' He sighed. 'This is all my failure as much as his.'

'Do you know, he's been acting so oddly that I even suspected him for a while. All that disappearing off for hours at a time – I still don't know where he was going. And then when Arnulf mentioned that he preferred to use his left hand …'

'Oh yes, I'd forgotten about that. Terrible time I had with him when he was a lad, always wanting to hold his sword and shield the wrong way round, though we sorted him out eventually. But you must know he wouldn't have done this?'

'He certainly wouldn't have killed William. But he was so angry with Ivo, and not for himself; it was for other people. His sense of justice. And with him being so changed as well, I just wondered if it might lead him to …'

Sir Geoffrey shook his head. 'Never. Roger can kill, of course he can – you no doubt saw that yourself a few months back. But he'd do it openly, publicly, with a declared intent. Smashing a man's head, in secret, in the dark? Never.'

'You're right. I don't know what I was thinking. But everything was so strange and so horrible that it was difficult not to suspect everyone. After all, I've been fooled before by thinking "it couldn't possibly be him".' His hand went to the thong around his neck.

Sir Geoffrey took one last look at the muddy water in the crater, crossed himself again and resumed walking. 'Oh, he hasn't done that badly, considering. He'll learn from it. I made mistakes too when I was younger, when I had my first command.'

There was probably an opening there to ask, but Edwin didn't yet feel comfortable enough in his position as stepson to enter it, so he said nothing.

'In hindsight it was a mistake giving him his first command in a place where men have known him since he was a little boy. It's always difficult to exert authority in circumstances like that.'

Edwin had plenty of thoughts on that subject himself, but he kept them to himself.

'Anyway, we don't want him going back to his manor and sitting there doing nothing. I've told him I'll ask the lord earl if he can be sent to one of the other estates, but he said he had "other plans". The cheek of the boy!'

Edwin smiled at the knight's apparent lack of awareness. 'Maybe it would help him, Sir Geoffrey, if you didn't keep calling him "the boy".'

The knight opened his mouth to bark out a retort to such impudence, but it died on his lips and he laughed. 'You're right.' He clapped Edwin on the back. 'I think we're going to get on all right.'

They had reached the outer ward. It was perhaps a little less busy than usual, with a few groups of men standing about talking, but there was still enough bustle to make it feel normal. Edwin tried not to smile at the sight of Jack Jackson raking the stinking muck out of the kennels.

They were drawn to the bright fire of the forge, where Crispin was busy at work. He used his tongs to hold up a glowing horseshoe, examined it, put it on the anvil and started hammering again.

Piled up under the smithy roof, to keep them dry, were a dozen or so of the castle weapons. Sir Geoffrey indicated them to Edwin. 'The state of those – don't think anyone's taken proper care of them while I've been away. But he won't have time to sharpen them today, I suppose. He hasn't had an apprentice since that other young fellow left him last year, has he?'

'No.' They drew nearer to the forge and held out their hands to the heat. Crispin saw them and nodded, but didn't stop working. Edwin listened to the rhythmic hammering.

'So, suspected everyone, did you?' said Sir Geoffrey, returning to their previous conversation.

'To start with. But then I had to apply some sort of logic or I'd never get anywhere.' Edwin watched the huge muscles in the smith's arms as he worked, and pointed. 'If Crispin had hit someone with a hammer, he'd have no head left, so it couldn't have been him. And Father Ignatius might even have been angry enough about people starving to have it out with Ivo, but if he'd killed anybody it would have been written all over his face.' He cleared his throat and wished he'd brought some more of the ale and honey with him. 'So that gave me two men I could trust. But as to the rest?' He shrugged. 'It was like madness. Like being caught in a nightmare.'

'Small communities can get like that, especially in the winter.'

'Yes. And of course everyone had secrets, and nobody wanted to say anything for fear of being found out, even if what they were trying to hide had nothing to do with the murders. But that made it all the more difficult.'

He'd said a little more than he was intending to, but Sir Geoffrey did no more than murmur his assent, so Edwin was saved from having to decide whether to give away any of those secrets. In most cases it wasn't his business, so he was glad not to.

After a few more moments staring at the forge, Sir Geoffrey asked, 'What about the fire?'

Edwin grimaced. 'I'd like to think it was an accident, that nobody could have done something so dangerous, but it's too much of a coincidence. I think we can probably lay that at Robin's door as well – he took extreme measures to get rid of the masons once he realised his attempts to blame them weren't having the success he hoped.'

Sir Geoffrey spoke with some vehemence. 'He'd better be dead already, or I'll make him live long enough to regret it.'

Edwin felt tiredness begin to wash over him again, and he didn't want to think about death. 'I should go home.'

That got the knight's attention. 'Home? You mean, to the cottage?'

'Where else would I mean?'

'Is the village your home any more? Really? Or are you more welcome here?' He turned to look at Edwin properly. 'Your lady mother is moving up here. Why do you and Alys not do the same? You're the lord earl's man and my family, so we could easily find household quarters for you. And your mother would be glad both of you and of the female company, I expect.'

Edwin was caught off guard. 'I'll think about it,' was all he could manage.

Sir Geoffrey gave him a look of sympathy. 'All right. You've had quite a day, I know, so off with you and we can talk more tomorrow.' Another clap on the back and he was on his way to the inner ward.

Edwin nodded at Crispin and drifted away from the forge, back towards the outer gate. It was still only early in the evening, but almost completely dark, and the thought of comforting food, fire and company at home was pulling at him. And he realised that despite the events of the last few days and weeks, the cottage was still the first place that came into his mind when he thought about 'home'. For now, anyway.

So acute was his sense of danger at the moment that he knew he was being watched as soon as he entered the village. He slowed, putting his hand to his belt before realising that he had not yet recovered either his dagger or his eating knife.

He tried to appear casual while looking surreptitiously around him. There was some light spilling out on to the street, for most houses had their fires lit, and their doors and shutters were not all well fitted. But that meant that the shadows were even darker, and although he could hear scurrying footsteps, he could see nothing.

He bent as if to attend to his boot, groping round to see if he could find a stick or a stone – anything – that he might be able to use to defend himself with.

Then he heard a sniff, and was filled with relief, and not a little irritation. 'You can come out now, Hal.'

The boy appeared from the gap between two houses and sidled forward nervously.

'Stand there, where I can see you.' Edwin pointed to a spear of light that ran along the ground. 'Now, what is it?'

Hal's voice was shaking. 'It's really you, Master Edwin? Not a ghost?'

Edwin's annoyance dissipated at the tone. 'Yes, it's me. And I'm alive, I can assure you.'

Hal couldn't hold back a sob. 'I didn't mean to, Master Edwin, it was all my fault, what with what I said at the trial, and then I thought you'd get out of it, but we all got called along to watch and they were going to hang you, and I thought ...' the rest of the words dissolved into tears.

Edwin took a step towards him, but then stopped as he saw the boy take a step back. 'It's all right, really it is.'

There was a loud sniff. 'Really?'

'You told the truth, and that was the right thing to do.' He thought of all the lies and half-truths he'd had to wade through during the last week. 'It's always the best thing to do.'

'So – you forgive me, then?'

'There's nothing to forgive, Hal, but if you want my forgiveness then you have it.'

'Thank you, Master.'

'Now, you'd better get home. And I don't think I'm your master any more, am I?'

'I can ask Pa if he'll let me,' came the hopeful reply. And then, 'But he probably won't. He says now I'm bigger I can help him, and we'll get more money if it's Ned that goes out labouring. I'd rather be with you, I would, really!'

Edwin wanted to deal with this, knew it would help the boy if he could, but he was just too tired. But as he opened his mouth to spout some platitude or other, a thought struck him. 'Your brother Ned, he's big and strong, isn't he?'

'Like an ox, Pa says. And much stronger than I'll ever be, he says that too.' He sounded mournful.

Edwin thought of the bright forge, of the incessant lifting and falling of the heavy hammers. Of the status of the smith in the community. 'Well, maybe we can get him something better than labouring, something that will help you all as you go along.'

'What?'

It was cold and raining, and Edwin didn't know how much longer he could stay upright and awake. 'Never mind. Leave it with me. In the meantime, get yourself home before your mother wonders where you've got to.'

He watched Hal pick his way along the street until he was lost in the shadows, and then took the familiar way home.

As he opened the door, he could smell the pottage and see the welcome sights of the fire and his wife. 'Mother and Cecily?'

'Cecily has gone home – she insisted. And Sir Geoffrey sent a man to escort your mother up to the castle.'

He laid his damp cloak over the kist. *Must sort that peg out.* He looked at her over the flames. 'Just us, then?'

'Just us.'

<hr />

Alys watched as Avice came out of the carpenter's cottage, followed by Edwin, Sir Geoffrey and Sir Roger. They all paused a few moments to talk, the soggy morning light slanting over them, and then the two knights turned in the direction of the castle while Edwin came over to her.

'Did she …?'

He nodded. 'Yes. Everything she said confirmed what I'd thought.'

'Good.'

'And I won't make the same mistake again: I'll remind myself to talk to more women from now on.'

'Will she be in trouble?'

'No. She should be, really – for soliciting as much as anything – but of course she had to do what her father said. And what purpose would it serve to punish her more? She's going to have her work cut out as it is.'

'And the rest of them?'

'They *seem* to have known nothing about it. The little ones didn't, of course, but I'm not sure about Young Robin. But there's no evidence, and I can't go around accusing him or punishing him just because I say so, otherwise I'd be as bad as everybody else, wouldn't I?' He paused. 'I'd like to have brought him to justice for … you know. But it would just be your word against his.'

'It's all right.' She kissed him, and was then distracted by a sight over his shoulder. She gripped his arm. 'Look.'

Four of the garrison were coming from the direction of the river, carrying a litter that was fashioned from poles and ropes. Lying on it was a corpse.

Alys had no desire to move closer, but she watched Edwin do so. He looked down at the body, nodded to the men and pointed towards the church. Others had by now noticed and small knots of people chatted and craned their necks to see, but without getting too close. Edwin said something to one of the soldiers, then took his place at the back corner of the litter while the man hurried off in the direction of the castle.

Robin's children, perhaps alerted by the exclamations, had all come out of the cottage. The older ones looked grim. Little Barty was as unconcerned as ever, too small even to understand what was happening, but Wulfric, the two younger girls and some of the other smaller boys all had tears on their faces.

Cecily had appeared next to Alys. She stood in silence as the little procession passed through the church door and out of sight, and then turned on her heel and disappeared again. A movement caught Alys's eye: Wulfric had made as if to run after her, but he was pulled back by one of the Berts.

It wasn't long before Sir Geoffrey and the sheriff appeared. They too entered the church, and Alys – along with several others – drifted closer to the open doorway.

'I say hang the corpse and leave it there, as a warning.' That was Neville, of course.

'Barbaric!' Father Ignatius.

'Hmm.' And that was Sir Geoffrey. Surely he couldn't be considering something so grotesque? And why didn't Edwin say anything? Although – she reminded herself – he could hardly want to exchange many words with the man who had tried to hang him yesterday.

She strained her ears. She could hear Edwin now, talking in a half-whisper. She caught the words 'Counterproductive … together … children.' Oh Lord, yes – how could those little ones possibly live with the sight of their father's body swinging from a tree?

Sir Geoffrey added his voice to the priest's in resisting the sheriff's idea, and eventually Neville made an exasperated noise. 'Very well. But you can hardly bury him in the churchyard.'

'Of course not.' That was Father Ignatius again. 'He's a confessed murderer and a suicide. We'll bury him at the crossroads, but at least he'll be in the ground and the village will be able to forget him.'

'And so,' said the sheriff in an irritated tone, 'I've come all the way here for nothing.'

'No you haven't.' That was Edwin, and Alys heard the slight pause as the sheriff reacted to being thus addressed.

'Your meaning?'

'You've come to see justice done, and you have. The man who murdered Ivo and William has been identified without doubt, and here he lies, dead.'

There was a short silence. Alys was so sure of what Edwin was thinking that she could almost hear it, but of course he wouldn't say it out loud. *So get out and leave us all alone.*

'I will include this information in my report – along with the fact that Earl Warenne's lands are lawless and out of control.' But that was a puny threat; even Alys recognised it, especially when she heard Sir Geoffrey's barely hidden derision.

'Get out, Neville. Get back to York and don't think you can harm a Warenne.'

'The Nevilles will be the equal of the Warennes one day, you mark it.' The sheriff must have known that he was losing the argument if he had to resort to such childish insults, so he said no more. Alys heard him coming towards the door; she moved back, along with everyone else who had been listening and who now tried to make it look as though they were standing around the church porch purely by chance.

As he stalked past them, Alys returned her attention to those inside.

'He's not fit to lie here, not next to William.' That was Sir Geoffrey again.

'They won't be together for long,' said Father Ignatius. We'll inter William this afternoon, and then I'll deal with this poor unshriven soul after dark tonight, if you will lend me the men to carry and dig.'

'Very well. And may God forgive him, because nobody else will.'

⟶•⟵

The whole of Conisbrough, village and castle alike, turned out for the burial of William Steward. The rain held off for a while, but the ground was soft and wet, the graveside muddy as so many people stood around it.

Edwin watched as the shrouded form was lowered into the earth. William had been his uncle, his friend, a constant fixture in his life. Many was the afternoon he'd spent in the old office, hiding from the world while he immersed himself in the accounts; and long before that, some of his earliest memories included William breaking the tip off a cone of sugar to keep him quiet as he sat under the table with his alphabet.

The body reached its final resting place, and Father Ignatius began to intone the familiar Latin. Edwin stared straight ahead, trying not to let the tears fall, as he reflected on how he might have prevented such a needless death. Another one. To his right, Sir Geoffrey stood lance-straight, and to his left Alys and his mother had their arms around Cecily, all of them weeping.

As the service concluded, Father Ignatius threw the first handful of earth back into the grave. Others did the same, including Richard Cook, with whom William had engaged in a running feud in life. He didn't often emerge from his kingdom in the kitchens, but tonight's meal at the castle was less important than paying his respects. After he had cast his soil he nodded briefly at Cecily before turning away, rubbing his eyes.

Eventually the crowd grew thinner, and the two men who helped out the priest when graves needed digging stepped forward. They began to shovel the earth, and soon the body was covered.

As well as their immediate family circle, a few others still dawdled. One of them was Wulfric, who was sidling up to Cecily as though approaching a raging fire. He stopped a few yards from her and waited to be noticed.

Alys saw him and pointed him out. Cecily's face hardened, and she looked down as he threw himself to his knees and grasped at the hem of her gown, tears making tracks in the dirt on his face.

'I'm so sorry, Mistress. I'm sorry, I didn't know it was him, and I couldn't … I mean, I would have … if I'd known …' the rest was drowned out in sobs.

Even in the depths of her bereavement, Cecily couldn't stand out against that. She helped him to rise, saying that she knew it wasn't his fault, before she finally took him in an embrace and cried into the top of his head.

Edwin turned away. A few yards away, on the other side of the grave, Osmund was trying to pull Gyrth away, but the youth was making distressed noises and refusing to move. Osmund looked apologetically at them and Edwin made a calming gesture to show him it was all right. The reeve, who was just leaving, patted Osmund on the shoulder. 'It's fine. He's a good lad, does his work well, and we all know God made him that way for a reason.' Edwin saw Osmund flinch, and he winced on his behalf, but said nothing. It wasn't his secret to tell.

And speaking of secrets, over the churchyard fence he could see Aelfrith, who had walked in for the funeral, chatting to a few of the young men his own age. A short distance away stood a gaggle of admiring girls, Rosa among them. But Edwin certainly wasn't going to get involved in that: he'd rather investigate ten crimes than have to wade into complicated matters of the heart.

Mother and Sir Geoffrey were leaving, and Cecily had finished talking to Wulfric; the boy wasn't exactly skipping as he left, but he certainly looked happier than he had done earlier.

Edwin turned to Cecily. 'So, what now? Will you go home, or come back with us for a while?'

Cecily took a deep breath. 'I'm on my way home, but only to pick up my salves. Then I'm away to the masons' camp – there's Alban to see to, and I'd like to check on Denis as well.'

'But …'

She looked at him, and he saw the pain in her eyes. 'I thought the world was going to stop, but it didn't. And so life must go on, and there's work to do.' She turned to Alys. 'Will you come with me?'

Edwin caught the slight wobble in her voice and was glad when Alys agreed. He watched them leave and surveyed the graveyard. Other than the two men shovelling, there remained only himself and one other.

He walked over to join Sir Roger, who was pacing up and down between older mounds.

The knight saw him. 'Remind me again where his family lies?'

Edwin didn't need to be told who 'he' was. He took a moment to orient himself and then moved a few paces nearer to the church. 'Here.' He indicated four graves in a row, almost flat now as they'd been there for years. 'His brother and sister,' he said, pointing at the two smaller humps. 'And these are his mother and father, though I don't know which is which.'

'Thank you.' Sir Roger knelt and drew his dagger; he began to dig a small hole between the two adult graves.

'What are you doing?'

The knight took something out from his purse and held it up for inspection. Edwin saw that it was a lock of hair.

'I couldn't bring him back, but I took this before we buried him so I could put it with his family.' Edwin watched as he placed the hair in the hole and then covered it up. Then he stood.

'You asked me where I'd been going, when I left here.'

'Yes.'

'Do you still want to know?'

'If you want to tell me.'

'I have been riding to Roche Abbey, to consult with the abbot and to try to get first wind of the news I was waiting for – you know tidings travel fast between monasteries.'

'Tidings about what?'

'Now that Sir Geoffrey has returned to take up his position here again, I will be going on crusade.'

Somehow, Edwin wasn't as shocked as he could have been. With such religious zeal as Sir Roger had always displayed, something like this had always been likely. Indeed, rumours about it had been floating around for some time. 'On your own? Isn't that dangerous?'

'No. That's the news I've been waiting for – now that the war is over here, the Earl of Chester is gathering a force to travel to the Holy Land, and I will be part of it.'

'But my lord earl …'

'This is something I discussed with Abbot Reginald, and also with the good Father here. Our hope is that the lord earl will approve of my going, as I can represent his interests in the affair, but even if not, he cannot stop me. The expedition has the blessing of the Holy Church, and that is a higher authority.'

Edwin said nothing.

Sir Roger obviously interpreted his silence as doubt. 'But don't you see? It's the best way. Here, everything is complicated, and it's difficult to see what the Lord's plan is. Out there it will be different, simpler. We're right and the heathens are wrong, and we must fight to drive them out of the holy places. I will be secure in the knowledge that I am doing God's work.'

The day was dull and grey, but the light of Sir Roger's enthusiasm was almost enough to illuminate it. 'Then I wish you well.' Edwin held out his hand.

Sir Roger shook it. 'It's time to move on.' He nodded at Edwin and walked away.

Edwin stood for a few moments, and then moved to his father's grave and said a prayer. And then he looked over to the part of the churchyard that he hadn't felt able to approach for the last half a year. There were two mounds there that dated from the same week as Father's; one larger than the other.

He crossed himself as he passed the small one, but it was next to the other that he knelt. He drew out the dagger that Everard had returned to him that morning, and, guessing approximately where the place was that would be over the heart, he scraped out a small hole. Then he took the thong from around his neck, took a last look at what it held, and placed it in the earth. He covered it up and gazed at it for a long moment.

Edwin stood up. He looked around him at the graves and the church, at the village, and then up at the castle that had loomed over him for the whole of his life.

'Yes,' he said to himself. 'It's time to move on.'

Historical Note

The war was over by November 1217, but the ramifications were still being felt across England. The chaos of the latter stages of King John's reign, followed by the French invasion, meant that established systems of law and order had in many places broken down. There was (or at least there had been) a national system of justice for serious crimes such as murder, with each county having a sheriff and a coroner to whom all violent deaths should be reported. However, Yorkshire suffered not just from the confusion of the conflict – there really were six sheriffs in the five years between 1212 and 1217 – but also from being one of the largest counties in England, meaning that distances and travel times could be an issue. The combination of these factors is why Edwin has not met a sheriff of Yorkshire up until now.

The sheriff in November 1217 was called Geoffrey de Neville, so I have used his name but created the rest of his character from scratch: unsurprisingly, we know nothing about his personality or what he looked like. Every other individual featured in *Cast the First Stone* is fictional, although, as in previous books in this series, they all represent people or professions who would have been easily recognisable to contemporaries. Most of the men in a village such as Conisbrough would have been labourers (either free men or serfs tied to the estate), who divided their time between working in their own fields and those of the lord according to a strict annual schedule of ploughing, sowing, harvesting and so on. However, more specialist jobs were held by individuals who would work on behalf of the whole village: the swineherd, for example, took everyone's pigs off to the woods as it would be impractical for each family to do the same just for a couple of animals each.

Village life was thus communal in some respects, and this was particularly true for the female inhabitants, who took it in turns to brew
ale for all (it was not economical to make ale in anything other than
large batches, but it went stale quickly) and who shared a communal
well and bread oven. Women led extremely busy lives, organising
and labouring from dawn to dusk in house and garden as they grew
vegetables, raised animals, cooked, cleaned, washed, span, sewed or ran
small businesses – all without the benefit of any labour-saving devices
and often while pregnant and/or caring for small children.

Hawise, the late wife of Robin the carpenter, is portrayed as having
given birth to fourteen children, something that was not all that
uncommon in the thirteenth century, and having all of them survive,
which certainly was. This would be a scenario worthy of comment
among the neighbours, but with some luck it would not be impossible, and in fact I took the example from an ancestor of my own: she
lived in the eighteenth century (obviously much later than our story
here, but as the wife of an agricultural labourer in a rural village the
conditions in which she lived were not actually much better) and,
according to a well-preserved parish record, she married at sixteen,
spent the next twenty-two years having fourteen children, and then
died giving birth to the last. The story of the three Berts is also an
aside to my family tree: I have recently been cataloguing my great-
grandmother's extensive postcard collection, a task made considerably
more difficult by the fact that two of her brothers and her fiancé were
all known as Bert.

A prominent lord such as the earl would have a number of officers
in each of his domains to whom responsibilities would be delegated.
Inside the castle the military lead was the castellan, while the senior
administrative officer was the steward; the wider estate came under
the bailiff and the local day-to-day management under the reeve. One
of the major differences between the two latter figures was that the

bailiff of an estate was chosen by the lord, while the reeve was elected by the villagers themselves, so he was their representative. Both would feature at the manor court, an event that was held regularly to deal with minor infractions, with every man or boy over twelve serving on the jury.

The question of local laws and customs was an all-important one to many ordinary people. Life was precarious, and the fee that had to be paid in order for grain to be ground into flour at the lord's mill could make a significant impact on family finances, as could matters such as the right to pick up fallen wood or to catch small birds and rabbits. Even the tension depicted in this book over the proposed relocation of the fair is entirely plausible: margins were so tight that something as simple as the extra dung on the fields might make a crucial difference to harvest yield, which in turn could be a matter of life or death over the course of the year.

Some of the Conisbrough court rolls from the Middle Ages survive and have been made available online (www.dhi.ac.uk/conisbrough/). The earliest, alas, dates only from 1324, over a century after the events of *Cast the First Stone*, but in it we can find villagers being fined for cutting wood, for brewing weak ale and for the damage caused by escaped pigs; and one unfortunate individual in that year was sentenced to hang for theft. In the thirteenth century there was no presumption of innocence in legal proceedings (the phrase 'innocent until proven guilty' is not recorded in print until the early nineteenth century, according to a research article in *The Jurist*), so defendants could be found guilty if sufficient jurymen found against them, regardless of the quality of the evidence.

———◆———

Masons were specialist craftsmen, itinerant and often foreign, and France was a particular centre of architectural development at this time. The keep at Conisbrough is based on the design of that at Mortemer in Normandy, both being built by Hamelin de Warenne (the father of the earl who appears in our books), so it is not unlikely that some of the same men, or their apprentices or sons, worked on both projects. Masons formed their own community at each place they worked, centred around their lodge, so they would not have been fully integrated into the life of the village – local people may well have seen them as 'outsiders' even when they had been working there several years.

The stone keep and curtain walls at Conisbrough had been complete for some years by 1217, and William de Warenne, Edwin's earl, continued the work by overseeing the demolition of the old wooden buildings inside the bailey and the construction of a kitchen, hall and residential accommodation in stone. The layout of the castle as described in *Cast the First Stone* is based on the real plan, except that (as in previous books) I have moved the chapel in the keep from the third floor – off the private bedroom – down to the second, so it is accessible from the council chamber.

Sir Roger's desire to head to the Holy Land on crusade was mirrored by many thirteenth-century contemporaries. The new king of England, Henry III, was not in a position to travel east himself – he had just inherited a broken kingdom and was only nine years old – so the English contingent (including Ranulf, the Earl of Chester, whom Edwin met in *The Bloody City*) joined up with a group of French noblemen when they set off in 1218 for what became known as the Fifth Crusade, against Damietta in Egypt. This alliance might seem odd in the context of the recent war in England, but what contemporaries saw as the fight for Christendom cut across national boundaries.

Finally, Denis and Edwin's survival of their ordeal is based on a number of real accounts from the Middle Ages and later. Hangings at this time were generally carried out by hauling the victims up, not by dropping them down from a height, and this meant that – unless the knot of the noose was very specifically placed and the pull on the rope very sudden – death occurred as a result of slow strangulation rather than a broken neck. Relatives and friends of the victim were sometimes, as a mercy, permitted to pull down on their legs to hasten their ends, but if they did not then death might take anything up to half an hour (this was later used as a specific feature of the method of execution known as hanging, drawing and quartering, where victims were deliberately cut down while still alive). Stopping a hanging part-way through could therefore result in survival, and there are documented instances of people living after being strangled for much longer than Denis and Edwin. Whether or not Edwin will end up thanking his rescuers, of course, remains to be seen.

Further Reading

Bennett, H.S., *Life on the English Manor: A Study of Peasant Conditions 1150–1400* (Cambridge: Cambridge University Press, 1938)

Coldstream, Nicola, *Medieval Craftsmen: Masons and Sculptors* (London: British Museum Press, 2004)

Dyer, Christopher, *Everyday Life in Medieval England* (London: Hambledon and London, 2000)

Gies, Frances and Joseph Gies, *Life in a Medieval Village* (New York: HarperPerennial, 1991)

Given, James B., *Society and Homicide in Thirteenth-Century England* (Stanford: Stanford University Press, 1977)

Homans, George C., *English Villagers of the Thirteenth Century* (New York: W.W. Norton, 1975)

Titow, J.Z., *English Rural Society 1200–1350* (London: Allen & Unwin, 1969)